EVERYTHING TO LOSE

Before turning to full-time writing, Andrew Gross was an executive in the sportswear business. Andrew has written eight novels, six of which were Top Ten bestsellers in the UK. He has also co-authored five *New York Times* Number One bestsellers with James Patterson. He currently lives in New York with his wife Lynn and their three children.

Novels by Andrew Gross

No Way Back
15 Seconds
Killing Hour
Reckless
Don't Look Twice
The Dark Tide
The Blue Zone

By Andrew Gross and James Patterson

Judge and Jury
Lifeguard
3rd Degree
The Jester
2nd Chance

ANDREW GROSS

Everything to Lose

HARPER

This novel is entirely a work of fiction.
The names, characters and incidents portrayed in it are the work of
the author's imagination. Any resemblance to actual persons, living
or dead, events or localities is entirely coincidental.

Harper
An imprint of HarperCollins*Publishers*
77–85 Fulham Palace Road,
Hammersmith, London W6 8JB

www.harpercollins.co.uk

This paperback edition 2014
4

First published in Great Britain by
HarperCollins*Publishers* 2014

A catalogue record for this book is
available from the British Library

ISBN: 978-0-00-748446-1

Set in Meridien by Palimpsest Book Production Limited,
Falkirk, Stirlingshire

Printed and bound in Great Britain by
Clays Ltd, St Ives plc

MIX
Paper from
responsible sources
FSC™ C007454

Prologue

The two of them lay together in the breezeless night on the banks of the Arthur Kill, overlooking the dark container ports of New Jersey.

He knew this was the last time they would be together.

This was their spot, on the blighted western shore of Staten Island, beneath the shadowy trusses of the Goethals Bridge and by the chained wire gate of the shuttered-up soap factory that years before had given Port Ivory its name. The ground around them was pocked with deep man-made holes. He'd always been told that the government had dug them, connected to a network of tunnels as part of a defense project during the Second World War. Now they were just the open, unhealed sores on the face of the abandoned landscape that protected him from the outside world.

The dark world that was encroaching on him tonight.

1

"You don't have to go," he said, his voice cracking as he stroked her apricot-smelling, honey-colored hair. His life was as gray and drab as the world around him. She was the only thing that added beauty to it.

"Yes, I do. You know I do. We've known that from the start. We both have to get out of here. Next year it'll be your turn."

His turn . . . He was poor; no one in his family had ever gone to college. With his father gone, how would that ever happen now?

"C'mon, you're smart." She smiled and stroked his face. "You'll go far."

Yes, he would go far. He felt it, no matter how everything seemed stacked against him. "I don't know."

And he *was* smart. Though sometimes he had trouble convincing his teachers, who were really stupid themselves and had no idea what was inside him. In a couple of days she was headed off to Canisius College in Buffalo. He'd known from the start that one day she would leave him behind. But now that the day had come, it felt no different from all the other hurt in his life. She was the first person he had truly known, who saw what was truly inside him. Not just the part he showed to others. Though they kept their time together hidden from everyone else. They made up names—she used his nickname, Streak. In the third grade it was given to him because he ran faster than anyone else. But since then it had morphed into something else, something his stupid younger brother had come up with that he hated.

Mean Streak.

For the kinds of urges that rose up inside him. Things he couldn't control. Things the family saw. But his brother was a lying little pest who he should have dealt with long ago.

He called her Cordelia, from this play he'd been reading. The most beautiful and truthful. And most loyal. Now he would have only the wincing smell of chemicals and gasoline and these lonely trestles to remind him that she was ever here.

"You know we could go away." He faced her. "College isn't so great. We could go out west. My uncle has a ranch out in New Mexico. I was there once. It's beautiful there. I could get a job. We could—"

"Ssshh . . ." She placed her finger against his lips. "No, we can't. We just can't. This is the way it is. Don't spoil this. I want to remember things as happy between you and me."

"You'll meet someone," he said. He felt something rise up in his blood. She would. Someone older. Cooler. Nothing will ever be the same.

"No, I won't." She giggled and leaned her head against his shoulder. "Not someone like you."

Yes, you will, *he knew, as clear as the lights were bright. Leave. Just like his dad had left. Back when he was six. He barely remembered him now. His mother always called it his fault. That he was just too much to take. Mean Streak.*

And then Mike, five years older, who enlisted in the marines and was killed in a copter crash at Camp Lejeune while still in basic training.

Like every person he had ever put his trust in had left him.

3

The night suddenly felt so sticky it seemed to cling to him like cellophane.

Yes, you will, he said to himself, certain. Leave.

He would never let that happen again.

"What?" She cocked her head, fixing on him. "You're looking at me funny."

He shook his head. "Nothing."

It was that nothing would ever be the same.

"It's late," she finally said. She pulled up her top and arched her back to wiggle up her jeans. "You're acting so strange tonight. Maybe we should just head back."

"Just another minute," he begged. He felt that tingling start to come over him. He willed it to go away. "Please."

"Okay, just one . . ." Her eyes lit up mischievously. "But you know what that always leads to, silly . . ."

He pulled her close, stroking her soft hair over and over, pushing the demons back, back into the hole where they crawled out from, his hand suddenly coming to rest on her shoulder.

A tanker went by, arcing into a wide sweep into Port Elizabeth, a sight they'd watched together surely a hundred times.

"It's beautiful, isn't it? I mean, it's so ugly it's somehow beautiful. There's a word for that somewhere. Much as I want to leave, there's something that I just can't leave behind."

"Yes, it's beautiful." His blood began to heat. But not in the way it usually did with her. In a different way. Why should someone else get to have her? Why should someone else get to feel what he felt? In a few months she would come back home.

Would she even call him? The little boy from the flats she'd left behind? When he saw her with someone else, would she even look at him? If he went up to her, she probably wouldn't even remember his name.

She was right about one thing, though, he knew. He would. Go far.

"Streak," she murmured, reminding him that it was time. But he just acted like he hadn't heard her and continued to stroke her hair. The things he knew so well: the apricot scent of her shampoo; the slippery feel of his thumb against the sweat on her neck that he would run his fingers over for the last time. Wanting her more than ever, just not wanting her to go, to leave, like they had all left, never coming back.

Suddenly aware of the parched, gagging sound that came from her lips, and how her eyes stretched to twice their size, searching out his in an incredulous and kind of accusing way. Everyone he'd ever loved, everything he wanted to keep for his own just once reflected in them—those wide, scared pools.

Not even realizing that his hands had come together with a seeming will of their own and tightened, a noose of last resort, around the nape of her long, bare neck.

HILARY

CHAPTER ONE

I read somewhere that every life is the story of a single mistake, and then what happens after.

Whether it's brought into the light and owned up to. Or left buried in the darkness of the soul where it all just multiplies in consequences and festers into something far worse.

One wrong decision that can't be taken back. Even the best of lives has one.

And thinking back on that night, on the backcountry road between Westchester County in New York and Greenwich, Connecticut, I felt my own life starting to come down around me like the intensifying drizzle that glared through the oncoming headlights, I could look back where I had run headfirst into mine.

Normally I wouldn't even have driven this particular

route to Jim's, my ex of four years, who's remarried now to Janice. It's a winding and poorly lit stretch with turns that can come at you pretty quickly if you're not familiar with them, or maybe distracted, as I might have been that night.

But I'd thrown a few bills to mail in the car and driven north on I-684, just to get out of the house and think, so I came back down and cut across from Bedford, which seemed the fastest way. These past four years had become a bit of a struggle to keep things together for Brandon and me. I'd never asked for much in the settlement, even when my lawyers were pushing me to rip the coat off Jim's back, which in his case meant the condo in Costa Rica where he went with his pals to go bonefishing and surf; whatever was left of his construction business, which by that time was on fumes and down to mostly house painting and a few remodeling jobs; and of course his perfectly restored '70 Porsche Targa, which, if he were ever honest, was the true love of his life.

I'd just wanted out, as quickly and painlessly as possible.

And four years back Brandon was the sweetest, slightly nonverbal three-year-old with soft blue eyes and a mop of sun-blond hair.

And also the healthiest.

Ahead, the brake lights flashed from the vehicle about fifty yards in front of me, the driver taking a curve a bit wide. I slowed my Acura SUV, staying several car lengths behind.

He was three when we first started noticing it. At least when we started admitting it. He'd always been slow to talk. When other kids were gushing phrases and cuteness, Brandon mostly stared distractedly and pointed at things he wanted. We had him in a Montessori Stepping Stones program and one day his teachers called me in and said he seemed to be having trouble interacting with the other kids.

What made me concerned was that the head of school, Ms. Roby, was at the meeting too.

"Well, he's always been a bit high-strung," I said. "He was high-strung in the womb. In our house, when you want to know the temperature, you can just check Brandon."

Their laugh was brief and polite.

They mentioned that he had difficulty writing—which we'd seen, of course—and completing his tasks. Switching from one activity to another, he would even throw fits. There were times, they said, when he became downright defiant.

They suggested that maybe he should see a specialist in this kind of thing.

What I was praying was just a heavy dose of ADHD was diagnosed as Asperger's syndrome, and not a mild case either. Though they claimed that Brandon's IQ, especially on the creative side, was sky high. They just weren't sure how to reach him. Clearly they didn't think they could do the job for him there, in such an open learning environment.

So I found a school, Milton Farms, in Greenwich, which specialized in severe learning difficulties. It was expensive, close to fifty grand a year. I went back to work to help with the costs. Not as the rising magazine executive I'd been before I left to start a family. Assistant publisher of *Modern Lifestyle* in New York. But as the comptroller for a small marketing firm in Westport, Connecticut. Not exactly the glamour job—the recession was in full throttle and publications were shutting down left and right or going digital, in any case, not exactly hiring. But it was reliable—Cesta Pharmaceuticals had been the backbone of their client list for the past twelve years. More important, it allowed me to stay close to home for Brandon.

I brought in just enough to make sure he could stay in school—which after a year or two was really starting to show results—and pay my share of the mortgage and the real estate taxes.

Which soon became *all* the mortgage and real estate taxes, as by then no one was really interested in Jim's eight-thousand-square-foot McMansions and his construction business was floundering. And Janice, the blond Greenwich divorcée Jim had taken up with barely a month after our divorce became final and married a year later, finally said enough to bankrolling the operations.

Not to mention the two perfectly preppy and *healthy* boys he'd inherited from her who now seemed to take up all of his attention. I also paid for Elena, who cleaned the house and picked Brandon up from school most days until I got home. And the weekly behavioral and language tutoring at $150 an hour. And the day camp Brandon went to in the summer for kids with disabilities.

Or the rare times we actually got away these days. Which soon became *what* time to get away . . .

For a while, my folks helped out as much as they could from their teachers' pensions. My aunt and uncle, actually. My birth parents were killed in an auto accident when I was eight, and Uncle Neil and Aunt Judy took me in, as they didn't have children, and I never felt for a second that I wasn't theirs. I even called them Mom and Pop. They'd bought a small boatyard on Long Beach Island and the recession had hit that even harder than the home building business. My dad's health wasn't what it once was and there were boats to pay off that hadn't sold, that they were paying interest on top of interest on to some finance company. Thank God I'd always kept a little savings separate from Jim from my working days. But now that was just about gone.

For the past year, Brandon and I had been living exclusively on what I brought in; Jim was MIA. Maybe I'd let it go on for too long. The couple of guys I got close to and who I might have seen something happening with both backed off when they got to meet my son. And in truth, he was a handful. I was thirty-six, an eyelash from being broke, months behind in my school payments, with a house my ex had left me that was now completely underwater and a son who ate up every cent I earned.

I saw what was ahead of me, the way the driver in a chase scene going ninety might see the upcoming cliff. Every night I fell asleep, my arms wrapped tightly around my pillow, knowing that all it would take would be one unexpected nudge to send us over the edge.

And how there was no one, not a single person in this world, to catch us.

I'd been there years before in my own life, feeling the terror of sudden abandonment and instability, and that was the last thing I wanted my own son to feel.

Yet somehow we always made it through. A bonus here, a tax refund there. And Brandon showed such clear signs of improvement, it made everything worthwhile. The little nudge that could send us toppling never seemed to come.

At least, not until yesterday, that is.

My boss, Steve Fisher, called a bunch of us into the conference room. It looked like most of the division I worked for. There was Dale Schliffman from accounts, and two of his senior managers. Dawn Ianazzone from Creative. She'd been hired about when I was. A couple of administrative people who worked on the Cesta account.

I knew we were in trouble when I saw Rose from personnel standing alongside.

Steve looked uncomfortable. "Yesterday Cesta informed me that they were going to be making a change . . . A change of agencies . . ." He shrugged sadly. "I'm afraid that means there have to be a few changes around here as well."

I heard a gasp or two. Someone muttered, "Holy shit." Mostly we all just looked around, suddenly realizing exactly why we were there.

An hour later, in my one-on-one, Steve shook his head, frustrated. "Hil, you know you've done nothing but first-rate work since you've been here. I wish there was something we could do."

"Steve . . ." I didn't want to beg, but I could barely stop the tears. "I have Brandon."

"I know." He let out a sympathetic breath, nodding. "Look, let me check one more time. I'll see if there's anything we can do."

Which ended up as just an extra week's salary for the four years I'd been there. And one more month on the health plan before I went on COBRA.

I was officially in free fall now.

Which explained why I was here tonight on this winding, backcountry road, heading to Jim's, which I hadn't been to in years other than to drop off Brandon for a weekend every couple of months. And even that had become rarer and rarer these days.

When I saw what looked like a deer dart across the road about fifty yards ahead, and the car in front of me go into a swerve.

CHAPTER TWO

It was a black Kia or a Honda or something. I was never the best at recognizing cars. It swerved to avoid the deer as it bolted past and then another car heading in the other direction.

Maybe the driver got blinded in the lights.

The front of his car spun out. He was going around fifty, and was headed into a curve. I watched him make a last effort to brake, then the back end drifted off the shoulder and suddenly the car just rolled.

A jolt of horror ripped through me.

The curve was at a steep embankment and the car plummeted over the edge and tumbled down. I hit the brakes, craning my neck as I went by. I watched it roll over and over until it disappeared into the dense woods.

I heard the jarring sound of impact as it came to a stop against a tree.

Oh my God!

I screeched to a stop about twenty yards past the crash site. I leaped out and ran back to take a look, my heart racing. I smelled the steamy burn of rubber on pavement and the smoke coming from the engine down below. I could see the car's taillights, still on; it had cut a path though the thick brush. It was clear that whoever was inside had to be badly hurt.

I was about to race down when another car backed up on the far side of the road, the one that must have passed it a moment earlier. The driver, a man with a round face and thin, reddish hair combed over a bald spot, put down his window. "What's happened?"

"Someone drove off the road," I told him. "I'm going down."

I headed down the incline, tripping on the brush and losing my footing in the damp soil. I fell on my rear, scraping my arm, and got up. I knew I had to get there quick. The car had spun over twice and come to a rest right side up, the front grill sandwiched between a couple of trees. I saw that the roof near the driver's seat was severely dented.

I could see someone in the driver's seat. A man. His door was wedged against a tree. I tried to open it, but it wouldn't budge. I peered through the window and didn't see anyone else. I knew I had to get this guy out.

He didn't seem to be conscious. He could be dying. He looked around seventy, white hair, balding, slumped against the wheel, blood streaming down one side of his face. He wasn't moving or uttering a sound.

The engine was smoking.

"*Are you all right*?" I rapped on the glass. "Can you hear me?"

He didn't respond. It was clear he was either dead or unconscious.

"Mister, are you okay?" I tugged on the driver's door one more time, but you'd have to rip it off or move the car.

From above, I heard the driver of the other car call down, "Is everyone all right down there? Do you need help?"

"Call 911!" I shouted back up. I'd left my phone in the car. "Tell 'em there's a single driver who's not responding. I can't get to him. The door's stuck, and I don't know, I think maybe he's dead. They need to send an ambulance."

I could barely catch a glimpse of the guy through the brush as he hurried back to his car. I looked at the smoking hood and had a sudden fear that any second the engine might catch fire. Maybe the right thing was to back off and wait for help, but with the guy non-responsive, the engine smoking, the stronger voice inside me pushed me to see if he was alive.

I ran around to the passenger side. The door there

wasn't obstructed and opened easily. I wedged myself into the seat. In front of me, the driver's head was pitched forward and a trickle of blood ran down his forehead as if it had been bludgeoned against the wheel. His eyes were rolled up. His white hair was matted with red. I reached across and pushed him back against the seat. "Are you okay? Can you hear me?" Again, he didn't respond. I'd taken a CPR course a few years back, but there didn't seem to be anything I could do for him.

There was a black leather satchel on the floor mat that must have fallen off the seat in the crash. I picked it up so I could squeeze in closer.

My heart almost jumped out of my chest at what I saw.

A wad of money. Hundred-dollar bills. Neatly wrapped together. I couldn't help but pick it up and flip through. There had to be a hundred of them—*Jesus, Hilary!*—bound together by a rubber band. A hundred hundreds would be what . . .? I did the math, ten thousand dollars. The satchel was open slightly at the top, and so far the guy hadn't moved or even uttered a sound. I couldn't help but satisfy my curiosity, unzipping it all the way open.

This time my heart didn't jump—it stopped. And if my eyes had been wide before, they surely doubled now.

Holy shit, Hil . . .

The bag was filled with similarly bound packets of cash. All hundreds! Reflexively I pawed through them.

There were dozens of them. This time the math was a little harder to calculate.

I was looking at hundreds of thousands of dollars.

I looked over at the driver and tried to figure out what some old guy driving a beat-up Honda would be doing with this kind of cash. Maybe the receipts from a business. No, that wouldn't make sense; they wouldn't be all hundreds. Maybe the guy's life savings that he'd been hoarding for years under his bed.

More likely something illegal, I speculated.

I pulled myself across the seat and tried to determine one last time if he was alive or dead. I even put my hand on his shoulder and shook him. He didn't move. I spotted a cell phone in his lap and picked it up. There was a phone number and a partially written text on the screen. "Heading back wi—"

Heading back with *what*?

Heading back with the cash, of course. What else would it be? The message hadn't been sent. On a hunch I looked for the time of that last entry: 6:41 P.M. It was 6:44 now. He'd probably been about to text that when the deer bolted out in front of him. That's why he couldn't control his car. Something that every father begs his own son or daughter not to do . . .

I put the phone back.

It was clear there was nothing I could do for him. The EMTs and the police would be here any second. The engine continued to smoke; I realized I'd better get out of

21

there. I pushed backward on the passenger seat and my eyes landed once again on the open satchel of cash.

In business, I'd made a dozen deals for this amount of money, but I'd never actually seen so much in cash. At least, not staring directly up at me. It might have been only an instant in actual time, but yesterday's events came flashing back to me: losing my job; the four-weeks' severance; how I'd had to beg for an extra month on the health plan. And how the past couple of years were such a struggle . . .

Then *this* . . . Enough to take care of so many things: Brandon's school, which was five months past due; a good chunk of my payments on a house that was now completely underwater. Even help my folks. Life-changing money for me. I'd never done a bad thing in my life. I mean, maybe smoked a little pot back in college. Stolen a book or two out of the library. But nothing like this.

Nothing like what was suddenly racing through my mind. *You must be crazy to even be thinking this, Hil . . .*

Suddenly the guy called from back up on the road. "They're on the way!" I still couldn't make him out through the brush. "I'm coming down."

Everything I'd been raised with, every code I lived my life by, every voice of conscience inside me told me just to let it sit. I didn't know who it belonged to. It could be gambling or drug money for all I knew. Possibly even traceable. Whatever it was, it damn well wasn't mine.

I just stared.

Then I felt my blood begin to surge. The guy was dead. Who would ever know? If I just got the hell out of here, didn't take it with me now, but maybe hid it, then came back another time? I'd gone to a few Al-Anon meetings with a friend back in my twenties, and I remembered this role-playing game they used, on how easy it was to slide back into past behavior—in one ear, there was the addict side, to whom they gave the name Slick, and in the other, the person's rational side. Slick, seductively whispering in your ear like the devil: "Come on, you can handle it; no one will know; it'll just be this once." On the other shoulder, your conscience countering, "*You'll* know. This will only be the start of something bad. Once you do it you'll never go back."

We all have a Slick inside, the exercise was meant to show.

And it all just caught me at a point when my life was crawling on this teetering sheet of ice. And I saw Brandon there, all the good work he had done taken away, on that ice with me, about to split into a hundred pieces beneath my feet. And nowhere to go but in. Into the black, freezing water.

And I'd been there before.

"*Shit*," I heard the guy cry out on his way down, sliding in the wet brush as I had.

23

"Be careful!" I yelled back. "It's dangerous."

If you're going to do it, you have to do it now, Hilary.

In that moment there was no offsetting argument or rationale. Not that it was someone else's money. Nor that it didn't belong to me. Or whether it was legit or dirty.

There was just Brandon. And the fear that I no longer could take care of my son. I didn't see it as right or wrong. Only that fate had given me a way out. And I had to take it. My heart felt like it was beating at a hundred miles per hour.

I zipped up the bag and lifted it out of the car. I hesitated a last second, almost hoping that the guy on his way down would suddenly appear and the decision would be out of my hands.

But he didn't.

I took the bag and hurled it as far as I could deep into the woods. I prayed it wouldn't be visible when it landed—sitting up there like a fucking neon arrow was pointing to it, and I'd have to admit to the police what I'd done. But it landed about ten yards in amid a thicket and disappeared into a clump of brush.

It was done.

The other motorist finally made it down. He seemed in his fifties, in a sports jacket, striped shirt, and loosened tie. As if he was on his way back from a hard day at the office. He had a flabby, ruddy face with thin, reddish hair combed over a bald spot.

24

"You were right. You could kill yourself getting down here." Wide-eyed, he focused on the wreck and then the driver. "*Shit*," he whistled, "*is he . . .?*"

"I think so. I tried to get at him, but he's completely wedged in. I couldn't even open the door. Not that I could have done anything anyway. He was already gone." I nodded toward the engine. "I think we ought to back away . . ."

"I think you're right. The police said someone will be here soon. I saw the deer up there. It took off into the woods."

The police. At the sound of the word, I felt my heart start to patter. If they found me here, I'd be a witness; I'd have to leave my name. There'd be a record that I'd been first on the scene. If the money was ever reported missing, it would lead right back to me. I glanced at my watch. Four minutes had elapsed. Others driving by might see our cars and stop to help.

"Listen . . .," I said, hesitating.

"*Rollie*," the guy said, pushing his hair across his brow. "McMahon."

"Jeanine," I said, in a moment of panic, knowing I needed to say something, so I came up with my middle name. "Rollie, I know this is crazy, but I really have to get out of here. I'm already late to pick up my son. He's in this basketball league. The cops will be here any second and, you know how it goes, they'll have me tied up for an hour. You said you saw the deer . . ."

25

He nodded. He seemed to think it over for a second, a round-shouldered, amiable dude. "I guess you're right. No worries. I'll wait for them. You can go on ahead."

"Thanks." I blew out my cheeks. Realizing that every second I remained here might get me in a load of trouble. "You're a lifesaver.

"Shit . . ." I looked at the body and grimaced at the choice of words.

"You ought to leave me your info though," he said. "In case the police want to contact you."

"You're right. I'll leave my card on your car. Under the windshield wiper. That okay . . .?"

He nodded. And glanced back at the wreck. "Like you said, it's not like there's much we can do for him anyway."

"I'm really sorry to run out like this." I looked at the dead guy one last time.

"Go on. Go get your kid," he said. "Raised three myself. I know what it's like. I'll wait here."

I waved thanks and hurried back up the slope, feeling like hell that I'd taken advantage of such a nice man.

On the street, a car going in the other direction slowed to see what was going on. I averted my face and waved him on like everything was okay.

Suddenly I heard the wail of a siren from behind. I turned and saw flashing red and blue lights through the trees, heading my way. *Shit.* I hurried to my car, climbed in quickly, and started it up. For a last second I questioned whether I should stay. Admit what I'd done now. Anyone might have been tempted. Probably nothing would even come of it.

I heard myself say inside that I could always follow it up. I could track it and see if the money was ever reported missing. And if it did end up rightfully belonging to the guy, I could send some kind of note, anonymously, to his family, about where it could be found. They'd be happy to get it back. No one would even have to know what happened. Or care, ultimately.

Right?

The siren grew louder.

I pulled away just as the police car came around the bend. I accelerated and looked back at it in the rearview mirror as the police car slowed.

A hundred yards ahead, I passed a poster on an electrical pole. An election poster that hadn't been taken down. BRENNAN FOR CONGRESS. In bold underneath his photo, COMMITMENT. INTEGRITY.

If I ever needed to come back, I could use it as a marker.

This time, Slick won out.

CHAPTER THREE

Jim and Janice lived in a colonial on a couple of acres with a pond in back.

Janice's house actually, whose CFO ex-husband had come through for her slightly more supportively than mine had for me.

Clearly, Janice had gone in the opposite direction when it came to Jim, who was, at heart, a big-shouldered, over-grown teenager. The truth is, there's not much *not* to like about him: he's always happy, usually finds the fun in life; always the last one to ever figure out that anything's actually gone wrong. Other than maybe he's way more of a dreamer than he is a provider, and a little light on the scale when it comes to family responsibility.

I met him when he'd just turned a couple of torn-down sixties ranches into brick and glass McMansions at the height of the housing boom. He took me sailing to Nantucket and up the coast of Maine on his motor-cycle, things I'd never done in my life, having grown up in the Bronx and majored in cultural anthropology at NYU. He was kind of a furry brown bear to me; that's even what I called him—Bear. No one I knew ever understood the match.

There was nothing particularly acrimonious about our split. We just grew apart. We still remained friendly mostly. I didn't even mind that as his business declined, the alimony and child support payments gradually petered out. It was just Jim being Jim, in my view, until he got back on his feet. The thing that was hard to swallow was how he seemed to enjoy being a dad to Janice's boys a lot more than he did to Brandon, who tried hard when it came to sports, but let's be honest, we were talking a different league. Janice's kids played squash and did moguls. At Milton Farms, the varsity basketball team was co-ed.

Not to mention, I didn't come with a couple of mil in the stock portfolio . . . And her kids didn't beat their heads against the wall until they turned blue when you took away their Xbox.

I pulled into the driveway and noticed the gleaming blue new Carrera parked in front of the garage. Jim's old Targa was like a relic compared to it. I parked, still reeling a bit from what had just happened on the road. Jim must have heard me drive up because he met me at the door on the wide front porch with his arms wide, as if I was bringing the beer to a Super Bowl party. "*Hey, Hil . . .*" He shot me that walruslike, everything's-cool-here smile through his thick brown mustache. "You're sure looking nice."

"Thanks." He put a hand on my arm, and we stood there awkwardly before he leaned in and gave me a kiss. "Thanks for letting me come by."

"Come on in." He was in painter's pants and beat up Cole Haans. He looked like he'd added an extra ten pounds. "You sounded anxious. The boys are upstairs doing homework. Pinot . . .?"

I would have loved a glass of wine. Shit, a couple of them would have gone down smoothly about now. My heart still hadn't calmed a beat. "No, it's okay," I said. "Thanks." I didn't want to be any more relaxed than I had to be.

"Come on in the study." He shuffled through the foyer that had a perfectly polished Biedermeier table and antique candelabra, framed pictures of the boys and Janice.

Who suddenly appeared as if on cue from the kitchen. Her blond hair in a short ponytail, in a form-fitting fuchsia lululemon yoga outfit, holding one of the boys' crested Brunswick jackets. "Hil . . ."

"Hi, Janice. Been a while."

"It has." She came over and gave me a kiss. "Sorry the place looks like it does . . ." I noticed a couple of suitcases at the bottom of the stairs. "The kids are on break Friday if we can get through exams and squash practice, and then we're headed out to Vail." She blew out a weary breath and wiped her brow as if she'd been shoveling the driveway. "Crazy, right?"

Other than the suitcases, the place looked like it was being photographed for *Architectural Digest* in the morning. And it was nice of her to frame so vividly how differently our lives had vectored. Brandon and I had gone to Epcot in Orlando two springs ago.

"Yeah, crazy."

"Well, I'll let you two go over whatever it is you're here to discuss . . . ." As if she had no clue in the world about what that might be or why I would be here. "How's Brandon, by the way?"

"He's actually doing great, Janice. Thanks. He's almost caught up to grade level in math and you ought to see what he's drawing these days. The place has really had such an amazing effect."

"That's so inspiring. We'll have to have him for a weekend when we get back."

"I know he'd love that," I said. Actually he'd hate that. He always felt like an outsider, unable to compete with her boys at almost anything. And over the past two years, those invitations had become fewer and fewer, always revolving around the boys' sports practices and family trips. Jim rarely even showed up at school on parents' day anymore.

Janice held up the jacket and sighed. "Doesn't anyone ever hang things up around here . . . Always nice to see you, Hil. Let's be in touch."

"C'mon," Jim, said, mercifully pointing toward the study, "let's go in here."

We went down a step into the sunken wood-paneled room with a brass-hearth fireplace that looked like something out of a Martha Stewart catalogue. The wall with the windows was painted a textured green, with two brass sconces bracketing each window. In between them hung a painting of a guy in an ornate Chinese robe with a Fu Manchu mustache down to his waist.

"Janice's side of the family?" I asked. Truth was, I couldn't find a single trace of Jim in the entire house. Except maybe in the back, in the McMansion of a play shed he had built, where I knew they kept a couple of small ATVs for the boys to race around the pond, the lacrosse nets and sticks, the pool rafts.

"Distant cousin." He chuckled. "You never met?"

"Somehow, no . . . Of course we didn't get invited to the wedding . . ."

"C'mon, Hil, you didn't drive all the way up here to take shots at me. Anyway, you sounded worried on the phone." He leaned forward, his beefy forearms on his knees. "You want to tell me what's up?"

"Listen, Jim, something's happened. I need to go over a few things with you."

"Brandon?" He actually sat up and seemed concerned.

32

"No, Brandon's fine. He's doing multiplication and division now. Everything's going real well. And you should see his artwork. He's doing amazing things, Jim. I think he's got a real talent."

"That's really good. I know I should come and see it. I mean to. It's just I'm always—"

"Look—I know he's not exactly the son you've always wanted. He's not exactly someone you can take boogie boarding at the beach or out to the driving range like Lucas and Trey. Though God knows he does try. But now I need some help, Jim. I don't know if I can cover the costs any longer. At Milton Farms. I'm four months behind in tuition and next year is coming up. I can't keep going back to Neil and Judy. They're getting on. Dad's starting to go downhill. They survived the storm okay, but they're underwater on a couple of big boats. They kind of zigged when the rest of the world zagged . . ."

"Guess I know how what feels like," he said with a glum smile.

"Anyway, they're gonna be needing whatever they have for themselves. And you're Brandon's father, for God's sake—" I gazed around.

Jim's eyes drooped guiltily and he sat back, the cat out of the bag now, as if it was ever really in. "I'm sorry about Neil. No one likes to hear that."

"Thanks. I appreciate that. My dad always liked you."

He folded his thick fingers in front of his face. "You know I had to close up Double Eagle, don't you, Hil?"

33

Double Eagle was his construction business. "No, I didn't. I'm sorry, Jim."

"I was gonna call you about it. Then I figured, *hell* . . . you'd probably just think I was trying to wriggle out of another check."

"I'm really sorry to hear that. I know that company was a big part of you."

I thought back to those early years when he was making three, four hundred grand a house, several times a year, much of which long ago went down the drain in the financial meltdown, the houses sold at a loss or borrowed up to the hilt against. "But, Jim—look at how you live. I need some help now. You can't hide behind that anymore."

His toothy smile turned downward. "I don't have to tell you the story here, do I, Hil . . .? Look, I understand how most of this has always fallen on you. I know you've had to change your life. And, no BS here, I admire you for what you've done. I do. It's just that right now . . . you're bringing in a helluva lot more than me." He snorted cynically. "Right now the UPS man is bringing in a helluva lot more than me."

"Well, as of the other day"—I fixed my eyes on him— "that's all changed."

"What do you mean, changed?"

I told him about Cesta and Steve having to cut things back. That I basically got four weeks' salary and a month on the health plan. "I'm behind on everything, Jim. We were basically living check to check the past year as it was. Now . . ."

He nodded, his mustache curling into a frown. "I'm really sorry, Hil. That sucks."

"It does suck. But that doesn't make anything go away. I've cut back on a hundred things over the past few years to keep everything together for Brandon and me. I hoped we had some equity still in the house, but there's zero in the current market. I had it appraised. The whole thing's underwater, which, let's face it, is pretty much how you left me. And anyway, what would be the chance of refinancing now with no job even if there was something to pull out? I've been working full time, putting everything toward our son, while you're what, zipping the kids off to squash practice in that new Porsche I saw outside . . ."

He rubbed the back of his hand across his mouth. "That's a little cold, don't you think, Hilary?"

"No. No, it's not cold, Jim. Look, I'm sorry . . . I know it's hard to close the company. I know it's like closing a chapter on yourself, an important one. I get that. But it was no picnic for me getting fired and seeing the past four years go up in smoke. My savings are shot, Jimmy. You're Brandon's father. This isn't about my fucking shoe allowance or jetting down to St. Barth's for my tan . . . Jim, I need you to stand up. I don't have anywhere else to go."

I was trying to hold it together. Promising myself not

to cry or let my emotions come through. But my eyes started to sting and there was no way of holding them back. "I can't go it alone anymore. I tried."

Jim reached over to the side table and pulled out a couple of tissues from a quilted Kleenex box. He handed them to me.

I dabbed at my eyes. "Thanks."

"So how much we talking about?" he asked. He leaned back on the couch.

"I don't know . . . The school alone is close to fifty grand. I'm so behind on the tuition plan they're starting to give me calls. There's still the mortgage and the taxes . . . Look, I see you have a new family and I'm happy for you. I am. But I have *my* family. And you're his father, Jim. I'm going to do whatever I can to do what's best for my son. *Your* son . . . Whatever that is."

His gaze grew a little harder. "Just what do you mean by that, Hilary . . .?"

"I don't know what I mean. I'm just asking you, please, don't make me beg."

We were kind of face-to-face, the tears cleared, my desperation out on the table. All of a sudden I could see what was turning through his mind. What must have been from the moment I called, because what other reason could there have been for me to ask to come over?

He'd have to go to Janice. He probably didn't have a dime apart from her anymore.

He probably didn't even own the Porsche parked in front of the house.

"Look. He cleared his throat. "Things aren't exactly rosy around here either."

"What does that mean, Jim?"

He shrugged. "Janice had to take a job. She's gotten her real estate license. At Pepper Loughlin's place. You know, it's on the avenue, where that stationery place used to be . . ."

I stared blankly.

"In fact, the whole damn house is up for sale. Trust me, her divorce settlement is just about enough to keep the kids in school and take care of our nut. Even the furniture's up for sale." He nodded to Fu Manchu. "Distant cousin on the wall included. And the fancy table out front, what's it called, Biedemeister, or meier? I never know. That as well."

"Jim, you're on your way out to Vail."

"Kind of like our last hurrah." He snorted. "I mean, you can't let the kids think things are bad. Not in this town anyway. You know what I mean. I'm tapped out, Hilary. The well is totally dry. Trust me, that Porsche won't even be in the driveway when we come back."

I felt a weight crashing through my chest. An elevator falling. The thought snaked through me that if I stayed here even a minute longer, everything would come crashing down and I'd start to cry. "All I'm asking for is what you owe me. Don't you even care about your son? Can't you—"

Suddenly the boys ran in. Lucas and Trey, Christopher Alexander III. Like marauding outlaws in *The Wild Bunch* riding through a Mexican town, except with Brunswick crests on their dress shirts. "Trey won't give me the Xbox stick," Luke, who was ten, whined. "And he called me a *douche*. Didn't you, Trey?"

"No, I didn't! *He's lying!*" Trey said defiantly, with a glare that read, *When we get back upstairs, you're dead, you traitor.*

"You know Hilary," Jim said, catching Luke by the arm. "Brandon's mom."

"Hi," Trey said, barely shifting his glare from his brother. "*Douche bag,*" he mouthed silently.

"Hi," said Luke, not even looking at me, just sticking his tongue out at his brother while in Jim's hulking grasp.

"Hi, guys," I said. "You're both getting so big . . ." All I could think of under the circumstances. I couldn't believe I came up with something so lame.

"I'm sorry, Hil." Jim shrugged, his expression hapless. "I hear things are starting to pick up in some places. Maybe I can start up again next year."

"Sure," I said, standing up, trying to hold it together. "Next year."

"Hey, dudes." Jim cackled. "Homework done? Time for one last game of Madden?"

"*Yay!*" the two shouted as one.

"C'mon, Jim, I'll take you both on. You and *douchie* here . . ."

Jim stood up too, carrying Luke like a sack of wheat with those ham-hocklike arms. "I'm really sorry about the job, Hil. How about I'll be in touch when we get back. Okay?"

"Don't worry about it. I can see you've got your hands full. Something will come up. Always does, right?"

I picked up my bag and made my way to the door.

"*Hey, Hil . . .*"

I turned, praying inside he'd had some change of heart and come to his senses; some realization of what he was putting me through.

Jim winked, holding Luke upside down. "You're looking good, Hil. You really are."

I knew if I didn't get out of there now, I was going to cry.

CHAPTER FOUR

Back in my car, any semblance of control completely broke down. Tears filled my eyes even before I put the key in the ignition. I could take the whole new family thing—Jim playing *über*dad—even though it did eat at me where the hell he'd been for the last four years with Brandon. I could even take the spanking-new Porsche, which alone would have paid a couple of years of tuition.

What I couldn't take was that he'd basically just washed his hands of us. When he could see I was falling. *How could you just look at me and say that, Jim?* I put my head against the wheel and shut my eyes. *About your own son?*

It was clearly all on my shoulders now.

I started the car and it took everything I had not to ram it headfirst into Jim's Porsche and leave it a mound of crumpled steel. I backed out of the driveway and almost made a U-turn a block away, then regretted that I hadn't.

You could sue his ass, Hil, I said to myself as I drove. There were deadbeat laws. No judge in the world would side with him. But I knew Jim's assets in his own name might even be less than mine. He was probably down to his ski jacket and a pair of Cole Haans.

And that would all take time. And lawyer's fees. Money I didn't exactly have right now. Even if there *was* something left to take. Whatever was left was surely now in Janice's name.

What I had to do was figure out how to get through the next two months.

I put the radio on, 1010 WINS news. A Pakistani minister had been blown up in a suicide attack. Residents of Staten Island were still angry over delays in storm relief. Something about a Connecticut politician whose wife had tragically drowned on a family vacation in South America. I winced, suddenly aware of my own blessings. Whatever I was going through, at least Brandon was healthy and alive.

It was 7:36. I'd promised Elena I'd be back by eight. Two things were going around in me.

First, that I would do anything for my son. Anything. Whatever it took.

Any mother would.

And the other, my mind drifting to the satchel in the

woods, was that I'd already made enough bad choices that had put me in this situation.

So what was one more?

Which was basically what I was dwelling on when I realized I'd already driven past the highway and was headed back toward the accident site.

As I got near, the road narrowed to a single lane, yellow police tape now marking off the site. Three county police cars and a tow truck were there, all kinds of lights flashing.

I slowed. I couldn't see if the Honda had been removed. It seemed that it hadn't. I figured there had to be all kinds of people getting things together down there. With everyone traipsing around, who knew if the satchel hadn't already been discovered?

Who knew if now they were looking for the person who had flung it there?

I went over what I'd told Rollie. *"I'm Jeanine . . ."* That was all. No Hilary. No last name. I knew I'd touched a couple of things—the car doors, the victim's cell phone—but even if they were able to remove my finger-prints, they certainly weren't anywhere in the system. Nerves suddenly wormed their way through my stomach on whether, if it came to it, Rollie could have ID'd my car.

No. I was sure. I'd parked a ways down the road.

I felt pretty safe.

Which didn't completely eliminate my fear that the

part of the county police force that wasn't currently on site here would be waiting for me at my house.

They weren't. Though I did let out a sigh of relief as I drove up the cul-de-sac Jim had developed and into my driveway. Only Elena was there, putting on her coat when she heard me come in through the kitchen door.

"How was he?" I asked, coming in from the garage.

"Eezy tonight, missus." Her English wasn't exactly the best, but she was devoted to Brandon and indispensable to me. Not to mention that my son adored her. "Heez in the bed." She grabbed her bag. "I be in tomorrow at ten. And don't worry, I pick him up at school."

"Elena . . ." I was trying to decide how I should tell her. That I was going to be around for a while. That I had no idea how long I could keep her on, with her present hours. She was like part of the family to me.

"*Sí*, missus . . .?" She looked at me with those round, trusting eyes.

"Nothing. I'll probably be here in the morning, okay?" I knew there had to be some kind of explanation. "Drive home safe."

She smiled brightly. "Good night, Miz Cantor."

I closed the door behind her and went through the large brick-and-glass neoclassic Jim had constructed, which was now buried in debt. I had tried to refinance it for years and pull out whatever equity I still had in it, but with home prices still down and Jim's credit a mess, it simply wasn't in the cards. Since Jim's name was still on the note, he was supposed to pick up half of the $1.6 million, interest-only debt, $4,290 a month, a parting gift from the days when lenders were throwing loans at his business. Even though rates had dived in the past year, now I'd have to disclose that I no longer had a job and that Jim's company had closed. God only knew what workout committee *that* would put me in. I was scared I could lose the house. In today's market, the place might go for only 1.6, $1.7. The truth was, I couldn't leave and I could no longer afford to stay. As it was, I was only praying that some loan officer wouldn't be reviewing the loan and call me to tell me they were foreclosing.

"I'm home, Brand!" I shouted into his room. "I'll be up in a minute . . ."

I went up to my bedroom. High ceilings, a Palladian window overlooking the pool. Which last year I didn't even open in order to save on the cost. I pulled off my sweater and jeans and threw on the pajama bottoms and yoga T-shirt I usually crawled into bed with. In the bathroom, I pulled my bangs into a scrunchie and took off my makeup. I had short brown hair, a small nose, and wide hazel eyes that I worried were starting to show the strain of everything. I was only thirty-six, had always been told I was pretty, Natalie Portman pretty. But my days of wishing for some handsome knight were over. Everything was all in my hands now.

44

I went into the kitchen and put on some water for tea, then back down the first-floor hall to Brandon's room. He was curled up in his bed, playing on his iPad. A design app called FLOW, which always intrigued him, muttering, "*Tie, tie, tie, tie . . .*" to himself, which he often did when he was in his own world.

"Hey, guy." I sat on the corner of his bed.

He didn't answer, just kept swirling the colorful arrows on the app with his index finger.

"Cool design!" I curled up on the bed next to him.

I always said there were two of him: Sweet Brandon and Mean Brandon. Mean Brandon was where he would say to people who were averting their eyes, "I want to cut off your head." No matter how many times I took him aside and scolded him, telling him that it was totally inappropriate. When he was four we had a dog, but I had to get rid of it because Brandon once tried to cut off its tail.

There was a time a few years back when I was really worried about him. Who he was inside. Who he would grow up to be. I'd read about these children with what they called C-U tendencies. Callous and unemotional. Kids who seem to carry the gene or the early dispositions that turn them into psychopaths. At times Brandon showed some of the signs. I read about things like the Child Psychopathy Scale and the Inventory of Callous-Unemotional Traits and the Antisocial Process Screening Device. In a particularly defiant stage, I even had him tested. But when everything was in, Brandon tested within only one standard deviation from the norm. Nothing to worry about, I was told.

Sweet Brandon won out.

"*Tie, tie, tie, tie, tie . . .,*" he droned to himself. I leaned down and stroked his hair.

Then all of a sudden: "Where were you?"

At times his questions seemed to come from out of nowhere.

"I was just out, hon. On some business." No chance in the world I would tell him that I was with his dad. "What'd you do tonight?"

He didn't answer, just kept swirling his finger around on the screen, making his squiggly designs. "I heard you tried to teach Elena how to play."

No response. Only a shrug.

"How did that go?"

He just kept swirling. "She doesn't even know what an app is, Mom."

"You remember, I didn't either not too long ago. Any homework?"

"Some math. And I had to do some sentences. They were boring."

"Well, one day you'll realize that what seems boring now is when you actually learn something . . ." He didn't look up and this time I couldn't even blame him. I couldn't believe I'd actually said something that trite and parental. I laughed at myself inside.

Once I came home and found him playing happily in the tub. These clumpy brown objects, floating amid the suds. At first I thought they were just some plastic toys he'd brought in. Until I realized in horror what it was. Feces. Brandon's own. He was smeared in it, having the time of his life. He could also beat his head against the wall if he didn't get his way. And bite his nails down until they bled. Luckily, a lot of this was in the past.

Before Milton Farms.

Now most of the antisocial behavior seemed to be under control.

"C'mon, let's climb into bed," I said, taking the iPad away, praying that he wouldn't grab for it back and act up. I couldn't handle that tonight.

But tonight he was Sweet Brandon.

He said, "I did a drawing. Wanna see?"

"How about I look at breakfast tomorrow? Right now it's late."

"I want to show it to you." He jumped out from under the covers, went over to his desk, and brought back his sketchbook. He could draw anything. He had a gift. He just saw things that way. The sketchbook was basically filled with the same kinds of drawings. Monsters and underworld creatures that looked as if they had crawled out of someone's ghoulish imagination. Mean Brandon, maybe. At first I was concerned. With how he acted sometimes and what was clearly going on in his imagination. It was all pretty dark. And always the

47

same things: these creatures. But the doctors all said it was just a sign of a fertile imagination and not to worry. This one had a horse's snout, the extended ears of an elf, two legs, scaly skin, and malevolent devilish eyes.

"Jeez, Brand, where do you come up with these things . . .?"

"He's called Polydragon. Someone at school said my brain is in another dimension."

"You're not in another dimension, Brand . . ." I took the sketchbook and laid it on the table, wrapped the covers back around him, and cuddled closely. "You're here. With me. I know that *I'm* not in another dimension. So you can't be either. Sorry, dude. Maybe once you could draw a picture of the house. Or me."

"I guess I could," he said. "But that would be boring."

I snuggled close to him. "Not to me."

He smelled so sweet, the purity of everything that I imagined was good in his soul, that would one day come out. For years he barely uttered a word. He'd ask for things by pointing; he wouldn't let go of crayons or Magic Markers. He'd simply grunt, cry, or babble gibberish. We didn't know what was going through his head. Then one day Jim and I had the TV on, and I said, "I wonder what's on next." And from out of nowhere Brandon blurted, "*CSI: Miami*, Mommy." We turned, flabbergasted, sure that this would open up a new chapter in our lives.

It was six months before he spoke another word.

Now look at him, drawing, holding a conversation. How could I possibly tell him he might lose it all: his school, his tutors? The only home he'd known.

"Do you ever think of going away?" I asked him, squeezing my arm around him over the sheets.

He shrugged. "I like it here."

"I know you do. I like it here too. I just meant, if you *could* go somewhere else, somewhere new. Different. Where do you think it would be? The beach? Like in California. Or the mountains? You remember we went skiing once."

He paused a while and closed his eyes, and I thought he had drifted off. Then he opened them again. "The North Pole."

"The North Pole? Wow. That's interesting. Why there?"

"That's where the Polydragons live. Underneath the ice."

"Oh, I see . . ."

He nodded into my chest, his voice growing sleepy. "But I don't want to go away, Mommy . . ."

"We won't," I said softly. "It was a silly thing to even ask. I like it just fine here too. With you."

"Me too," he said, closing his eyes.

He yawned and I felt him snuggle his face in my chest. "Nighty-night, Brandon."

He didn't speak for a while, and I stroked his hair, a tear rolling down my cheek. This is what I had, I realized. *All* I had. This is what God gave me to protect, to keep safe. To help grow into a whole person so he could one day go out into the world and prosper, which I was sure he would. This wasn't his fault. He didn't choose how he was. Life did. And I wasn't going to let life set us back. With whatever options I still had.

Brandon's voice trailed off one last time. "I love you, Mommy . . ."

I drew him close, knowing what I had to do. "I love you too, honey."

Sweet Brandon.

CHAPTER FIVE

Charles Mirho nursed a bourbon at the end of the bar in Stamford, Connecticut, waiting for the call that never came.

He was supposed to have heard back by nine. That would have given the old man time to get back home and do what he had to do.

But now it was ten fifteen and the phone still hadn't rung; the two calls he had placed back to him from his throwaway phone had gone unanswered. He was starting to feel pretty certain something had gone wrong.

That or he was being set up—and not even a fool would do that.

Even an old fool.

The local news was on the TV. Something about a

51

four-year-old who had fallen out of an apartment building in Stamford.

It left two options, and either one meant he was going to have to earn the money he was being paid. Mirho had spent three years as a sergeant in the military police before moving into intelligence. His specialty was interrogations. He was the guy they brought in when all the "new age" shit didn't get anywhere. Not that that assignment lasted long. A couple of drunken brawls and a messy sexual harassment charge got him a general discharge, hastening his new career. Now he was in private practice. With one highly notable but confidential account. His new specialty was digging up dirt on people. Or creating it when there was none.

Though there was always something, if you pulled up the rock and looked under.

Mirho tossed a twenty on the counter, and had gotten up to leave when something on the overhead screen caught his eye.

A car accident. By the looks of it, a bad one. It was the headline that grabbed him.

FATAL ACCIDENT NEAR BEDFORD
IN WESTCHESTER COUNTY

He stopped and said to the bartender, "Mind turning that up, Al . . ."

"An old-model Honda, with only the driver inside . . ." was what he heard.

Then the camera zoomed in on the car and Mirho realized things had just gotten a whole lot more complicated.

In the parking lot, his cell phone rang. Mirho glanced at the number. Only one person it could be. He answered, not relishing how it would go. "Mirho here."

"Do we have it?" the caller asked. Mirho was supposed to have gotten back to him by now as well.

"No, not yet." Mirho sighed. "There's been a complication."

"What do you mean by 'complication'? You met with him, didn't you?"

"I met with him," Mirho acknowledged. He'd worked for a lot of tough men in his day. But this was one who knew how to use the hammer. Someone you didn't want to be feeding excuses to.

He laid the whole thing out for him as best he could.

"So where's my money, Charlie?" his boss replied indifferently.

"I don't know, maybe in a police station somewhere," Mirho said, until something else occurred to him. "Unless someone got there first."

"Someone got there first? Well, that wouldn't be good for business, would it, Charlie?"

Mirho opened his car door. "Or for them."

"Find that money, Charlie. And more important . . ."

"I know what's more important," Mirho said.

But just to make sure, the caller added, "More important, you find me the rest of what we're looking for as well."

Mirho's father, an oil lease salesman from East Texas, always had a saying that selling didn't even begin until the customer said no. In this trade, it was more like it wasn't work until something went wrong.

Mirho shut his door and started up his car. "That's what you pay me for."

CHAPTER SIX

The next day I started sending out e-mails to see what might be out there for me. The first was to Steve, my ex-boss, reminding him to keep his antennae up as he had promised. How Brandon and I were in a real bind. Then I started sending them to people in the industry. Some had already heard and were shocked; others offered to help. Finding a new job was Priority Number One.

I tried to put the accident and the money out of my mind.

I poked around the employment sites. Looking at openings for advertising sales managers, media planners, corporate comptrollers. Nothing seemed on the money. I envisioned crowded cattle calls for positions I was totally overqualified for. Going up against young Ivy

League grads with resumés far deeper than my own. Standing in lines at job fairs in front of junior-level human resources managers just out of school.

I pulled my old resumé up on the computer. It seemed woefully thin. I updated it for what I'd been doing these past four years, but it still had this pretty wide gap for the time when I'd just been at home being a mom. I even called the admissions director at Milton Farms, hoping I might qualify for financial aid. They loved Brandon there. They'd never let me have to pull him out.

I was told she was at a conference and would have to get back to me.

As much as I tried to ignore it, the thought of last night kept drifting back.

Taking a break, I went online to the local newspaper's site up there, the *Bedford Record Review*. I needed to know who the crash victim was. What kind of person was he? A solid citizen? Or dirty? Had I taken someone's life savings? Or a bundle of cash no one would ever even know was missing?

On the paper's website, I scrolled past articles on safety in the Pound Ridge Elementary School and one about a Bedford investor who had been bilked out of millions in an insurance scam.

There was nothing on the accident.

Sipping my coffee, I switched over to the Westchester *Journal-News*, which I knew had a daily police blotter.

The big story of the day was of a Yonkers teenager

who'd been eliminated from the TV show *The Voice*. And something about the second in a series of home break-ins in Chappaqua and Mount Kisco.

I kept scrolling down, passing over dozens of local stories, until under the heading of "More Top Stories."

Then I saw it: "Fatal Crash on Route 135 near Bedford."

My heart kind of spurted up, then became still. I told myself that whatever ultimately happened, I didn't cause what happened to take place and the only reason I'd gone down there was to help. I put down my coffee and clicked on the link.

A man, identified as Joseph Kelty, 65, of Staten Island, New York, was killed last night at approximately 6:40 P.M., when his Honda Civic, driving east on Route 135 between Bedford and Fairfield County, drove off the road and down an embankment, rolling over several times and striking a tree. Mr. Kelty was the only passenger in the car.

Sergeant Neil Polluto, of the Bedford Hills Police Department, said an eyewitness spotted a deer cross the road just before Mr. Kelty's car began to swerve. It was possible the deceased had been texting at the time of the accident. Mr. Kelty was described as a retired line maintenance manager with the New York City Transit Authority, and it was not known why he was in the area at the time of the accident.

My first reaction was relief. There was no mention of any missing money. No mention of anyone else being on the scene. I'd covered myself well.

My next thoughts were about Kelty. A retired line manager with the New York MTA. I brought back the lifeless, bloodied face. So he wasn't a criminal. A job like that paid what, I guessed only seventy to eight thousand a year? So what would he be doing carrying that kind of cash? And all the way up there? In rural Westchester.

I'd promised myself that if the money was legitimate, I'd find a way to get it back.

Fate had intervened. For both of us, I guessed. Before I decide to could keep it, I had to find out as much as I could about him.

I went back to the article.

Funeral services for the deceased are being made through Dellapone Funeral Home in Midland Beach on Staten Island.

CHAPTER SEVEN

That same day two men stood near a construction site on West Forty-fourth Street in New York City, just off Times Square.

One was large, with bushy dark hair in a black leather jacket that he wore open, as if he didn't feel the February chill. He was devouring a sausage in a bun from a nearby food cart.

The other was in a blue-and-orange New York Knicks jacket, his baseball cap turned backward.

"Seventy thousand dollars is quite a sum," the large one, whose name was Yuri, said in a heavy Russian accent. "I tell you that Sergei Lukov is patient man. He shows you restraint, out of respect for your circumstances. I think you know what I'm saying, right? But even a starving whore stays at home when her *putchko* is aching . . ."

"Meaning *what* . . .?" The man in the Knicks jacket put his back against the scaffolding.

"Meaning everyone has their limits," the burly Russian replied. Then he shrugged. "Maybe the saying was not so good."

The other man took a sip of coffee. "I think I get the routine."

"'Course you get routine. Your people invented routine, right? You probably seen this movie a thousand times. Hey—you sure you don't want one of these?" The Russian showed him the half-eaten sausage that looked small in his meaty palms. "I come all the way from Brooklyn just for these. You're missing something good."

"Thanks, but I never eat anything that would have killed me if it was alive."

Yuri furrowed his brow. "Pig are so vicious over here?"

"Boar," the man in the Knicks jacket said. *"Cinghiale* means wild boar. It's Italian."

"Oh." The Russian looked askance at what was left of his sausage and chomped another large bite off nonetheless. "Boar, huh? Anyway, you know it goes up, Thursday. Three days. Eighty thousand then. Pig or boar."

"Like the national debt." The man in the cap pointed

60

to the digital sign on a building high above them, the numbers racing. "Except with a Russian accent."

"Ha! Good one! Except is Ukraine . . ." Yuri elbowed him good-naturedly. "Back home, you could get knife in skull for that. Or radiation bath. Chernobyl cocktail, we call it. Very popular at home today. *Here*, Ukraine, Russian . . . Like pig and boar, no one knows difference. No harm, no worry, right?"

"No harm, no foul," the man in the Knicks jacket corrected him.

"Yes. Sorry my English is, how you say, work in progress." Yuri shrugged. "But my math is still good. And real meaning is, what you don't want is for this loan to become even more expensive. By that I mean you have no way to pay, so we need to collect, how you call it . . . *in trade*. Maybe at your job. I think you have strong idea what I mean by this."

The man looked at him. Neither of them were laughing now. He nodded. "I have a strong idea."

"Good. So then you know how life gets truly fucked up for a good guy like you. Where loan gets really expensive. Then it's not just money—money you can always find. It's kind of life loan, if you get what I'm saying? And you keep paying and paying. Clock never stops. Tick, tick, tick, tick, tick . . ."

"I get it," the man in the Knicks cap said.

"I know. Because people like us, once we get in your life, we don't leave so easy. We like cousin from Tbilis

61

who stays on your couch. Your wife cooks for him, mends socks, washes clothes. Then one day you come home and catch him fucking your wife on your couch. And he looks at you with pants down and says, 'Fuck are you doing here . . .?' You see my point? Like that, but whole lot worse. Anyway, I'm trying to do you good turn here. Even though I offer to buy you lunch and you turn me down. I still try to give you good advice."

"You seem to have a lot of sayings, Yuri." The man in the Knicks cap crumpled his Styrofoam cup and tossed it in a bin.

"Is true. And I have one more . . . You don't need beard to be philosopher. And I'm glad you appreciate"— Yuri chortled and elbowed the man— "because Thursday, seventy thousand becomes eighty. Then goes to ninety. Then . . ." He wiped his chin with his napkin. "Don't keep Sergei Lukov waiting too much longer." He backed away, winking, but a wink that no longer had mirth in it. More like a warning. "Because next time, pig or boar, won't make one piece of difference, understand what I mean, Lieutenant?"

CHAPTER EIGHT

It had been three months since the driving winds and unchecked tides from superstorm Sandy swept over Staten Island, battering the middle-class communities of Tottenville, Oakwood, and Midland Beach, situated along New York Bay.

A lot of us who lived in the area never fully appreciated the full impact of the storm. In Armonk, thirty miles to the north, it was mainly a wind event—downed trees and mangled power lines blocking the roads for weeks, resulting in close to two weeks without power.

The heartbreak of the Jersey shore and Staten Island seemed a million miles away.

But driving across the Verrazano-Narrows Bridge three days later and seeing the devastation for the first time, it looked to me as if the storm had just happened yesterday.

Homes along the shore were split wide open. Streets were still blocked with whatever the tides and winds had thrown around. A tanker was aground, with the famous message written on the hull: FEMA CALL ME! There were mountains of random debris. From the bridge I could see boats and cars still piled in streets and driveways like discarded toys. Power lines twisted at right angles. My mind flashed to the angry residents who appeared on the news, screaming about how FEMA hadn't even come around yet, how insurance companies were ignoring them, how they were living in cramped, remote motel rooms, unable to even gain access to their own battered homes.The rebuilding hadn't even begun.

I swung off the bridge onto Hylan Boulevard. Midland Beach was about two miles south.

Where Joseph Kelty had his home.

I was lucky to even make it to St. Barnabas's, ignoring what the GPS was telling me, searching for any street that was even open. I had to walk the last three blocks on foot. The church was on Rector Street, a few blocks inland from the demolished shore.

There was a line of people leading into the church, an old red-stone Romanesque-style structure with a bell tower. I took a seat in the back and waited while the pews filled in. Finally the organist played a hymn and people turned; the family began to file down the main aisle. I saw a nice-looking man in his mid-thirties with his arm around the shoulders of a young boy. He had to be Kelty's son and a grandson. He followed a woman who looked around my age with her husband and two kids. They took their seats. Maybe a hundred people were there. The organist stopped. Finally the priest stood up.

"O God, you are my God, I seek you,
My soul thirsts for you;
My flesh faints for you,
As in a dry and weary land where there is no water.

So I have looked upon you in the sanctuary,
Beholding your power and glory."

"We are here today to celebrate the return of our friend and neighbor Joseph Kelty to his immortal father."

A few people wept in the first rows. The priest went through his blessings and prayers, and when it was time to remember the deceased, he called Kelty "a little rough around the edges, except where it counted—in his heart and in his deeds." He called him a "salt of the earth, good-hearted man, who came into this life without much and would have left the very same way were it not for the bountiful blessings of his family he had built up."

A co-worker stepped up to the altar, a round-shouldered black man with a graying beard who introduced himself as "Carl. From the tunnels," who said, "Joe Kelty was as solid and dependable a man as any who ever worked the lines." He said he would pick up any shift when someone called in with a problem, rain or shine. "Except for his grandson Chris's birthday. We all knew *that* day, June seventh."

Several people in the pews laughed.

"And when he worked his way up to supervisor, even becoming our union rep, Joe didn't lead by bossing people around. He had a quiet way of leading by example. He'd as soon grab a pick as quickly as any of us 'tunnel rats' down there. Show you how it was supposed to be done."

Carl said they had a kind of ritual in the tunnels that when someone who had spent his life working the lines died, someone they wanted to honor, they named a section of track after him. And that "a quarter mile of the Staten Island Railway between New Dorp and Midland Beach would from this point on be known as Joe Kelty Way."

People clapped.

"'Course, only those people who work in the tunnels will ever know that." Carl laughed. "But to Joe, those were his family. After his beloved Paula, Patrick, Annette, and his grandkids. We'll miss you, man."

Carl sat down, and the man I'd noticed coming down the aisle stood up and went to the altar.

"I'm Patrick," he said—a pleasant voice, short dark hair, nice build—"in case you didn't know. And my dad was one of the quietest, most stubborn, good-hearted, but *exasperating* men I've ever known." Several people in the pews murmured their agreement. "It was hard to get a good word out of him. 'Course, it was hard to get *any* word out of him at times," he said, which drew more laughs. "That was just the way he was. Old school. He'd rather break an arm than break his word. If he told you he'd be there, he'd drive through a snowstorm for you, as he did many times when it came to his beloved MTA, to which he devoted his life. My father always said he didn't have much, and he was right. But he always gave whatever he had. When I was young, he used to drive me out to the island for CYO hockey . . . even up to Boston, and we'd ride up together in his Ford—he always bought American!—and we'd barely exchange a word on the trip. Maybe around New Haven he'd turn to me and say, 'Y'know, you shouldn'ta passed on that shot! Next time take it.' I thought we were going to have this conversation, and then he wouldn't say anything again for the rest of the trip."

A few in the crowd chuckled.

"When Mom got sick . . ." He hesitated and cleared his throat. ". . . When my mom got sick, he took early retirement and he went with her, two times a week, every week, to the clinic. It ate up a lot of his pension, certain medications, getting her home care. Anything she needed. He didn't flinch. And then it was his turn . . .

"I think everyone here knows, after the storm, even in his condition, there wasn't a person who worked harder for his neighbors. For Mrs. O'Byrne . . ." He looked

67

around for the person he was referring to. "Right, Mrs. O'B? I know she's here somewhere. Her house was devastated and he practically cleared it by himself, brick by brick. When he went to my graduation from the academy, I know that his was the proudest face in the crowd. And he *still* didn't say much!" That brought more laughter. I even found myself joining in. "But what he *did* say, what always stuck with me, was 'You're a cop now, Patrick. Be a good one.' It was exactly who he was. Right?

"And if any of you want to honor his name, you can make a contribution to the Hurricane Sandy Relief Fund. Or better, come out and volunteer and join the rest of us down on Baden Avenue. We're all pitching in to get these homes back in order. He'd love that. He really would.

"So bless you, Pop. You and Mom both. Whatever you were doing up there when you went off that road, I know it was for someone's good. But I'm sure Mom is probably yelling at you now, *'Why the hell did you even have to go up there . . .?'* " He glanced apologetically at the priest. "Sorry, Father Steve . . ." More chuckles.

"Well, you can work that out with her for eternity, Pop. Down here, bless you for who you were. We'll miss you."

He sat back down and the mass finished up. At the final hymn they wheeled Kelty's simple casket back up the aisle, the family following behind.

His son glanced appreciatively from side to side as he went past, recognizing most, shaking a hand here and there, thanking them for being there. He stopped for a second to give a hug to someone in the row in front of me.

As he passed by, he even gave an appreciative nod to me.

As I ride back home, conflict rattled my thoughts. On one hand, I felt guilty, hearing what a down-to-earth, honest guy Joe Kelty was. A guy who would rather break an arm than his word.

And I'd taken his money.

On the other hand, I didn't hear a thing about anything missing from the crash site. About Kelty having lost his nest egg or his retirement funds. No appeal to the person who had taken it to turn it back in. Patrick said his father had spent the large part of his pension on his wife, who had cancer.

So where did this money come from?

No one seemed to have any idea what he was doing up there all that way from home. With half a million dollars in cash.

A salt-of-the-earth guy, I thought, as I crossed the Verrazano-Narrows heading back to Westchester.

Still, one thing I knew:

Joseph Kelty may have been the Rock of Gibraltar to his family or in the New York City subway tunnels.

But aboveground, he was definitely hiding something.

CHAPTER NINE

Twice a week, I take a kickboxing class at a gym in White Plains in the afternoons. That Friday I wasn't exactly eager to go.

Finally I just decided that the best thing I could do for myself was to let off some steam. And there was nothing that did that better than delivering a spinning roundhouse side-kick combination into an eighty-pound bag.

I'd always kept myself fit. I grew up playing soccer and running cross-country in high school. In my twenties, I moved on to spinning and hot yoga. I took a little break when Brandon came along. But nothing I'd tried made me feel as strong or as empowered, or let out the stress when I needed it to, or built up the sweat like an hour of spinning, grunting, gut-crunching sidekicks—kicks that sprang not from my legs, but from my core, from deep inside my abdomen. I may be only five feet four and 115 pounds, but I've put my instructor, Maleak, who's cut like an linebacker, on his back plenty of times. "Damn, girl," he'd say, shaking his head from the mat, "there's a whole lot of anger in you."

"Divorce'll do that," I'd reply, helping him back up.

After class, I'd sometimes catch a latte with Robin, who was forty-five, and whose husband bailed on her five years ago while she was in the process of going through chemo treatments for ovarian cancer, leaving her with two kids in high school and a failing party-planning business. She was able to beat it, and was in remission now, and she'd somehow built her business back up after declaring Chapter Eleven. Now both her girls were in college. We'd gone out a bunch of times. For drinks or to the movies. Robin was pretty and funny, but also one of the toughest women I knew.

That day we had started talking about Brandon, and then about some guy who had asked her out, when I caught her looking at me and she finally stopped and asked if anything was wrong.

It took about three seconds for me to blurt out what was happening. Not everything, of course. But losing my job and how my finances were crashing down on me, and how desperate I was to keep Brandon in school. I'd always prided myself on being a person who could hold it together when things got tough. But I just couldn't there. In my damp tights, my hair a sweaty mess, my makeup smearing, it just all came out of me.

"You're preaching to the choir now, honey." She took my hand. "We all hit bottom, but you're a gorgeous, capable woman. And smart. I know it sounds like a cliché, but they're only clichés because they're generally right. You just have to suck it up and pull through."

"I'm sorry," I said, dabbing my eyes with a napkin. "It's all just kind of crashing down on me right now, and I haven't talked about it to anyone."

"You know what they say . . ." She grinned. "The world always looks bleakest through a double mocha latte and a Starbucks napkin. Or maybe it's at three in the morning and through a glass of vodka? I do forget."

"Is that what they say?" I sniffed in and laughed. "You mean it's not just me." I took another sip of coffee and picked at a muffin. "I can adapt to anything. But it's Brandon. I mean, what do we do, give the house to the bank, pull him out of a school that's totally making a difference in his life; file for bankruptcy . . .?"

"No. You definitely don't want to go down that road. That's your last resort."

"Without a job, I can't afford to even stay in Armonk, Robin. Even if I did put him in public school."

"Hil—" She took my hand again. "It took me six years to build myself back up. My health. My credit rating. And I'm not even talking about who I was inside. What about your ex? Can't he come to the table?"

I shook my head. "He's broke. He's closed down his business. I guess we're both broke."

"Shit—I'd call a lawyer on his deadbeat ass anyway." She chortled. "Trust me, beats kickboxing any day for getting the endorphins going."

"Jesus . . ." I blew out a sip of my latte, laughing. "Remind me not to get in your way."

"Think I'm joking? For two months, I had my girls at my sister's and I was sleeping in our warehouse," she said, her eyes fixed on me. "Getting myself to chemo twice a week. For years, who do you think it was I visualized every time I was hitting that hundred-pound bag?"

"It was hard, huh? I mean, obviously what you went through with your health . . . But the rest. Watching the life you built up around you fall apart. Losing everything you counted on?"

Robin looked at me. This time she wasn't smiling. "Killer. Hardest thing I've ever gone through. And I hope you're not looking for any fairy tale, take-home nuggets like it was all worth it in the end. 'Cause it wasn't. It sucked. You just do what you have to do. And first order of business, you protect your cubs, right? That's what drove me. I'd do anything I could for them. And I did. And you will too."

"What if there was something you could have done . . .?" I put down my cup. "Something you didn't want to do, but that you had kind of in your back pocket, that could have changed things. Changed everything. I mean, financially . . ."

"You got some rich dude who wants to marry you you're not telling me about?"

"Not even a broke one," I said. "Just if somewhere I could find some money . . ."

"Legal?"

I just looked at her.

Her eyes narrowed. "You're not thinking about putting yourself out there, are you? In that case I change what I said. Try Chapter Eleven first."

I laughed, and shook my head. "Gimme a break. Of course not, Robin."

"You'd be surprised. There're a lot of suburban moms who are finding all kinds of ways to pay for Pradas these days."

"Well, that's not me. Yet."

"Good." She took a sip of coffee and then shrugged. "Look, there's this . . . and then there's the other side of the road. I've been on both sides. And it's dark over there. Short of maybe killing someone or robbing a bank . . . I'd do whatever you had to fucking do to take care of yourself and Brandon, Hilary. No one else will."

She took a last gulp of her latte and there was only the slightest hint of humor in her eyes.

CHAPTER TEN

In terms of money, things were only getting worse. I threw myself into finding a new job. Steve Fisher knew someone in the market for an ad manager. I just hadn't done that kind of work in years. All my contacts from back then had mostly moved on or were ancient history by now.

Someone else told me about someone who was looking for an accounts payable manager for a local wine distributor. The problem was, it paid only around half of what I'd been making. Enough to pay the mortgage, but no way I'd be able to cover Brandon's school. Anyway, they were looking for someone with an accounting degree, and mine was in cultural anthropology.

I called up Karen Richards, the head of school at Milton Farms, to see if I could qualify for some financial aid. Brandon was one of their success stories and I always tried to pitch in on school events. The past two years I paid tuition on an extended monthly plan, the only way I could handle it even when I had my old job. But now I was hopelessly behind. And the spring payment months were coming up.

"Hilary, I'm afraid it's just too late for this semester. Our funds are all allocated. And to be honest, our financial support isn't really designed for your sort of situation anyway."

I hesitated. "My sort of situation . . .?"

She cleared her throat. "I'm sorry, but look at the home you live in, Hilary. Your ex-husband comes here on Father's Day driving a new Porsche. I know I don't really know what's going on, but I honestly think the best solution is to work this out with him. I wouldn't normally say this, but I noticed you're several months behind in tuition payments . . ."

"That's why I'm calling, Karen."

"Look, you know we love Brandon. We've all seen the improvements since he's been here. But this is something you need to address. I've already spoken to the tuition company. I can only keep them at bay so long. You understand what I'm saying, don't you, Hilary?"

"Yes. I understand." The vise was closing.

"We're a needs-blind school here, when it comes to aid. But I'm not sure I can run with you if this continues into next semester."

"I hear you. I'll figure something out," I said.

I told Margaret Wheeler and Eileen Pace, Brandon's social behavior and physical therapy tutors, that we'd have to put things on hold for a while.

"But he's doing so well," Margaret said, her disappointment clear. "Look, if this is what it's about, you don't need to pay me right away. We'll work something out."

Margaret was a retired special ed teacher. Her husband was a cop. Ten days ago I was bringing in more than they did together.

"Just for a couple of weeks, maybe," I said. I hugged her. "Thank you, Margaret."

I put together a balance sheet of my finances. You didn't have to have an accounting degree to see that it was bleak.

I had twenty-six thousand left in the bank, including the thirteen and change I'd received in severance. Forty-two hundred was due every month for the mortgage. And zero chance of refinancing that now. Utilities were another six hundred. Not to mention the sixty-five hundred due next month to the town of Armonk for property taxes. Jim used to pay that, like the mortgage. But no longer. If I made Brandon's school current, that left me only ten thousand.

The house payments alone would eat that up.

I couldn't go to my folks again. They owed as much in unsold boats as I had in debts and it was bleeding them dry.

I could cut the tutors, all the stuff for me I'd always fit in—mani/pedis every couple of weeks and facials every couple of months and the trips to the mall.

That was all history now.

I could cut back on Starbucks, along with eating out. I could even cut back on the barre method and my kickboxing, though sending a spinning, grunting side kick into a sixty-pound bag was about all that was keeping me sane right now.

But I saw the wave that was coming at me. Like someone in the path of a tsunami coming onshore with no chance of getting out of the way. Maybe not this month, but certainly the next. It was going to crash over me and snap me in two. Me and Brandon. Like matchsticks. And even if I did find another job, and quickly, the math still didn't add up.

I looked at the numbers and saw what any person would have seen a while ago.

Everything was falling apart.

It wasn't Slick anymore who was whispering on my shoulder.

It was survival.

Something had to change or I wouldn't last another month.

CHAPTER ELEVEN

"Jim . . ." I had to try him one more time. I had to try anything.

"Hil . . .?" His voice was cool and reserved, clearly not delighted to hear from me. "Hil, we're out in Vail. Can't this wait until we get back?"

"No, Jim, I'm sorry, it can't wait. Not any longer."

I heard him whisper to someone, an exasperated tone, like his hysterical ex-wife was on the phone and can you believe he had to deal with this out here, with ten inches of fresh powder on the slopes and an Irish coffee in his hand?

Maybe I *was* starting to grow hysterical.

"Jim, I've only got a month's cushion to my name. I don't know how I'm going to pay the mortgage. Not to mention Brandon's school. You said you'd think it over and get back to me, but all that's past. I need your help, Jim. Now. Not for me, but for your son. I don't care where you are right now . . ."

"Hil, hang on," he said. I heard him excuse himself and there were a few seconds of silence. When he got back on, he was probably outside. "Listen, Hil, I thought I told you we're pretty much in the same pickle."

"I don't care about your fucking pickle, Jim. You're out in Vail. Your pickle is keeping your wife's name in *Greenwich* magazine and holding on to your Porsche. I'm doing what I can to protect our son."

He was silent.

"Jim, look, through everything we've always dealt with things pretty reasonably. But I don't have the luxury of being nice anymore. You owe me for over a year of child support. You bailed out of Brandon's school. I can't sell the house. I won't get a fucking nickel from it even if I could. And I can't even sue you—it would take too long, even if there was something I could get from it. Jimmy, please . . . you know I don't beg easily, but I'm begging. I'm trying to save ourselves . . ."

I was also begging for him to save me from doing the one thing I didn't want to do.

"Look, I shouldn't even say this . . ." He cleared his throat. "Maybe there is something I've kept aside. But we're not talking much, Hil."

"How much is something, Jim?"

"I don't know." He paused. "Maybe five or ten thousand. Max . . ."

"Five or ten grand?" The blood pretty much stopped in my veins. The math ran over me like a train had plowed into my car. Ten thousand would barely get me past March. No more.

"I had to pay off some obligations with the company. Otherwise, I was headed to Chapter Eleven, Hil. Anything else is Janice's. And you know, that gets complicated."

"Jim, that's only a month, maybe two, of Brandon's school. I'm not asking for anything for me, but—"

"Anyway, it's going to have to wait until I come back. This isn't exactly sitting in my 401(k). And, Hil, all I can say is that this isn't going to get any easier. I know you don't want to hear this, but we really are going to have to consider putting Brandon in public school. I'm told the programs are really good up in Chappaqua and Bedford."

"Chappaqua and Bedford . . .?" The words fell off my lips like heavy weights.

"I checked. Bedford has a separate special ed school. And Ridgefield, I know that's in Connecticut, but it's good too and it's tons cheaper to live up there as well."

"Screw off, Jim." Tears flooded my eyes. I couldn't hold it back. I'd never said those words to him before.

"Hil, please . . ."

The phone in my ear, I flashed back to the day we

were married. Me, in my white lace dress, my hair in braids. Jim, nervous, clumsy, a big, cushy walrus, fumbling for the ring. I knew he wasn't the safest of bets, even back then. Just a big, overgrown boy with his toys. But what I did think was at least I had a partner. Someone who loved me for me, whether it worked out in our marriage or not. Someone who would always be there for Brandon if I ever got sick or was in need.

"Why don't you just keep it, Jim? I'll find another way."

"Hil, c'mon. I'm trying my best to—"

"Just keep it!" I hung up on him, and with it the hope that anything was coming to my rescue.

"There's this," Robin had said, *"and then there's the other side of the road."*

I threw on a jacket and asked Elena if she could stay another hour.

Then I drove back out to the accident site that night.

CHAPTER TWELVE

The night was clear, the roads mostly empty. Every stop sign, I told myself I could always turn around. *You don't have to do this, Hil. There has to be some other plan.*

I never turned.

On the Bedford–Greenwich road, the landmarks grew familiar. A stone barn I'd passed ten days before. The apple and vegetable farm. I remembered following that Honda, my life in a shambles, watching him swerve, seeing him spin off the road. I slowed, passing a bend in the road that looked familiar. *Was it here? That curve? Or farther along?*

The police tape was gone now. Everything looked back to normal.

It wasn't until I passed the election poster that I realized I'd driven right by.

I turned at the first chance about a quarter mile past it and headed back around. There was a hole in the dense brush about the width of a car where Kelty's car had gone through. I drove on about a hundred yards and found a turnoff with a chain blocking the drive and a NO ACCESS sign. Maybe for a property someone was hoping to develop.

I pulled my Acura in maybe twenty yards from the road. There was a long time between cars going by. I turned off the engine. I made a promise to myself that I wasn't going to use a penny of it for my own needs. Only for Brandon. And keeping a roof over our heads.

For a while I just sat there, telling myself that there was this one last chance to drive away. I looked at my face in the mirror. It wasn't my current face I saw, but strangely, the eyes of a child. Remembering the uncertainty I'd gone through as a nine-year-old, everything I loved and counted on ripped away in an instant.

It had taken me years to learn to trust life again.

I wouldn't let that happen to my son.

I took my flashlight, and this time my face was filled with resolve.

Welcome to the other side of the road.

CHAPTER THIRTEEN

A car sped by in front of me and I ran across the road. I found the break in the bushes and shined my light and still saw the tire marks on the pavement, fresh as if it had happened yesterday.

I made my way down the slope.

I slipped this time as well, sliding a few feet down. The brush had been flattened by the path of Kelty's car as well as all the emergency vehicles and personnel that had been down there. I made it down, casting my light on the tree where Kelty's car had ended up, now pitched at a forty-five-degree angle. I stood where I was sure I'd been when I climbed inside his car, only a bare patch now. I shined the light over the area in the woods where I had flung the satchel.

I didn't see anything there.

A flash of fear stabbed me: what if someone had found it? One of the emergency crew who went down there. Or maybe a policeman traipsing around. What if all this had been for nothing and now it was gone?

A week ago that might have given me some kind of relief. That the decision had been taken from me. But now I was more like a wolf who'd left a stash of food for her cubs that was now gone. As if that money was mine all along, not Kelty's, and someone had stolen it from me!

I started to walk through the brush, sweeping the light in all directions, knee deep in dried branches and dense weeds. I'd spent so much time conflicted. Now there was no longer any doubt about what outcome I was hoping for.

Where the hell was it?

I kept walking, casting the light about haphazardly, nerves kicking up in me. I got to the spot where I was sure it had to be. Ten days ago, I'd seen it sink there amid the leaves and brush.

"Where the hell are you?" I said aloud.

I started to think how maybe I'd made someone else rich. How I was someone else's lottery ticket. Some lucky Joe who was probably dragging a towline around. I wondered if he'd declared it. Or turned it in. If the police had it now.

No, if they did it would've made the news, Hilary. I would have seen it.

Angry, I used my light as a large stick, swatting brush

and branches. Then I almost tripped over something. I looked down and didn't see the bag, only the leather handles peeking through a blanket of leaves.

Thank God! I let out a grateful sigh of relief.

I bent, a bramble tearing at my hand, and pulled it out, the bag resisting for a moment. Then there it was! The same stuffed leather case, as heavy as when I'd hurled it into the woods a week before.

There was no pretending I felt anything but joy.

I took it back to the clearing and set it on the ground. I pulled open the zipper and shined my light in it. My skin tingled all over at what I saw. I was staring at the same bundles of wrapped bills, Ben Franklin's wise, nonjudging face over and over and over, alit in the yellow, beatific light.

My blood surged ecstatically.

"Forgive me," I said. To whom I wasn't sure.

To Kelty. To the police. To my own conscience.

"I'm sorry."

I zipped it back up, the taste in my mouth bitter and bile-like. I knew the expression, how one bad act opens the door to many others. Acts that flood the world with a hundred awful consequences you could never foresee.

All from a single mistake.

This was mine, I knew. No hiding it.

You're not just a thief, I told myself as I lugged it back up the hill.

Congratulations, Hil, you just stole a half million dollars.

CHAPTER FOURTEEN

The heavyset blond-haired clerk in the Bedford Hills police station looked up at him from her desk. "You said insurance adjuster, right?"

"Yes, that's right," Charles Mirho nodded affably.

Not that he was an insurance adjuster at all, of course. For him, the whole concept of risk management was simply about staying alive. He'd merely had the business card printed at Kinkos, one he'd used many times in his real line of work, which was mostly uncovering dirt on people who crossed his boss and kicking a little ass when it was called for. And sometimes when it wasn't. He'd simply embossed the Farmer's Insurance Group logo in bright red lettering on the front so it would look as real as if he'd passed the insurance licensing exam with flying colors.

Mirho smiled at the clerk. Maybe a tad chubby, but she had huge breasts under her pink sweater, and maybe a little too much mascara around those pretty, maybe a shade too trusting eyes. He didn't see any wedding ring.

"In the vehicular accident division," he said. "Claims subrogation. You know, two parties put in counterclaims and ultimately the two insurance mammoths go to battle and somehow it gets resolved. Boring stuff."

Except in this case, there weren't two parties at all—only one, and the one was in his grave. But Mirho figured his smile was good enough to charm her into getting what he needed. And the gal, whose desk plate identified her as Chrissie, probably wouldn't know the difference between claims subrogation and how to figure out the interest on her bank statement.

"You say you want a copy of the case file?" she said.

"That would really help me out." Mirho smiled.

"And you said the name was Kelty? Joseph."

"That's the one. You know, the guy who went off the road up here a week or so ago. Let me see, claim number, I have it right here . . ." He glanced at his notepad, but it was basically just useless scribbling. "606-410BN . . . Of course, that's *our* number, not yours. We're one of the coinsurers on his life insurance policy. I just happened to be up here on other business and thought I could save all parties a little time."

"Of course. Poor guy . . ." Chrissie exhaled

sympathetically. "That stretch of road is always a problem at night." She wheeled her chair across to a computer screen and Mirho got a glance at those wide-load thighs. He always liked women with some meat on them, and tits like calf bladders.

Chrissie punched into her computer. "Let me see what I can do."

It was a standard request; case files were routinely shared between the police and the insurers. Usually by a formal request from one of the claimants, but in this case, there was no criminal aspect to the case, only lawyers arguing against lawyers. Insurance bigwigs negotiating it out. It was no big deal.

"Found it," she said. "Officer Polluto was first on the scene."

"Polluto," Mirho said. He already knew that. "Maybe I can talk to him as well."

"Neil's out on patrol. I saw him earlier today." Chrissie punched a key. "Photocopy or PDF?"

"A hard copy would be great," Mirho said appreciatively. "This sure is saving me a ton of work."

"You, maybe." Chrissie chuckled. Her boobs jiggled as she stood up. "Be back in a flash."

Mirho winked and took a seat on the edge of her desk. He picked up the photo of two smiling teenage girls.

He knew how to manipulate people. It all started with that easy way he had, and conveying what he

90

needed without blinking an eye. Extracting information, that's mostly what he did. Rule Number One: the more brazenly you asked for something, the greater the likelihood you'd get it. Boldness created its own trust.

No dad in the photo, he thought. Maybe a single mom. Or they could be her nieces.

It took six or seven minutes, but finally Chrissie shuffled back holding a manila envelope.

"You're lucky. It's not a very large file. Otherwise you wouldn't be able to wait." She handed it to him.

"You're a gem!" Mirho knew he wasn't exactly George Clooney. He was big shouldered and large, with a round head and short shaved orange hair. A ruddy complexion. But he knew he had that smile. Women trusted him. At least they did for a while. "Maybe I'll see you next time," he said. "When something else comes up."

"Something else . . .?" Chrissie laughed. "This isn't exactly the South Bronx up here." She placed her ass back in that chair and smiled up at him. "But I'm always here."

"Then we'll just have to see about that." Mirho waved the envelope at her with a wink as he backed away.

Back in his Escalade, Mirho opened the envelope and pieced through the file. Photos of the accident—the Honda a mangled wreck. He'd watched Kelty drive away with the cash not thirty minutes before. Shit, he'd handed the fucking thing to him. The guy probably got a woodie for the first time in a decade, carrying around that kind of cash, and couldn't handle it. Popped through his pants, hit him in the face, then he slammed headfirst into a tree.

There was an eyewitness report. The police case write-up. He saw that a deer had bolted across the road. That much he'd been able to pick up from what he'd read in the papers.

Sergeant Neil Polluto, Mirho underlined in the report. Maybe it would be worth paying the good officer a visit somewhere down the line if nothing else panned out.

Only one eyewitness, Mirho noted. That made the job easy. He knew his next call might prove a bit more troublesome. But anything was doable with the right kind of persuasion.

He centered on the name, from Briarcliff Manor according to the report. The witness, the first to arrive at the scene.

The only one on the scene.

He underlined it, knowing his next stop wouldn't be quite so social.

Roland McMahon.

CHAPTER FIFTEEN

He was always a difficult child.

As a two-year-old, if he didn't want to eat something or wanted to get down, he would bang his G.I. Joe milk cup so hard, he actually shattered it once and needed ten stitches in his hand. Hardly a day would pass when he wouldn't tell me how much he hated me; a minute later he'd look up at me with the most contrite and innocent eyes and say, "Give me a hug, Mommy. You didn't think I really meant all that, did you?"

Did I?

It makes me ashamed to admit he always scared me a little. Of what he would grow into one day.

He always had a dark edge, my son, from the day he was born.

What a thing, living in fear of my own child.

Sometimes he got so angry I had to lock him in his room,

but he would only tear up his bed and rip down all the books from his bookshelves. Break his brother's toys and smash his little wooden chair against the door. A hundred times. Until he ran out of strength. And then he'd whine in that repentant voice of his that he would never be this way again.

But when he was good, he was the most lovable and likable boy any of us knew. We called him Curious George. Because he was so smart and needed to understand everything. It just seemed, somehow, his brain got ahead of his heart, his father always said.

He'll grow out of it, I would say. He will. You'll see. Just wait.

Until he left.

One day he just said he couldn't handle this anymore and I never saw him again.

Once, when he was six, I had him in the bath. It was just me then, and the two kids. Todd was just two. He had a laugh, my Todd; that boy's giggle could leave the whole family in tears.

His brother was in a good stage at that time. I grew to trust him more. Things had changed in the two years since Todd was born. I was always busy with him, feeding, changing diapers. Tickling him under his chin, trying to produce that giggle. And I had work.

His older brother suddenly had to work to get everyone's attention. The tantrums grew louder and more frequent. He was always stealing things; then somehow they would miraculously reappear. He always looked to be the hero.

I remember he was supposed to watch over Todd that day. "C'mon, Toddie," I recall him saying, "c'mon in here with me 'till Mommy gives you your bath."

I ran after some laundry that needed folding and he brought in one of Todd's favorite toys. And I heard the two of them playing in the tub. That infectious giggle.

And I remember thinking for once, that's so, so nice. Could it be he's finally growing out of it? It had been so long since he'd gone off in a big way. Maybe it was just like I always said.

And I allowed myself to imagine a world in which he was a normal boy. Where we were a regular family. Instead of living in fear and worry about the next outburst . . Always hiding things.

"Look, Toddie, it's Mr. Duckie . . .," I heard him saying. In that singsong voice he used when he wanted to be nice. The little one cooing and giggling. Water splashing.

Then after a while not laughing or giggling.

Just quiet. Damning quiet.

Then for a long time, nothing at all.

My gut told me something had gone wrong. I ran up the stairs.

"Where's Todd?" I burst into the bathroom. He wasn't there. He wasn't there. *That boy could sneak away at the drop of a dime once he learned to crawl. Fear seized up in me. "Where's the hell's your brother?"*

He merely looked up at me in the tub. "We're just playing, Mom." from

95

I saw an air bubble pop up from under the water. It took a second until it dawned on me—bludgeoned me!

"Oh my God, Todd!"

I dove to the tub, but he lifted the baby out of the water like he was a toy. "Here he is!" he crowed.

Todd was blue. At first I was sure he wasn't breathing. My worst fears rose in me. I screamed.

But then he was suddenly crying and spitting water out of his lungs.

"You're okay, you're okay, baby . . .," I said to him, patting him against my shoulder, tapping his back as water leaked out of his mouth. But he was crying and spitting, and his eyes were somehow clear. The color came back into his face. I could see he was okay.

"What were you trying to do?" I screamed, wrapping Todd in a towel, staring at his brother in the tub as if he was some kind of monster. "What kind of person are you?"

He just stared back with that innocent look of his, as if he didn't understand.

"Don't be mad, Mommy," he said. "I just wanted to see what it was like when someone drowns."

CHAPTER SIXTEEN

I stared at it for most of the night.

I put the satchel on the ottoman of the upholstered chair in my bedroom and never touched it again for the rest of the night.

I never even counted it. The money was kind of an abstract thing that part of me didn't want to admit actually existed as much as another part needed it to solve my problems. The conflict I felt in having taken it was real.

Not taken, I had to remind myself. *Stolen.*

I just let it sit, partially feeling a sense of relief. That I could breathe now; that for the time being my son could stay at Milton Farms. That I could pay the mortgage, the house taxes, and get out from under this cloud. That if I wanted to I could even help my folks get out from under theirs. I kept telling myself I'd won the lottery. That no one had actually been harmed by taking it because it was probably ill-gotten gains and no one seemed to miss it or even know it was there.

At least no one I knew, right, Hilary . . .?

But I hadn't won the lottery. I'd taken something that belonged to someone else. I was sure I'd crossed the legal line. Tampered with evidence. A foreboding crept in, like in the movies when the bass track starts to drone and the unsuspecting girl opens the back door, letting the killer in. As if the same urge to save my son had also put him in danger.

No matter how victimless it seemed. Someone would miss it.

Someone always missed it.

At some point I dozed, and in the morning my eyes blinked open. Brandon was by my bed, staring at me. "Remi wants to go out."

Remi. Our caramel-colored toy poodle. I glanced at the clock: 6:41 A.M. I'd probably only gotten a couple of hours of sleep.

"Let her out the back, sweetie," I said, and shut my eyes again. The yard was totally closed in back there. "Mommy will be up in a little while."

"You're going away?"

"No, I'm not going anywhere," I said.

Then I realized what he was talking about.

Brandon's eyes were on the satchel. My heart lurched,

praying that I hadn't left it open and he had peeked inside. The last thing I needed was him going on at school about this or to a teacher. Or worse—if it ever happened at some point—to Jim.

I shot up out of bed.

With relief, I saw that the zipper still was closed.

"No. I'm not going anywhere, sweetheart," I said, my heart regaining its normal pace. "I'm staying with you. Forever. And you're staying with me, right?"

"I guess." He just sort of nodded blankly. "I'm going to watch TV."

"Let Remi out!" I yelled after him.

As soon as he'd left, I jumped out of bed and threw the satchel in my closet. I had to find a place for it. Elena had access to all the usual storage areas and I didn't exactly need her to inadvertently come upon it either.

I grabbed a nylon ski bag from the basement, shut my door, and transferred the cash from the satchel. If I ever got caught, that leather satchel was the only thing that could tie me directly to Joe Kelty's car. An hour later, after breakfast—it was Saturday, no school—I lugged the nylon bag outside and around the back of our deck.

It was freezing. The ground was covered with a fresh layer of frost. I was just in moccasins and my robe. I opened the latticed wooden door that led underneath the deck, where we stored the outdoor furniture for the winter. I crawled inside and dragged the bag amid the chaises and pool toys—the crawl space was less than five feet high. A large red Styrofoam drinks cooler was lying next to a folded-up outdoor umbrella. I kneeled and opened the nylon bag. For the first time I started counting what I had. As I'd thought, the first, elastic-bound packet of bills contained a hundred hundreds. Ten thousand dollars! The rest all looked about the same. One by one I took them out and stacked them on the tarp next to the umbrella. I counted fifty of them. $500,000! The sight of so much money filled me with both awe and fear. Fear that I had already crossed a kind of line. Though I felt certain I'd covered my tracks well. I hadn't given Rollie my name. And he was the only one there. I was just being paranoid, I told myself. Anyone would be. Still, I packed the money back into the nylon bag and zipped it shut. I opened the cooler tub and packed it all in. Then I wedged the whole thing behind a stack of chaises and shut the top.

No one would find it in a million years.

Later I drove down Route 22 toward White Plains until I spotted a house under construction. I got out—no one around—and hurled the black satchel into the half-filled Dumpster. I was glad it was gone. I drove to a Family Discount store and bought a padlock, and when I got back secured the latticed door under my deck.

Maybe it was wrong, I thought, but the real wrong had already been committed. Over a week ago.

I didn't go back for it again for ten days.

PATRICK

CHAPTER SEVENTEEN

Patrick Kelty put down the debris-filled wheelbarrow and caught his breath against the February chill.

It had been more than three months since Sandy destroyed his family home, along with much of his neighborhood. Three months since the bay swept over Father Capodonna Boulevard that terrible night, filling up Midland Beach like a giant tub, reducing the place where his family lived to an abandoned, demolished war zone and the house he grew up in to rubble.

Three months and still no power, apart from generators. No settlement from the insurance companies; not a dime yet from FEMA to help any of them build back their lives.

It was on the way, he was told. Always on the way. Congress had just approved an aid bill. Last night it snowed and people were shivering in their homes, protected only by taping blankets over their windows to keep out the frost. Those who hadn't had their homes torn apart by the sea.

A few of the heartiest returned as soon as the waters had receded. Amid the morass of mud and bricks, cars washed into others' lots; downed trees and power lines; boats tossed around like bath toys. There was the overwhelming deflation of having everything you had in your life ruined. Every possession; every item of value; every memory, lost. Those who hadn't lost their parents or friends. No shelter or clothing against the cold.

Most of them had nowhere else to go. For weeks no one could even get near their gutted homes. Midland Beach, like Tottenville to the south, and Oceanside, was barely more than a debris-filled lake. For a week, the only way to even get around was by an inflatable raft or a small powerboat. When everything finally receded, there was nothing for the eye to see in every direction but ruin.

Patrick took a leave of absence from the NYPD. His career didn't matter now. Not as much. Everything he knew, had grown up with, traced his roots to, was in shambles. His father was in failing health and completely on his own. The rebuilding was massive and slow. And it wasn't just Patrick's home. It was the whole block, Baden Avenue. The entire neighborhood. Everything was down. Friends he'd grown up with, those he'd gone to Father Aquinas with and mass at St. Margaret Mary's; played CYO hockey and touch football with on Midland Field. All down. A lot of those who were left behind were older and couldn't fend for themselves. Like Mrs. O'Byrne. She'd lost everything. Everyone felt cold and abandoned. There were mouths to feed. The Jersey shore and the Rockaways, where that terrible fire razed a hundred homes, captured all the attention.

The world seemed to forget they were even here.

The way Patrick figured, it wasn't just homes that had been battered and destroyed. It was their lives. Everything they had all grown up with and looked at as a way of life. Their history.

Like the Giorgios two houses down, who were in their eighties and whose kids had long moved away. Or the Flynns, who bought the white Queen Anne across the street and whose son suffered from Down syndrome.

Who would help them rebuild?

Or his dad. A proud man who'd never taken more than a week off at work until the day he called it quits. Who now picked up scattered photos of his wife, their home in ruin, holding back tears. "Just feel blessed that Paula is no longer around to have to see this." He shook his head. She'd lived on Baden Avenue for forty years.

So Patrick had volunteered to come back. That had always been his way. He'd gone to Cornell on a hockey scholarship, majored in government. Then it just seemed right to join the force after he graduated, a year after 9/11. There was such a gaping hole in the world and he felt it was his calling to help fill it in just a bit. He went straight into the Street Crime Unit and not too long after, married Liz, who he'd known in college, but she didn't see life going quite the same way—the force, Staten Island—and it didn't last. A couple of years later he moved into social services as an NYPD liaison to the mayor's office, specializing in community relations. Before he left he'd been the department's point person on the controversial Stop and Frisk program.

He'd put in a solid month helping his dad, believing that by now they'd be able to start the rebuilding.

But to date, whatever had been done had been borne solely on their own backs. And money. The building department still hadn't even finalized the new requirements for how many feet homes must be raised to ensure this wouldn't happen again.

So they pretty much just cleared—their houses and their neighbors'. In place of cranes and bulldozers, they had shovels and Dumpsters. They found their own people to help pitch in: carpenters and electricians, neighbors and volunteers. Patrick watched his father age in front of his eyes—angry and heartbroken.

But mostly it was like it was today. Shoveling rubble into trucks against an endless tide of debris. Handing out blankets and food to those who remained on the street. Helping whoever needed help, like making sure

Mrs. O'Byrne's portable generator worked or that her food delivery had reached her.

Then ten days ago his dad said he had something to take care of up in Connecticut and he never came back.

It was sad. His father was a proud and lonely man who kept trying to find a reason to live without his wife or his job. Then the storm took the rest out of him. Who knew what he was even doing all the way up there? Joe had grown withdrawn and secretive over the past few weeks, and Patrick was so wrapped up with the house and helping out, maybe he hadn't paid the closest attention. His dad had made it his mission to try and help Mrs. O'Byrne, who'd lost everything. For thirty years, he and Paula and Tom and Sheila had been the closest of friends. Patrick grew up with the sight of the four of them playing euchre on Friday nights, going to Mets games, and putting their American flags out on Fleet Week when the ships sailed under the bridge into New York Harbor.

What had Mrs. O'B said when Patrick told her about the accident? "Then it was all for nothing," she said. "Nothing." Then closed the door and went back into her shambles of a house.

Now he could see in the cleared-out streets the houses starting to be framed again. Families coming back—even those still living with portable heaters and plasterboard covering the windows to protect against the cold.

He could see that there finally would be an end to

107

this. That one day Midland Beach would be back like it was—that was the type of people they were. With rebuilt homes and kids playing ball in the parks again. The flags flying. But the task was endless. Every home was freezing and damp. Everyone was wearing down.

Patrick bent and noticed something under a pile of bricks. He dug with his pick and pulled out a child's teddy bear. Filthy and soaked, one beady black eye missing. These things that had washed ashore turned up all the time.

"Hey, guy . . ." He wiped off the caked mud and grime.

Yes, the storm had cost them all a lot. Most everyone in Midland knew someone who had died.

But when he looked around—the rubble, the broken lives, the now empty house he had put his own life on hold to rebuild—Patrick knew that while his old man might not have been washed away that night like so many others, or struck down by a falling tree, the storm had taken something personal and vital from him that could never be rebuilt.

He propped the bear up against a post on the porch and waved. "Keep an eye on things for me, Joe, would ya?"

It had taken his dad.

CHAPTER EIGHTEEN

It isn't exactly easy to convert a large amount of un-reported cash into money you can spend.

The Patriot Act of 2002, and the subsequent Bank Security Act that followed, regulated the amount of cash that could be taken out of the country, deposited into a bank account, or even paid for goods and services at $10,000.

Anything larger was likely to show up on someone's radar.

I checked online, on the IRS's website under federal statutes for money laundering. It only reminded me of what I already knew.

There were various ways to get around this. I could make deposits in banks in amounts under ten thousand dollars; that was the simplest way. But then I'd have to make a lot of them, and I wasn't sure if the IRS or some regulatory agency checked that kind of thing, or looked for trends. Who knew if they had the means of tracking someone going around the region opening multiple new accounts with cash?

I could go to a casino. Mohegan Sun and Foxwoods were ninety minutes away. I could convert several thousand dollars into chips, play an hour or two of blackjack or the slot machines, and leave. Then come back a week later and cash them in.

But again, how often could I do that? Twice, three times, before my face was known and on some kind of visual recognition list? This was high-stakes poker, so to speak. I'd only been in a casino maybe twice in my life and the thought of having my picture flashed at a cashier's window or people behind screens following my moves didn't sit well with me.

I wasn't exactly a pro at this.

There were money orders. I could drive around to bodegas and post offices, handing over cash and coming back with money orders that I could deposit instead of cash.

And then there were prepaid credit cards. They were everywhere now. Every CVS, every big box retailer, every tobacco store. I could plunk down several thousand and walk out with something akin to cash. I could even pay down the mortgage with them.

I knew I had to do this cautiously and in small

amounts, so as not to attract attention. And only when the need became dire. Justifying how I took the money was one thing. Explaining to the feds how I'd broken umpteen federal laws was another!

I started with my own bank. The local Chase in Armonk. They knew me there. The day after I took out the cash I brought in $8,600. One of the managers there, Desi, who'd handled a number of transactions for me over the years and who had two kids herself, was happy to handle it, counting out the cash in front of me, eighty-six hundred-dollar bills with random numbers and in varied condition. I told her I'd just kept some cash around the house since the divorce.

I was nervous to begin with, watching someone count out thousands of dollars that I knew, if it came out where I had gotten it, could land me in jail. But sitting there keeping it all in my heart began to pound through my chest. I suddenly had the fear that the entire cache was stolen. Kept track of by traceable numbers on some FBI hot list somewhere. Some junior agent just out of Quantico would be flagging my deposit within the hour. My eyes kept darting to unsuspecting Desi and then back to the cash, one hundred-dollar bill at a time, trying not to show the unrest that was raging inside me.

I finally reassured myself, *No, Hil, that scenario was totally unlikely.* Kelty, by all accounts, was no bank robber or kidnapper who'd be carrying around marked bills.

Keep it together, I told myself, smiling at Desi, acting as if this was the most mundane thing in the world, while all the time my heart was doing somersaults.

"Eight thousand, six hundred and fifty dollars, Mrs. Cantor," she wrote on a deposit slip after counting it three times. "In your money market account, you said, correct . . .?"

"Yes, the money market," I confirmed.

The second time it went easier. I waited a few days, and when no one had come to arrest me, I went to the Webster Bank in Rye where I'd opened up a checking account two days earlier and put in $9,000. As long as I stayed under $10,000, I was pretty sure I was okay.

Then I opened accounts at two more banks, in Harrison and Greenwich.

At the same time I went on a job interview, for the chief comptroller of a Westchester-based TV station. The personnel manager seemed interested. I thought it went pretty well. My work at the ad agency was perfect for it. I knew my way out of all this was to start bringing in money, then downsize. I kept seeing numbers that showed the local housing market improving. If that continued, maybe I could sell the house for something above the mortgage, then rent something smaller. Maybe apply for financial aid for Brandon next year.

A day later I took thirty-five hundred dollars to a CVS in White Plains and walked out with a loaded prepaid card with Magic Johnson's face on it. I repeated that at a drugstore in Rye and a food market in Chappaqua.

As I stood in the parking lot, placing the loaded card back in my wallet, I told myself, *Congratulations, Hil.* I looked at a mother and her daughter around the same age as my son going in. I wasn't just a thief. Someone who had walked off with a bag full of money that wasn't hers. I'd moved on to federal charges.

I was a money launderer now.

CHAPTER NINETEEN

"So, *Rollie* . . .," Charles Mirho said, looking up at him. "You don't really mind if I call you Rollie, do you?"

Rollie McMahon couldn't answer. His eyes bulged from up on the beam he was suspended from in the family room of his colonial in Briarcliff Manor. His mouth was taped, his hands were bound behind him, and a noose was looped around his neck. The rickety wooden side table, which was all that held him from cracking his neck, wobbled gingerly.

Rollie nodded with a grunt, but to Mirho it wasn't altogether clear whether that was a yes or just a reaction to the predicament he was in, which indeed was dire. He'd probably shit over himself next.

Rollie muffled a garbled, indecipherable response.

"I'll take that as a yes," Mirho said. "Good. That way

we can really talk and come to some kind of under-
standing about whether I'm going to kick over this piece
of shit table here . . ." Mirho jiggled his foot on the side
table. "Or if we're gonna actually get you out of this
little pickle. Understand what I'm saying . . .? Now Rule
Number One of finding yourself in this particular situation is, whatever you do, don't be jumpy now. Got it?"

This time Rollie, bug-eyed, nodded demonstratively.

"Good. Now that's the kind of response I like."

It hadn't taken much to disable Rollie after Mirho
watched his wife leave, probably to her book club or maybe
a movie with a friend. A squirt of pepper spray and then
a nose full of chloroform easily did the trick. The real work
was hoisting the fat tub up over that beam. And praying
it held. The visual of Rollie's red-cheeked, chubby face
when he came to and found himself dangling from there
was worth the price of admission in itself. Mirho stepped
up and ripped the strip of adhesive from the tubbo's mouth.

"What do you want from me?" Rollie said, gasping
for needed air. "Take anything we have. It's all yours.
Why are you doing this to me?"

"We'll get to that soon, Rollie. I promise we will. In
the meantime I just want to establish some ground rules.
I'm going to ask you something *once*." Mirho held up
his index finger. "Okay, twice maybe, but I promise, a
third time and it won't be fun. And if I don't hear the
answer that I'm looking for, I'm afraid your poor wife's
gonna come home from her book group or wherever it

is she's at and find a pretty messy pile of shit in the ol' family room, if you know what I'm saying." He jiggled the table again, sending Rollie's heart through his throat. "Scare her right out of that Fair Isle, right . . .?"

"Please, please," Rollie begged, tears starting to come down his cheeks. "I didn't do anything. I don't know what you want from me. You see I have a family . . ."

"And a nice-looking one it is, Rollie. Two big, strapping boys, and look at that gal. Would be a shame to leave them like this, wouldn't it now?" Rollie started to sweat. Large beads tracking down his ruddy cheeks. "*Wouldn't it?*" he said, firmer. "I didn't quite hear an answer . . ."

"*Yes! Yes!*" Rollie shouted. He twisted and turned, as if that might possibly free him, until his feet slipped on the tabletop, nearly making it worse.

"That won't help, guy. I promise. I've seen it many times before. But glad to hear we're on the same page at least. So look here . . ." Mirho picked up a photo from the credenza behind the couch. "Always the Good Samaritan, I see. Head of the Rotary Club. Pharmacologist of the Year, 2007. What are you, Rollie . . . Some kind of doctor?"

"I'm a pharmacist," Rollie answered. "Please . . ."

"Dispense drugs, huh? Well, what do you know . . . Then there's the time you ran to the aid of that guy in the car ten days ago. Up on the road that night between Bedford and Greenwich . . ."

Rollie didn't answer. He only looked at Mirho confused, the color draining out of his face.

116

"You remember that night, don't you, guy? The police report said you were first on the scene. That you even saw that deer dart across the road. You said you saw the car roll down the embankment, right?"

Rollie nodded fitfully. "Yes."

"And what did you do? You didn't just drive on by. You stopped to help, right? What was the poor guy's name . . .? The victim. Oh yeah, Kelty. Joseph Kelty, right? You even ran down to help him. Not that by that point there was much you could do. I mean, the guy's face practically went through the steering wheel, right? It was a bloody mess. Quite an effort for a big ol' guy like you. I went out to look at the spot myself."

"What about it?" Rollie asked, trying to put together what this had to do with anything. His feet buckled and the table wobbled for a second, Rollie emitting a terrified squeal.

"*Careful!* You sever that neck cord of yours, you should know it could take about five to ten minutes for you to die. Not sure we've quite got the height to do this humanely. You basically suffocate. But before you do, your brain swells up and you turn all blue. Probably mess up all over the floor . . ."

"Please, please," Rollie begged. "What do you want to know? I'll tell you anything. Just let me down."

"Not sure I can do that, Rollie, just now . . . So remember—one, two chances. That's our agreement, right? Otherwise it'll be shitsville, okay? So let's get

117

back to that wreck. You're down there doing your thing. You call 911. The police arrive, maybe what, according to the report, four, five minutes later?"

"I don't know. That sounds about right, I guess. Who cares?"

"I care, Rollie. I care. And that's all that should be mattering to you about now. Okay? But somehow there's something missing from the car. I know it was in there because I saw Kelty place it in there myself, not twenty minutes before. And you were the first one there, the only one according to the report. So it stands to reason it was either you . . . or that cop. Polluto, right? He was the next one there. But I'm betting on *you*, Rollie. Because you're such a Good Samaritan and all . . ." He tossed Rollie's Pharmacologist of the Year award on the couch. "We can just put it down to a moment of weakness . . ."

"I don't know what you're talking about." Rollie shook his head. "*What* was missing?"

"Now that's *one . . .*" Mirho frowned, shaking his head. "Didn't like that answer at all . . . Don't want to get two more. Did I hear you say you needed a hint? Okay, here it is. We're talking about this black leather bag that was in the car. It was right on the passenger seat. I watched Kelty put it in there myself. Funny how it never showed up in anyone's account of the accident. Not in your eyewitness statement. Not in the police report.

"Now the bag was nice—cow-grain leather, zippered top, flap pockets on one side . . . I'd even let you keep it if you liked it. But it was what was inside that I'm really interested in. But, hell, I bet you already figured that out for yourself. So you didn't have just a little extra curiosity while you were down there? While you were checking to see if poor ol' Joe was dead or alive? Maybe just a little peek?"

"*No, no!* I swear, I don't know what you're talking about," Rollie pleaded. "Please."

"Now that makes two!" Mirho exhaled a sigh of disappointment. "Two chances gone." He put his foot back on the side table. "I told you, all you get is three. I'm suddenly not exactly liking your odds now at all. I'm not . . ." He bumped into the table as he walked around him, eliciting a gasp. "One chance left. I may have to go at this a completely different way."

"No—no, please!" Heavy tears ran down Rollie's cheeks and he thrashed his head back and forth in desperation.

"You *were* the only one down there. So it had to be you or that cop. And the EMTs arrived just a few seconds after him. Which makes me think it had to be you." He wobbled the table. "Last chance!"

"No, no, please. Please! *Wait!*" Rollie seemed to be thinking. "There was someone else down there. I wasn't alone! She was actually there first."

"She? Someone else? Now that's a new one, Rollie. And a bad time to spring it on me. I didn't see anything in the police report."

"I don't know, maybe I never said it—but there was. A woman. She saw the whole thing happen too. She was down there ahead of me."

"*A woman?* You saw the accident, Rollie. You called the cops. This other woman thing, coming out of the blue like this . . ." Mirho scratched his head. "I don't know, it all sounds kind of fishy to me . . ."

"No, please, I swear! She didn't have her phone with her. That's why I made the call. I remember, she went into the car. She said she checked out the guy. The driver's door was wedged. By the time I got down there she was already out. It was clear he was dead. I don't know what you're looking for—this bag, whatever—but it must have been her. She has to have it."

Mirho balanced his foot on the edge of the table, rocking it slightly, Rollie's legs buckling precariously. "*Please!* Please! I'm not lying. I swear. Let me think. Her name was Janie or something. No—not Janie. *Jeanine. That's it.* I swear!"

"*Jea-neen,*" Mirho snorted skeptically. "Jeanine *who*, Rollie? Start filling me in, guy. Quick now!"

"I don't know! I don't remember her last name. I'm not sure she told me. She was supposed to leave her info on my car, but she never did. She said she was in a hurry. To pick up her son from school or something. Football practice, I think."

"Football practice . . .? Football practice ends in November or December. Rollie?"

"Then basketball! That's what she said. She just said that she had to go. She was in a hurry. So I just waited for the cops myself."

"So exactly what did this Jeanine look like, Rollie?"

"I don't know . . . Pretty. Brown hair. It was pulled up. She was in jeans and maybe a short leather jacket or something. You know, quilted."

"Quilted, huh? And you just let her go?" Mirho shrugged, shaking his head. "Just like that?"

"Why not? There was nothing we could do for the guy. He was already gone. I couldn't have taken anything if I wanted to. Even if I did see something. Which I didn't. The cops arrived as soon as she left. I swear."

"Once again, playing Mr. Good Samaritan right to the end, huh?" Mirho shook his head. "Except it's just not a very convincing story line. And that does make three now, doesn't it? I have to go back to the rules." Mirho kicked the table. Rollie pushed on his toes, trying to plant them more firmly. "What to do with you, Rollie. It just all sounds . . ."

"She had to have taken it! She couldn't wait to get out of there. Maybe she hid it somewhere." Rollie's face grew flushed with panic and sweat. "*Wait!* There was something. I *do* remember something."

"I'm listening. Now would be a good time to say it, pal."

"Her car. It was an Acura, I think. An Acura SUV. Silver."

"An Acura SUV? You're sure?"

"Yes! I'm sure."

"Silver, huh? And what about the plates?"

"They were New York. I can see them now. I can't recall the numbers. But it was definitely a silver Acura SUV with New York plates. She couldn't get out of there fast enough."

Mirho just kept staring. He'd gotten about all he could now.

"It had some kind of school decal on the back. I couldn't read it, 'cause I never got that close. But I think it began with an M. I don't know, Morgan or Monmoth . . ."

"An M, huh?" Mirho said. He was pretty sure that no one would become such a slobbering mess, hold out for so long, basically shit his pants if there was something he was hiding that could save his life. At least, not an everyday joe like Rollie here.

Jeanine. A silver Acura SUV with New York plates. Who lived in Westchester.

"You're gonna let me down now, aren't you?" Rollie said, a hopeful, tear-mashed mess. "I mean, that helps, right? It's something to go on. I told you all I know, I swear. You said that was our deal."

"Yeah, that was our deal, Rollie." Mirho agreed. He placed his foot on the stool one more time, and jiggled it, even more precariously than before. Mucus was running down Rollie's chin. His face was red and hopeful.

"That was indeed our deal."

CHAPTER TWENTY

The further I got away from having deposited the money, the more relaxed with it I was starting to feel.

Brandon was paid up in school through the next semester. Our house was current. I even got a call from the TV station I'd interviewed with that they wanted me back for a second time. Okay, the job paid forty thousand less than what I was previously making, but if I could get the house out from under me, and maybe rent something smaller, closer to Brandon's school, the savings on taxes and expenses alone would make up much of the difference.

I was beginning to feel that there was an outcome for us here other than total disaster. I still checked online every day for anything that might've come up on the missing money or on Kelty. If he'd been implicated in anything that might shed some light on it.

But so far it appeared he hadn't been.

I did find one mention in the *Staten Island Advance* about a fund that was being set up in his name. By his son to help people in Midland Beach, the proceeds coming from a softball game in the spring between policemen and firemen on Staten Island. And there was also a memorial fund started by his fellow MTA workers.

I gradually began to convince myself that I might just get away with it. No one seemed to be looking for it. No one even seemed to know. It was actually as if this lifesaving cache had simply fallen into my lap. That Joe Kelty was my guardian angel. I knew there were people connected to him who needed this money even more than I did. And I swore to myself, as soon as I was back on my feet, with a new job and a trimmed-down over-head, as soon I could create some distance from what I'd done, I'd find a way to get a good part of it back to them. Anonymously, of course. Maybe through that fund his son was setting up.

And it made the wrong feel better that ultimately I would put it to good use. Help people rebuild. Become a kind of guardian angel myself.

Yes, the further it all faded into the past that feeling put some peace in me.

It just didn't last for even another day.

CHAPTER TWENTY-ONE

"Guess what Mommy has tomorrow?" I said to Brandon. We were at the kitchen island; he was working on his homework; I was on my iPad, doing my daily check for any articles connected to the accident.

He didn't answer.

"Did you hear what I said?" I glanced away from the iPad. "I asked if you knew what I've got happening tomorrow?"

I could see he was off in one of his little worlds.

"I've got a job interview," I said, trying to steer him back to the conversation and away from his mood. "Not just an interview, a *second* one. I think maybe they like me."

"Who?" he said distractedly.

"This local TV station. It's in White Plains. So it's close by."

He looked up from his notebook. "This is stupid, Mommy. Why do I have to do this?"

"Because you have to, Brandon. Just stick with it. You're almost done."

"So you're going to work in TV now? No more advertising?"

"I told you, the advertising job is over, honey. And that's if they hire me. I'm sure there are lots of other people they're talking to who are just as qualified. But you never know."

"They'll hire you," Brandon said, his face down at the level of the notebook, sketching out one of his wild-looking monsters.

"Well, that's good to know. I wonder if I can get you on the hiring committee? I could use someone on the inside."

"*Tie, tie, tie, tie, tie . . .*" he began to drone.

"I thought that was funny," I said. "Why don't you put aside what you're doing and get back to your math. That's what you're supposed to be doing now, right?"

"I like drawing."

"I know you like drawing, Brandon. And I like your drawings. But it's math time now."

"*Tie, tie, tie . . .,*" he said, tuning me out.

"Brandon, please . . ."

He started drawing jagged lines through his math page, jerking his pencil in defiance, defacing the homework.

"Brandon, stop! *Now.*"

126

"Tie, tie, tie . . ."

"Brandon, you heard me." I reached for his hand. "I said stop!"

He tightened the grip on his pencil without even looking up, continuing to scrawl his angry lines. I finally pulled it out of his grip and he looked up at me, like I'd stolen something from him, and I saw a wildness I knew.

Mean Brandon.

"Why would they want anyone else? If they do, I could go over and kill them."

I looked at him in shock. "Brandon, you know that's not funny!"

"I don't mean it to be funny, Mommy. I'll send Polydragon. He can do that, you know! He can go over and eat them, like Chicken McNuggets, if I tell him to. M'wom, m'wom, m'wom!" he said, making loud chomping noises.

"Brandon, stop that now!" Sometimes he just said things, things he knew were inappropriate and would make me angry. Sometimes it was something else that he just couldn't control.

He suddenly looked away before he could get a reaction and the fierceness was gone. "That was just a joke, Mommy. I'm not really going to do it."

"Well, it wasn't funny," I said. "You know better. You have to watch what you say."

"I'm going to watch TV."

"Brandon!"

127

He got up, leaving his schoolbook on the counter. Most any other time I would have brought him back, put the math book back in front of him, and made him stay on task. But tonight I just exhaled, spent and not up to the effort.

For years, we couldn't get him to even look at his at-home assignments. He would just stare at the page, muttering his persistent, distracting phrases. Or scribble illegibly, even though he knew exactly what to do. Or sometimes hurl the book in anger or rip pages out. And if he received a time-out and was sent to his room, he would go in the bathroom and slam the toilet seat up and down for an hour.

At least that was the old Brandon.

I went back to the iPad and continued my search. First I put in "Joseph Kelty," as I always did. Then "Bedford, New York, auto accident."

Nothing.

On the *Journal-News* site I did find another article on the continuing string of home break-ins, the third in the Mount Kisco area, not so far from us. I also saw something about a new exercise studio opening up in Armonk dedicated to the barre method, which I'd been dying to check out.

I was about to exit when it caught my eye:

Pharmacist Tied to Fatal Auto Accident Found Dead in Briarcliff Home.

My heart came to a stop. I clicked on the link and began to read:

Roland McMahon, a pharmacist with the CVS company, was found hung in his Briarcliff Manor home, an apparent suicide.

"Oh my God! *Rollie.*" I exhaled. I felt my stomach fall.

The body was discovered by his wife, Annemarie, Wednesday night after she'd returned from an outing with friends. Attempts to revive Mr. McMahon by paramedics proved unsuccessful and he was declared dead at the scene.

There was a photo, the image there of the guy I recalled: ruddy-faced, soft around the belly, his tie undone and acting a little squeamish at the sight of Kelty in his mangled Honda.

I leaned closer:

Coincidentally, McMahon, 58, who worked at the CVS store in Bedford as their chief pharmacist, was in the news in the past month as the only eyewitness of a fatal accident on Route 135 in which Joseph Kelty, of Staten Island, New York, was killed. No one was criminally charged and Sergeant Richard

Toomey, of the Briarcliff Manor Police Force, insisted, "There was no reason to consider the two incidents as related in any way."

Annemarie McMahon, being consoled by her daughter, said, "We're all in shock. I'd just left him. He was staying home to watch a game. He never once showed any sign of depression or anything like that. It just makes no sense that he would do something like this. We were leaving on a cruise of the Caribbean in two weeks."

A family member said McMahon had no known financial problems and was in good standing at work. He leaves behind a wife and three grown children. He was a member of the Pharmacological Society of America and was voted Westchester Pharmacist of the Year in 2007.

A knot tightened inside me. *He'd hung himself?*

I read the article again, and it didn't get any less troubling. I didn't have a clue if what had happened was connected in any way to the crash. More specifically, to the money I'd taken. Meaning, my imagination started to run away with me—whether he'd actually killed himself at all. *Or . . .*

I shuddered as a presentiment of fear wormed into my brain. Or, if someone was trying to track the money. *Oh, God, Hil . . .*

Maybe it would come out that he'd had cancer; or

that he'd lost his life's savings in a kind of speculative investment; or that he was being treated for depression; or that he was having an affair. You hear about these things all the time. I thought back to what I'd told him at the site. *"I'm Jeanine . . ."* That was all. No last name. No way to find me. I'd been careful, I reassured myself.

And even if something *had* happened, something unimaginable, crazy, he had no way to trace me. But it all tingled terrifyingly on my skin.

Poor Rollie. Could he really have killed himself?

I thought back through everything I could remember from the moment he came down the slope. There was no way anything could point to me if, as insane as it sounded, this somehow wasn't a suicide after all.

Right?

Inwardly, I think I knew it from that very moment. Despite what the obituary said. Despite the police saying that they weren't looking at the two events as being related.

Why would they? They didn't know.

But I did.

As far as anyone else would be concerned, Rollie would have been the first person at the accident.

The only person.

The only person for anyone who might be on the trail of what had happened to that money.

You're thinking crazily, Hilary. I tried to bring myself back to reality. *You're watching too many detective shows . . .*

131

But if it wasn't—I pressed my fingers to my forehead—if what happened to Rollie wasn't a suicide at all, but the work of someone who had managed to track him down, let's say from an article in the newspaper, or from the cop who came on the scene just as I took off. *Polluto*. Or from the fucking police report, for all I knew. That was all possible, right . . .?

Someone looking for that money . . .

Then I'd basically set him up. He was killed because of me.

I was the one they were really looking for, not him.

My stomach went into free fall.

Suddenly I noticed Brandon back at my side, the defiance gone. "What's wrong, Mommy? You're all white."

"Nothing, baby," I lied, drawing him close to me.

I'd saved the biggest lie for myself. That in trying to help my son, had I now put him in danger? If Rollie had been murdered for what he didn't know, for what he had no idea had taken place, what would they do if they found me?

"Nothing," I kept repeating, stroking Brandon's hair over and over, terrified inside. "Nothing's wrong, honey."

CHAPTER TWENTY-TWO

The whole thing happened so quickly, Tom O'Byrne thought to himself as the basement window burst open and the bay began to pour in; there wasn't even time to say good-bye.

Everyone knew a heavyweight of a storm was coming in. But there had been a lot of storms before, and nothing had caused more than a nuisance of flooding. Midland Beach was the kind of place where you not only knew everyone on the block, but likely knew their parents too. And *their* parents. Houses were passed down for generations, where married children still lived with their parents: construction workers, Con Ed supervisors, cops and firemen. These were people who were used to downed trees and flooded basements. Storms had come and gone. They'd all been there before.

What they weren't used to and didn't fully under-stand, Tom included, was that the streets they'd grown up on, played on, drove back and forth on every day, lived out their lives on, were in a bowl. A topographic bowl, dipping a few feet below sea level from Father Capodonna along the bay all the way up to Hylan. So they stayed, even though it was designated as a group one evacuation area. They stayed because they'd always stayed, and nothing had happened before.

By 11:00 P.M. the winds were ripping off the bay. A few trees were down, power lines; it was battering the clapboard houses pretty good. But no one was prepared for the swell, which by midnight had swept through the bungalows along the beach and over Father Cap Boulevard.

It took only minutes for Midland Beach to become part of New York Bay.

Tom knew it was time to get the family out a little before eleven. He'd spent his entire life in this old blue Victorian. It was his father's, and you didn't just run away. He got their son, Rich, to take his mom to the Bonanos, who lived on higher ground up on Todt Hill. Tom waved them off, saying he just wanted to grab a few documents out of the basement, just in case, and he'd be right behind. While he was down there, stuffing his will and his deed into a briefcase, the fifty-foot oak in their yard came crashing down into the house, slicing a ten-foot gash in the sunroom that faced the bay. By

134

the time Tom tried to come back up, the first floor was under three feet of water.

He went back down and called Sheila on her cell, as water burst through the storm window under the porch and into the basement. It was too small to crawl through and the water was beginning to come in. He tried the stairs one more time, but the current was so powerful it knocked him back down. He called 911, but it wouldn't go through. They must be overrun. He called his wife again and left a message she didn't receive until much later. "Hon, this isn't looking so good."

By two A.M. the wind and tide had carried away their back porch and the first floor of their once proud home had become part of New York Bay. It knifed through the creaking eighty-year-old planks, engulfing every memento of their once happy lives. Four hours later it receded, like a dark thief, taking everything the O'Byrnes had accumulated in their lives back out to sea.

It took the armoire his wife's grandmother had brought over from Trieste. Her collection of antique ceramic boxes, and her filigreed old frames with the early photos of their grandparents and her parents' wedding. It took the pictures of Rich's graduation from the fire academy, guaranteed to bring a tear to Tom's eyes.

It took the oil painting of the Verrazano Sheila's brother had completed just a week before he passed. From lung disease, which he'd contracted as a first responder on 9/11. Tom's antique filigreed cigar box. The boxing shorts Muhammad Ali had worn when he knocked out Leon Spinks.

It washed away every memory. Every celebration.

And days later, Tom laid to rest, as Sheila walked through the gutted remains, shuffling through the mud and shattered glass and rotted wood that was now all that was left of their lives, she discovered something else the storm had taken: the hand-painted lacquer box that held the baby hair and photos of their daughter, Deirdre, the things closest to Sheila's heart.

Along with something else of their daughter's they kept inside it. Something they hadn't looked at in a long time, but that now, though it wasn't clear right then, would turn out to be the most valuable possession in their lives.

CHAPTER TWENTY-THREE

"Patatas pimentón . . .," Charles Mirho said, pushing the plastic menu across the table at the taquería in downtown Yonkers. "They're basically potatoes in kind of an omelet, lots of garlic and paprika . . ."

"I'm not really hungry," Dennis Finch replied, glancing around uncomfortably. The motor vehicles clerk was the wrong side of fifty, with the pasty coloration of someone who had spent the last decade behind a counter in a government office and wire-rims that seemed a size too large for his narrow face. "Why don't we just get on with it?"

"Suit yourself." Mirho shrugged, taking another bite. "Empanadas are good too."

"Look," Dennis said, "I narrowed the information you gave me down to four names." He took a manila

137

envelope from under his jacket. "First name Jeanine, a recent-model Acura SUV—it's called the MDX, by the way—and a Westchester address."

"Lower Westchester," Mirho said, not looking up while eating. "You sure I can't interest you in something here?"

"You realize I could lose my job for what I'm doing?" Dennis hissed under his breath.

"You want me not to call you again?" Mirho shrugged, dipping a forkful of potato in oil. "Just say the word. You don't think there's a dozen underpaid dweebs—one probably in the booth right next to yours—who'd be thrilled to make a couple of grand for half an hour's work? Next time, you oughta think about things like that when you push your kid to go to law school."

The clerk glared and pushed his glasses higher on his nose. This would have been the time to get up and take what he had back with him, which was probably what he should have done in the first place.

Instead, he sighed, "Look, let's just get on with it." He pushed the envelope across the table. Mirho wiped his fingers clean and opened it, pulling out what was inside.

Four printed-off pages.

"First, I think you owe me something," the DMV clerk said, putting his palm over Mirho's hand.

Mirho's gaze settled on Dennis's hand. "Three . . . two . . . one," he counted and lifted his eyes to meet

138

Dennis's. "And trust me, Dennis, you don't want to find out what happens next."

Slowly the DMV clerk removed his hand, Mirho's jaw barely twitching into a smile that read something like *Right decision, pal*. He sifted through each of the four identities, each with their vehicle info and driving history and a grainy, printed-off photograph.

The first was Jeanine Farancino. Not bad looking. A 2009 MDX. But she was from all the way up in Peekskill, definitely too far north, if Rollie's version of what happened down there was true. Anyway, according to the records she was twenty-four, and as per Rollie, his Jeanine had a kid old enough to be at basketball practice.

The second was a Jeanine Lisa Kramer. She was from Dobbs Ferry, which definitely made her a possible.

But Rollie called the woman at the accident site "pretty," and with her square, pressed-in face and chopped-off hair, this Jeanine looked like she wouldn't be able to get herself laid on a prison conjugal visit.

Mirho turned the sheet again.

Jeanine Ann Jackson. Thirty-one. New Rochelle. Another possibility, he thought, or would have, until he saw the photo. Black as freshly laid tar. Not sure exactly what ol' Rollie went in for, Mirho thought, but while he was shitting himself up on the rafters, that fact might definitely have come up.

"So are we square?" Dennis pulled the top of the sheet down. "I have to get back to work."

"Sure. We're square, Denny boy." Mirho stared back at him.

There was a kind of ice in his tone that said to Dennis maybe he shouldn't have said that, but Mirho just took out an envelope from his jacket and slowly pushed it across. Dennis put his hand over it and surreptitiously brought it back in.

"You said it was debt collection, right?"

"Debt collection . . .?" Mirho was giving some consideration to taking the guy behind the restaurant, stuffing him into a garbage bin, and slamming his head flat with the metal cover. And taking the two grand back, which at this point looked like it might not have bought anything of value.

"You said this was about a debt? Someone owed a friend of yours rent money?" Dennis asked again, pushing up his glasses.

"Sure. Debt collection," Mirho said, chuckling. "Whatever gives you a good night's sleep. Now, toodleoo, Dennis, get yourself back to your desk. There must be a line waiting for you."

The DMV clerk stood up and stuffed the money into his jacket. "Enjoy your meal."

Mirho waited until he had left the diner and then looked at the last sheet.

He exhaled, disappointed. Jeanine wasn't even her given name, but a middle name.

This might not pan out at all.

140

But she was pretty. And about the right age. Thirty-six. And the records said she lived in Armonk. Not too far away.

He stared at the name again. Hilary Jeanine Cantor. Didn't hurt to check it out.

CHAPTER TWENTY-FOUR

I spent the next few days looking into whether Rollie McMahon had actually killed himself.

I searched for whatever obits and follow-up news stories I could find. I found a family Web page on bereavement.com and scanned the postings—mostly stunned friends and relatives who couldn't believe what had happened, testimonials from outsiders who had gone through something similar. I even thought for a second about going to the funeral. Then I decided, on the chance that there was any truth to what I feared, that this was the *last* place I should be. I didn't know who might be there as well. Checking it out. While nothing I found contradicted Rollie's death as being any more than it appeared—a sudden, unforeseen tragedy—the complete bewilderment of those closest to him, the fact that no motive had emerged—no depression, no financial reversal—coupled with what only *I* knew that connected him to what went on at Kelty's accident, did nothing to calm my own fears that someone looking for that money had found their way to him.

The only thing keeping me together was that there was no way anyone could get from him to me.

Over the next few days I did my best to get my life back to normal. I went on that second interview—which went well, I thought, though I was told there were several candidates under consideration. I made an appointment for Brandon at the neurologist's. We even went to the circus at the Westchester County Center in White Plains on Thursday night.

Which was what we were on our way home from, he in a red clown's cap and greasepaint, stuffed with cotton candy and twirling around one of those green-and-red plastic lights. Still laughing about how the elephants had stood up on their hind legs and circled around when the pretty trainer gal was being held captive by a lion.

"It was like, you mean . . . *me*?" Brandon said, mugging a funny, wide-eyed face like the poor elephant in the skit.

"Not much of a hero," I played along. "Remind me never to call in an elephant if we're ever in danger."

"We don't exactly have an elephant, Mom," Brandon said. "Only Remi."

"Yeah. And all she'd do is lick to death anyone who wanted to harm us."

He kept laughing. It was nice to see him happy and

enthusiastic like any regular kid. I wished it happened more.

We pulled into our driveway and I opened the garage with the remote. "You go in and get ready for bed. It's still a school night, okay?"

"Okay, Mommy."

"And send Remi out. I'll bring out the trash."

It was a Thursday, recycling night. Elena usually took care of it before she left, but she'd had to go home early to take her son to the doctor, so I lugged the two bins of newspapers and bottles and cans up to the end of the driveway as Remi shot out to pee.

We had two acres at the end of a cul-de-sac. The house next to us was barely visible, down the hill and around a curve. Jim had developed the entire street off Whippoorwill Road—six homes, high-ceilinged, lots of glass and windows, with large family rooms and designer kitchens in a neoclassic style.

Remi ran up to say hello. We had an electric fence and she was trained not to go beyond the boundaries.

"Do your business," I exhorted her. She squatted down on the grass in the way she always did a tinkle. "Good girl!" She gave the mandatory barks at some imaginary foe in the woods. This time she did it more than usual. Must be something out there, maybe a deer. "C'mon, let's go inside."

We went back in through the open garage and the kitchen. I threw my bag and coat across a chair at the kitchen table, took out a tea bag and some calcium and magnesium I took at night.

I noticed the doggie fence we used to confine Remi to the kitchen was up. I didn't recall putting it up before we left. Then I almost stepped in a pee on the Mexican tile floor. "Damn. Remi—*bad girl!*" It was strange; she almost never made mistakes like that. We'd only been away a couple of hours.

Her ears went back apologetically and she slinked into a corner. Blotting it up, I had the strangest sense that something wasn't right. I looked around. The door to an antique hutch where I kept my china was open.

And my iPad, which I was pretty sure I had left on the island before we went out, suddenly wasn't there.

Then I noticed an old majolica plate on the floor in pieces, and another, now just a hole on the shelf, that was missing.

Someone had been in here.

I stood up cautiously at first in disbelief, then with a feeling of fear beating in my chest. My first thought went to Brandon.

"Brandon!" I called. He didn't answer. "*Brandon!*" I yelled again. He was probably already upstairs.

I hurried through the dining room and into the foyer, where I almost ran into him. He was in front of the stairs, strangely calm, but with his eyes wide and fixed on the living room.

"Someone's been here, Mommy."

CHAPTER TWENTY-FIVE

The room was turned upside down. Ransacked.

My hand shot to my mouth. *"Oh my God!"*

The couch pillows were strewn everywhere, cushions from the couch upended. A framed photo of Brandon and me was knocked off a side table onto the floor. A painting on the wall hung crookedly, to the side. Jim and I used to collect antique Chinese ceramics, and I noticed that a Ming plate and a scalloped blue and white serving bowl were missing.

"Oh, Jesus, Brandon."

Brandon's eyes were wide as moons. And confused. "What's happened, Mommy? Who did this?"

I looked around in a state of stunned deflation. "I don't know. Stay here," I said.

I went into the family room. It was the same in there.

Total havoc. A row of books were flung onto the floor from a bookshelf, as if someone was systemically looking behind them.

For what, a wall safe, maybe?

Remi was barking crazily.

I suddenly grew nervous. A terrifying thought rose up in me. *What if whoever did this was still in the house?*

"Brandon, I want you to go back in the kitchen," I said, pushing him in that direction. I hadn't noticed a vehicle around, even on the street that led up to the house, but now, feeling a draft, I saw that the sliding glass door to the back deck was cracked open slightly. Maybe that was how they'd gotten in. I was praying they had left the same way. Living all the way out here, sometimes I didn't lock it as I should. I listened carefully. I didn't hear a sound. I'd read about the string of home robberies in Westchester, but they were all up in Mount Kisco or Chappaqua, far enough away. I never thought for a second that it would be me. I admonished myself for not putting on the alarm. I rarely did. Only if we were leaving town for a few days. And Armonk was one of the safest communities in the county.

"Mommy, who's been in here?" Brandon said again, not heeding my request. I didn't want to go any farther in the house with him around. "I want to see my—"

"Brandon, just *go*, please!" My heart started to pound. "Just listen to me this one time. Go back in the kitchen and stay there with Remi till I know what's going on! *Now!*"

"Okay." He headed back in and I stood there, not sure what my strategy was now.

The right thing, of course, would be to call the police. Take my son and get out. Before I took another step. But then I flashed to what I had under the deck, and I got nervous that the police might be the *last* people I wanted here right now. I didn't hear a sound anywhere in the house. The deck door was ajar. I was starting to feel pretty certain that whoever had been in here was gone by now. I'd read about these break-ins. Mostly in affluent neighborhoods. I hadn't heard that anyone had been hurt in one, or even confronted, so far. They were pros.

My mind flashed to the money hidden under the deck. I was pretty certain no one in a million years could possibly find that.

"Brandon, stay in there. If you hear anything, I want you to run. Run to Meg and Taylor's." Our closest neighbors. "Okay? I'm just taking a look around . . ."

His voice was responsive yet mildly disappointed. "Okay, Mommy . . ."

I didn't care.

I went down the first-floor hall and into the guest bedroom I used as my office.

Christ . . . My stomach plummeted.

My desk drawers were all pulled open and rifled

148

through, files strewn about, a locked filing drawer where I kept our passports and insurance policies jimmied open. An identify thief's dream. I kneeled down. I was shocked to find my passport was still there. And my checkbook was still on my desk, where I'd written one to Elena a few hours earlier. Then I remembered how burglars didn't go for things like that, things that could tie them to a particular location. What they wanted were things of value they could pawn or sell quickly without a trace. My computer was a four-year-old Apple, not exactly state of the art. They'd left it. Maybe I'd gotten off lucky.

That was when my mind flashed to my ring.

My engagement ring. Not that the sentiment behind it meant anything now, but it was still about the most valuable thing I owned. Close to four karats and really good quality. Jim had sprung for it after he sold a big home. I still wore it every once in a while. In fact, I'd had it on yesterday for my job interview. I usually locked it away in my safe upstairs, but I suddenly remembered that I hadn't done that yesterday. I'd just tossed it in the change dish on my dresser.

In plain view.

Shit. A burglar in his first day on the job couldn't have missed it.

"Brandon, I'm going upstairs," I yelled. "Just stay in there till you hear me call."

He didn't answer.

"Did you hear me, Brandon? Please answer me. I just want you to say okay."

"Mommy, okay . . .," he called back, irritated.

I headed up the stairs, Remi following me, my heart ricocheting back and forth against my ribs.

I figured if anyone was up here I would have heard the creaking on the floor by now. I had most of my valuables here: pearls my mother had given me that had come from her mother; a gold and diamond Roberto Coin bracelet that was an anniversary present. The Cartier Ballon Bleu watch I'd sprung for myself a few years back. I was certain they had to be history now. A part of me was angry to have been so unlucky. Another part was even angrier that I hadn't turned on the alarm.

A last part was still wrestling with the thought that someone might still be in the house. And I was walking right into it. *What then?*

I went along the bridge that connected the stairs to my bedroom wing and paused at the doorway. My heart still, I listened for any sign of movement.

Nothing.

"If anyone's in here, please, just get the fuck out!" I yelled. *"Please . . ."* Knowing that didn't exactly sound threatening.

Nothing came back.

My nerves buzzing, I stepped inside my bedroom. I expected the same scene as downstairs. Drawers open. Things ripped apart. The contents flung everywhere.

But it wasn't.

The bed was still made, my clothes, the things on my night table just as I'd left them a few hours earlier. Amazingly, everything seemed to be okay.

Maybe I'd come home and surprised whoever it was before they'd had a chance to get up here. Maybe they'd run out the back just as we arrived. That was why the door was left cracked open. That gave me a creepy feeling as well.

I stepped inside the master closet. It was large, like an airplane hangar, I always joked—one of Jim's big selling points: the fancy master suite, with its built-in dresser drawers and a tower of shoe shelves Imelda Marcos would have gushed over.

The dresser drawers were open—but I was pretty sure, open as *I* had left them. Everything seemed to be in place. My jewelry box was there as well. Open. But after a quick inspection, everything seemed to be there. I saw my watch, my pearls. I let out a huge sigh of relief.

My ring?

I went over to my dresser and I saw it. Not in the dish where I was pretty sure I had left it. But right there on the dresser top.

Staring up at me.

"*Thank God!*" I blew out my cheeks. It definitely looked as if no one had been up here.

For the first time since I'd come home I allowed

myself to relax. I went to pick it up, thanking my lucky stars.

That was when I noticed something else, sitting directly under it, in plain view, and the elation I was feeling leaked out of me like water down a drain. In its place I felt an icy stab of fear.

My eyes fixed on the spot where I had found it. Not in the change dish, but on the dresser.

Sitting there for anyone to see.

And a face was smiling up at me, one I'd seen a lot these past ten days.

Ben Franklin's face.

My ring was sitting on a crisp new hundred-dollar bill.

CHAPTER TWENTY-SIX

From the woods, Mirho focused on the house through a set of night binoculars.

He had no idea if this Hilary Jeanine Cantor was the woman Rollie was with at Kelty's crash site.

Or even if she was, if she was the one had taken the satchel of cash. She did fit the description: the right age, the right area where she lived, the Acura SUV. And not a bad looker either, he confirmed through the yellowy lens as he followed her and her son into the house.

He certainly seemed a little shrimpy to be playing basketball.

Until he could be sure, it wouldn't have been wise to wait for her inside. Not like Rollie.

Not with the kid. The kid made it all messy. And would draw a lot of attention to something he wanted at all costs to keep quiet. All he could do was to get her attention. Which he was now sure he was about to get pretty good.

Three, two, one . . .

Through the lens, he followed her from window to window. The lights went on; he saw her son run ahead. He heard barking, the dog flipping out. If she was smart, seeing the fence up, she probably already knew.

Then she appeared. It hadn't been hard to get inside. The kind of slide lock on the glass doors leading to the deck he could've opened while getting a blow job. She made it all the easier by not activating the alarm. Most people didn't, he found.

Mirho watched the lights go on in her office. *There ya go, doll* . . . A sight of her through the shades, over her desk, looking through the disrupted files.

He enjoyed the anxiety and worry she would be feeling. And the fact that she had no idea what was actually happening yet. It gave him a tingling sense of control.

Then he saw the lights go on upstairs. She was heading to the bedroom. She'd be distraught, confused. Angry at herself for not activating the alarm. All that fine jewelry, it had to be gone, right? She was probably on the verge of tears . . .

He couldn't see in, but by now he knew she had seen what he had left for her.

Bingo.

If it was her, he knew, her mind would be going a mile a minute and she'd be going crazy with panic. Trying to figure out what to do next. How she was going to get out of this.

That, or else she'd be thinking she was simply the luckiest burglarized person in the world.

Mirho waited.

He checked his watch. It would sure make things a lot easier if she would do something stupid. Like retrieving that satchel. Maybe even getting in the car and leaving with it, taking it somewhere else. That was what an amateur did. Panic. And she wasn't exactly accustomed to this. That was how you could catch them.

Panicking.

But that didn't happen.

Twenty minutes later he was still keeping his eyes trained. She didn't leave.

An hour.

Maybe she didn't have it here. Maybe it was in a safety deposit box somewhere. Or maybe she'd already gotten rid of it—found someone who would take on the risk of the cash in exchange for something she could more easily deposit. They were out there.

Or maybe she wasn't even the one. Maybe he was out two grand. Maybe she didn't even have it.

Though he was pretty sure she had already told him she did.

He took out the GPS device he would affix to her car.

Not by anything she'd done. Other than why else would she not have given Rollie her real name?

But more by what she hadn't done.

First there was the sticker on the back of her car.

"I couldn't read it because I never got that close," Rollie had said, hanging there. *"But it began with the letter M."*

Mirho squinted on it through the scope. Milton Farms.

And the other thing . . . that made it kind of certain. She hadn't done the one thing a person would do if they had nothing to hide. If their home was broken into.

She hadn't called the cops.

CHAPTER TWENTY-SEVEN

I don't know if I ever fully understood the meaning of the word "petrified" until I stayed in that house with my son for the rest of that night.

I was certain whoever was looking for that money had somehow found me. I just couldn't figure out how. I stared at that bill for long minutes, the hairs raised on my arms, trying to come to grips with whether I was reading something into this, or if not, just what it meant.

It meant that someone out there knew I had it.

It also meant that Rollie McMahon hadn't hung himself at all.

The sweats came over me, staring at that bill, Ben Franklin's knowing smile. I almost threw up in fear.

I ran around the house and made sure every outside door was locked. And double-locked. I pulled Brandon into his room and made him stay there. I threw the house back in some kind of order as best I could.

I didn't want Elena to know.

How could anyone have gotten to me? It was a message; that was sure. But it was also a message that whoever it was wasn't completely certain. Otherwise I was pretty sure I'd be just like Rollie. Tortured until I divulged something. Dead.

Brandon too.

Of course there was also the very real possibility that I was imagining all this. I sat down in the kitchen, going over and over it again. Had anyone actually been up there? It surely didn't seem so. Nothing else was disturbed. Truth was, I wasn't 100 percent sure where I had even left the ring. *Think, Hilary* . . . Could that bill have been mine? Maybe Elena had put it there. I did usually pay her in hundreds.

Think. What you do next may determine whether you and Brandon make it out alive.

Part of me wanted to grab Brandon and just get the hell out. Go anywhere. To a hotel. To a friend's.

To the police.

But if I did, what did I really have to tell them? A break-in that may well have been just that. A murder that all the facts said was just a suicide. A ring that wasn't stolen. In plain sight. A random hundred-dollar bill.

A warning that only I would understand.

158

And then what, turn myself in and admit what I'd done? Who knew where that would lead? I'd likely be arrested. I might be separated from Brandon. Over what? All these things that didn't fully add up to anything. I kept coming back to the fact that whoever had broken in here couldn't be 100 percent sure. Otherwise they wouldn't have sent me a warning. They'd have had me up on the boards like poor Rollie.

They'd be trying to find their money.

I made Brandon sleep next to me. I lay down with him in my bed, my arms around him, maybe squeezing him a bit too tightly, my heart throbbing. The last thing he said before drifting off was to mutter sleepily, "Mommy, don't call the elephants in."

"The *who*?"

"The elephants, Mommy. Like at the circus." The reluctant heroes.

"No, honey . . ." I put my arms under the sheets and hugged him. "Don't you worry, we won't. We won't call them."

As soon as he was asleep, I gathered my nerve, grabbed a light, and went outside to the back deck. I went down the steps and found under the gardening table the key I'd hidden that opened the door to the crawl space.

Which at least meant that no one had been down here—that the money was still intact.

No one knew for sure.

Which also meant if someone wanted me to know they were on to me, they were likely trying to scare me into doing something reckless and showing my hand. Like maybe running with the money or re-hiding it somewhere.

Which meant they might be watching the house even now.

I looked around into the woods and felt myself shudder with fear.

If . . . I forced myself to come back to reason, if this wasn't all just what it appeared to be on the surface: Part of the string of Westchester home burglaries. Stuff was missing. My iPad. Some antiques. My files were all broken into. Someone was clearly searching for valuables. It just seemed they hadn't made it upstairs.

Back in the house I scanned the outside from the kitchen window, pushing back the feeling that I was being watched, that someone out there was just waiting for me to make a move. That I should just put the satchel out on the doorstep and let them take it, and then the whole thing would go away.

No, it wouldn't go away.

I'd already used a healthy chunk of it, $60,000. What about that?

What I kept coming back to over and over was how anyone could know. I hadn't given Rollie my real name. And I was sure I'd left no trace of myself back at that crime scene. Even if someone had dusted for prints in

Kelty's car, they might have found mine. But my prints weren't even in the system. And who was I kidding, this wasn't any kind of official investigation. The police likely didn't know a thing about any missing money. If they did, there would be flashing lights in my driveway and cops at the front door. Not upended furniture and an open back door.

I lay there, my son breathing innocently next to me, going over what options I had.

The clock read a quarter to two.

Clearly I'd committed a crime. I'd taken the money. Possibly from a crime scene, because at that point it might well have been a crime scene until foul play was ruled out. I'd tampered with evidence. Who knew where a half million dollars in the front seat might have taken the crash investigation?

Maybe a prosecutor would forgive me for that. I'd never committed a crime before. And anyone might have been tempted. But then I'd used part of it. I laundered it through the banking system. That was a federal crime. Surely that wouldn't just be brushed aside.

And worse, what I did might have led to the death of a completely innocent man.

My thoughts whirled in a hundred different directions. I felt the urge to run to the toilet and hurl.

I tried to calm myself, in the face of everything, by the fact that I didn't know for certain if any of this was even true. What if I went to the police and turned in the money—"*What money?*" they would want to know. No one had any idea there had even been a crime. I'd have to return whatever I'd spent. Milton Farms might be willing to give it back. But Brandon would be out of there that same day. And I'd be a felon. I'd be risking my son being taken from me. I was all he had.

And even if I *did* turn myself in, even if the district attorney overlooked all that I'd done, if someone was truly hunting me, for the money, if my fears about Rollie and tonight's break-in were true, then the people responsible still wouldn't have what they wanted.

Their money.

The police would have it.

They'd killed Rollie just on the suspicion that he had it. Knowing I had taken it and lost it, what would they do to *me . . .?*

My thoughts caromed wildly. Nothing ever looks very pretty in the middle of the night. I watched the clock turn three.

I decided I had four choices.

One was to just wait and see. Do nothing. It might all blow over or never ever come to pass.

Of course, if I did that, I could also wake up with a gun at my head one morning. And put Brandon at grave risk. At best, I'd never have a calm night's sleep again in my life.

Second, I could take off with the money and move out to Montana or something. Take Brandon out of his school.

Leave Judy and Neil. No, that was just the hour talking. Crazy. My life had been ripped apart at Brandon's age when my folks died. How could I possibly do it to him?

My third option was to turn myself in. Hire a lawyer; work out some kind of deal. As a first offender they might forgive much of what I'd done.

The problem was the very real possibility that the only actual crime that had been committed so far was mine. That the break-in tonight was exactly what it was—the work of the same people who had done the other three. That Rollie hadn't been murdered, he'd killed himself.

That I'd be turning myself in for nothing.

I could end up in jail. Then who would take care of my son? That would destroy him. His world would fall apart in an instant. He counted on me. I'd be bringing on him the same terror and abandonment I'd felt as a child. Exactly what I always tried to protect him from. Not to mention that if the money was illicitly gained, whoever wanted it back, whoever had killed Rollie, wasn't about to let me get off with just a few months in jail. They'd come after me.

It was going on four when a last option entered my mind. One that just kept nudging itself forward.

I had to find out where that money had come from. And who might be looking for it. Was it dirty? Were they bad guys? Did I have to be afraid? Where had Joe Kelty gone that night?

Before I completely tore our lives apart.

Not to mention, it occurred to me, that there might be someone else out there I had put at risk. Who, like Rollie, had no idea there had even been a crime.

Which all explained why at a quarter to four in the morning my thoughts drifted to Joe Kelty's funeral.

CHAPTER TWENTY-EIGHT

That damn dog never stopped barking.

His name was Jerry. The neighbors' white-and-black Jack Russell. Mr. Halverston always left him in the yard late into the night, and you could hear him, yip-yipping at the occasional car that drove by, people taking a stroll. Maybe the moon. And first thing the next morning he was out again. His mother always said you could set your clock by it. That barking.

He grew up with that yip-yip-yipping from across the chainlink fence.

He was a good dog mostly. Once you shut him up. He was happy and liked to fetch, and he'd come back with anything, a Frisbee, a Spalding ball, wagging his tail. His brother Todd always went over and walked him when he came home from school. He would toss him treats across the fence from their bedroom window.

"Why are you doing that?" he would always ask Todd.

"He's my friend," his little brother would say. "Why else? You shouldn't worry about him so much. The dog's just lonely."

They'd moved here and switched schools that year. Mom had a new job, working in some office of a garment manufacturer's in Manhattan. She had to take the ferry early in the morning and then a train. She always came home after dark. For a while it seemed they had to grow up by themselves. Every once in a while, their uncle Clifford would watch them. But he was a weirdo. Once, while they were watching TV in the basement, Clifford touched him in a way he knew wasn't right. It made him hard and he was ashamed of it, being just twelve. "Don't tell your mom," Clifford said. "She's damn well got enough to worry about without this. You don't need to upset her more. It'll be our little secret . . ."

He nodded, thinking to himself that one day he would take one of those screwy things his mom used to open a wine bottle and drive it into Clifford's eye.

But his mom did have a lot to do. Then, as soon as she put the dishes away and finally relaxed at night, there was always the barking.

"Someone should do something about it," she would say.

"Maybe you should talk to Mr. Halverston."

"God knows, I've tried. Lucky it's a cute little thing," she would say, holding back a smile, "or else I might well just put it out of its misery."

Then one night he was home alone doing homework. Mom and Todd were at Todd's elementary school for a parent-teacher night.

The yip-yip-yipping began. He waited for it to stop. It never did. He opened the bedroom window and looked down at the dog.

"Shut up."

Jerry just looked up at him, barking even louder.

"Shut the fuck up," he said.

Maybe thinking he was Todd up there, the dog continued to yelp, standing on his hind legs, looking up at their window. Probably hoping for a biscuit to come down.

Someone ought to do something, *he heard his mother say.*

He went into the jar on Todd's desk and took out a couple of treats. Then he went downstairs and out the back into their tiny yard. Jerry barked at him across the wire fence. He looked at the Halverston house. He didn't see any lights on inside. He knew they liked to play bingo at the church some nights.

Yip. Yip. Jerry was barking.

He went over to the fence and tossed a treat into the Halverstons' yard. Jerry went for it. He climbed over the fence.

"Here, Jerry. Here, boy . . ." He held the second biscuit out for him to see. "Come here."

The dog ran up, tail wagging. He looked around and went into the open garage. Mr. Halverston didn't really use it for his car. He parked his car out on the street. He used it as a kind of workroom. He had lots of tools and a large freezer in there. He liked to fish. Everyone knew he would go out sometimes at midnight on the bay and always catch something. He'd clean them and cut them up and give some out around the neighborhood. Thick fillets covered in ice shavings. His mother always looked forward to them.

"Come on in here, Jerry. Come on, boy," he said affably, showing him the second biscuit. He led him into the garage.

He'd had a dream once. Of what he might do to shut him

up for good. His mom would be happy. The entire neighborhood would be. He'd be doing everyone some good.

"Come on, boy . . .," he said. He opened the freezer door.

There were a couple of frozen fillets stacked on the top shelf, but the bottom was completely free. "Here, boy. Here, Jerry . . ." he said, waving the biscuit in front of the dog's nose. He tossed it into the bottom freezer bin and the stupid pooch climbed right in.

He stayed just long enough to enjoy the sound of him whimpering and scratching at the door.

It was two days later when they finally found him. He was frozen like a big dead fish. With a skinny tail.

For two days everyone figured Jerry had gotten out somehow and run away. Instead of barking, all you heard was old man Halverston and his brother going up and down the neighborhood. "Here, Jerry! Here, boy!" calling for the dog.

"Don't worry," he said to his mom while she was doing the dishes. "I fixed it, Mommy."

When they finally found it, there was wailing and shouting across the street. His brother ran into their room and punched him in the face. "I know it was you. It was you!" The police even came and talked with him.

His mom never said a thing.

It was nice, not hearing that stupid barking anymore.

But it wasn't too long after that his mom came and made them pack up their things and they had to move away again.

CHAPTER TWENTY-NINE

Driving across the Verazzano-Narrows Bridge the following morning, this still seemed like the most viable option.

I dropped Brandon at school. Later, Elena would pick him up and take him to her house. He stayed with her for a day or two from time to time if my folks were in Florida and I was out of town.

I was way too nervous for either of us to go back to my own house right now.

I turned off the bridge and wrapped onto Hylan Boulevard, as I'd done to go to the funeral two weeks ago.

This time I turned onto Midland Avenue in the direction of the bay. Patrick Kelty had said this was where anyone could find him if they wanted to come and help. The money rightfully belonged to him more than it did to me. I had to know where it might have come from, if someone was after me or not. Whether Rollie had been killed for it. Before I completely brought my life down for it.

And Brandon's too.

Every house I passed was still in some state of disrepair. The street was passable; what debris was left had been cleared to the side. Several houses still had boarded-up first-floor windows and blankets or insulation covering them where they were exposed. What were once pleasant and colorful Victorians and beachy bungalows now looked like gutted and abandoned slum houses.

Baden Avenue was a middle-class street that back-ended into the drive that went along the shoreline, Father Capodonna Boulevard. Several homes had work crews in front, volunteers pitching in, dump trucks and Dumpsters.

I pulled up across the street from number 337. It was a blue Victorian with a tower on the third floor. Most of the houses seemed in decent shape, though closer to the bay, a couple of others looked like they'd been gutted. I'd read that a few people from this neighborhood had died, and many of the homes were no more than tiny wooden bungalows, below sea level. I waited for a while in the car, not sure what I would say. Only that the wrong reaction on Patrick's part could land me in jail. Finally I just blew out my cheeks and thought, *Hil, let's just go*. The one thing I couldn't live with was the thought that I had possibly contributed to an innocent man's death, and that if my fears were right, Patrick could be in danger too. I spotted him on the front porch, directing a couple of workers who were hauling lumber. I heard the sound of a chain saw from inside.

I got out of the car.

The cold wind coming off the bay lashed into me, and I was probably a second away from turning around and calling this a bad idea, when he came down the front steps, lugging what appeared to be a rotted window frame. He was handsome, in a rugged way, wearing a blue New York Rangers sweatshirt and jeans, worn work boots, auburn-colored hair cut short and flecked with red. He almost bumped into me. I'm sure I had one of those dumbstruck, I'm-not-sure-what-the-next-word-out-of-my-mouth-will-be looks on my face, but I knew I definitely didn't look like I belonged here.

"I hope you're with FEMA," he said, heading past me to a pickup truck on the street.

"*Sorry?*"

"FEMA." He balanced the frame on his thigh and pulled down the latch for the cargo bay. "But I don't see any briefcase, so I think not. And you're probably not with Penn Mutual either."

"Penn Mutual?'

"Our insurance carrier. Who we haven't seen here since we first filed. Three months ago."

I shook my head and shrugged kind of apologetically. "No, I'm not."

"And you certainly don't look like you've come around to pitch in. So I guess that probably leaves you as some kind of local press down here to see how we're all holding up, which is barely.

"Which would actually be fine," he said, looking at me, "because we need whatever attention we can get. We're not quite the story line the Jersey shore is, God knows why. As you can see, there's a bunch of us still living like the storm was yesterday." He threw the rotted window frame into the truck's cargo bay.

"Sorry." I shook my head again. The icy wind whipped in from the bay.

"Well, that's three." He shut the cargo door. "Three *sorries*. Publishers Clearing House lottery maybe? I won the grand prize? We could certainly use it."

"None of the above, I'm afraid. I was actually just looking for a word with you. You're Patrick Kelty, right? Joe Kelty's son."

"That would be me." He headed back up toward the house.

"My name's Hilary Cantor. I just need to talk with you for a few minutes," I said, keeping up with him. "I know you're busy. Do you have a couple of minutes?"

"I do have a couple of minutes." He stopped. "I just don't have a couple of minutes anywhere that's warm. We could go inside, but it's drafty enough you might

172

as well be in a boat out on the bay." The chain saw whirred with its earsplitting whine. "Then there's that. We're finally demolding the first floor."

"Out here will be fine."

"Not out here. I can see you're freezing. Down here we call it 'the Father Cap breeze.' Balmy, right? C'mon, I can give you a cup of coffee at least? Courtesy of Dunkin' Donuts up on Hylan. They keep us pretty filled day to day."

"Sure." I smiled appreciatively. "Coffee would be great."

"Come on up then."

I followed him up onto the front porch. The drone of industrial-size drying fans and the hammering of drywall being stripped hit me from inside. "Milk, okay? Sugar?"

"Just milk," I said. "Thanks."

"Be right back." He went inside and I looked around at the neighborhood up close. A once happy family street, a block from New York Bay, in the shadow of the Verazzano. Now it looked as if a missile had hit in dead-on. A few of the homes had work crews at them and construction vans; others hadn't yet begun. A couple of the homes looked as they must have the day after the storm hit.

Patrick came back out with two Styrofoam cups. "If it's not right, don't complain to me . . ."

"I won't. Thanks." I wrapped my hands around it

and instantly it warmed me. I took a sip. "So how did you know I wasn't here to volunteer?"

He chuckled. "You're kidding, right?"

"No. I'm not."

His eyes drifted down to my moccasins. "People who come to pitch in don't usually show up in Tod's. Dead giveaway."

"Oh." I nodded guiltily. "Anyway, they're not. Tod's. Tod's knockoffs maybe."

"Anyway, you look like you should be volunteering up in Greenwich or Rye or something. Not that that's so bad. So what's up? You actually look familiar." He stared at me. "Why do I think I've seen you somewhere before?" My hair was pulled back and I had only a hint of makeup on.

"I was at the funeral," I said.

He slowly nodded. Then he jabbed his index finger at me. "That's where it was. You were in one of the back rows. I remember."

"That's pretty good under the circumstances. I'm really sorry about what happened to your dad."

"Thanks. He was a good guy. So you knew him then?" He smiled. "People he worked with generally don't wear Tod's either. Or the knockoffs."

"No. I didn't know him." I took another sip and drew in a steadying breath. "I was actually at the accident site."

He blinked. That seemed to take him totally by surprise. "Up in Westchester . . .?"

I nodded.

"Well, that wasn't what I was expecting to hear. So you're from up there?"

"Armonk."

"Ah, now I get the shoes." He rotated his coffee cup. "I actually didn't know there *was* anyone else at Pop's accident site. Just this one guy . . ."

"Rollie," I answered for him. "Roland McMahon."

Now he nodded. "My sister spoke with him. Now that I think of it, maybe he did mention someone else being with him there at first."

I waited to see if that seemed to mean anything to him. If the friendliness in his eyes suddenly shifted to suspicion. If behind them was the question of where the hell half a million dollars had gone that was in his father's possession at the time of his death.

I didn't see anything.

"I know this is kind of weird," I said, "but I don't know if you heard . . . He died."

"Yeah, we actually did hear that." Patrick leaned his weight against a column. "Suicide, we were told. The police contacted us, to see if he'd maybe been in touch after our initial conversation. Which he hadn't. Kind of a strange thing, though, given how he was ready to run down and help my dad, then not even a week later . . ." He shrugged. "So you were there?"

"Actually, I was there *first*," I said, putting my own cup down on the railing. "I saw your father's car go out

175

of control. A deer ran in front of it. You probably already know that. But he was gone by the time I got down there. I'm sorry, I really wish there was something I could have done. I just couldn't wait around. I have a son who I was late for and Rollie was there, so . . ." I shrugged. "There wasn't much either of us could do."

"No need to explain." Patrick smiled. "I understand." He sat down on the railing. "So I guess we've come to the part of the conversation as to what brings you all the way down here?"

We had. Did I just let it out right here? *There was half a million dollars on the front seat that might have belonged to you, and I took it.* This was the time. But Patrick didn't seem to be fitting into any of my concerns. His demeanor hadn't changed. He wasn't probing me for details. I was also thinking he probably didn't need to be going through this again so soon after the funeral.

"I don't know, I guess I just wanted to let you know that I was there," was all I said, feeling my courage ebb. "I was wondering if you ever figured out what your dad was doing up there? You mentioned at the funeral that you hadn't?"

He looked at me. A liveliness in his warm blue eyes. Earnest, trusting. "No. We still don't," he said. "I was going to dig into it, then I figured, what would be the point? What happened, happened. He'd mentioned something about some building supply outfit he was going to see up there. For kitchen tile. Anyway, it may

176

not look it, but what's left here is still very much alive, and it's pretty much taking up everything I have lately."

"I can see that. It's overwhelming."

He shrugged. "At times it seems that way. You just do what you can. Anyway, look, I appreciate you trying to help up there. My dad would have been the first one to pitch in himself if it had happened to someone else."

"So I heard." I wanted to tell Patrick exactly why I'd come. Why I was at the funeral. But the words stuck in my throat. I suddenly felt panic, mixed in with a bit of shame. I felt if I stayed there any longer he'd see right through me. I realized that Patrick Kelty's father was involved in something that his son knew nothing about. And there was likely nothing good connected to it. And the more I talked, the more it would come out. He didn't need to hear it.

I felt I had to get out of there.

"Look, thanks for the coffee." I stood up. "You're busy. I probably should head on."

"You're not just being modest and you're actually a whiz with a chain saw by any chance, are you?" He smiled.

"No. Wouldn't know which end was the chain and which was the saw."

"Figured. You didn't exactly look the type. By all means come see us again if you ever do figure one out."

"I will. Thanks for the coffee." I went back down the stairs. I motioned to a ragged stuffed teddy bear that was perched on the steps of the front porch. "Night security?" I asked

Patrick smiled. "Keeps out the looters. I found him washed ashore in a pile of rubble. Happens every day down here."

"What's his name?" I put my hand over my eyes as Patrick was suddenly in the sun.

"Joe." Patrick picked up the coffee cups and stacked them together. "He doesn't say very much, so I named him after my dad."

CHAPTER THIRTY

Patrick watched her drive up the street until she disappeared around the corner.

He wasn't sure just what had brought her down here. Maybe she felt guilty that she'd been unable to help his dad. Maybe just that she had been at the scene. On the job he'd encountered dozens of situations where witnesses would come back to the spot where a tragedy occurred. Or leave flowers when someone died, just to feel connected to it. Still, he couldn't help but feel that she was holding something back. Whatever her reasons. He couldn't put his finger on it.

The whirring of a chain saw inside stole back his attention. He took the cups and went to head back inside when someone called from the street *"Lootenant . . ."*

Patrick turned, instantly knowing who it was from

the gruff voice and familiar accent, his gaze falling on the black Range Rover that must have come up while he was talking to Hilary. Then on the large-shouldered man in the black leather jacket who stepped out of the passenger seat. Someone Patrick was not happy to see, and especially not here.

"No time for me?" Yuri asked, extending his upturned palms in a questioning manner. "And I come such long way."

Patrick went down to the street, his blood simmering. He didn't want him on the property. He didn't want him anywhere in the entire neighborhood. He didn't want to be seen with him, a Russian *Vors* as clear as any in the movies, on a collection call. Everyone within six square blocks knew Patrick worked for the NYPD. And you didn't have to be a detective in organized crime to figure out who Yuri worked for.

"*Girlfriend?*" Yuri nodded with an approving roll of the eyes. "Very nice. Little too thin, perhaps. More to grab, more to love. You know that saying? I think you have here too, right?"

"Why the hell are you here?" Patrick went up to him.

"Why I am here?" The Ukrainian bunched his thick lips. "I want to take trip on the Staten Island Ferry. Boris has never seen Statue of Liberty. Why you think I am here? Another week. Not even dime. I told you last time, clock is ticking. Tick, tock. Tick, tock . . ."

"And I told you then there are claims in the works and you'll be paid. Maybe you heard that Congress just appropriated relief funds. When I get paid, you'll be paid. I promise, you'll be the first to know."

"Government, eh?" Yuri grunted cynically. "At home we say little thieves are hanged, but great ones go into government. In a week, will be over hundred thousand dollars. You borrow from yourself? So tell me, Lieutenant, with what will you rebuild your house?"

"That's *my* worry. Your worry is to back off and leave. You'll be repaid."

"No, that is not your big worry," the Ukrainian said. "Big worry is that clock runs out and only way for you to repay is to make a call and poof, a particular case file disappears. Or maybe gun in evidence closet is no longer there. Or else, all hard work to rebuild house here and house goes up in ball of flames. *Poof!*" He snapped his fingers. "Know what I mean? That would be my worry, Patrick Kelty, if I were you."

"I want you the hell out of here now."

"Or what? You want to pick fight with me, Mr. Police Official? You want whole neighborhood to watch like on *Showtime*? Listen, we all know this debt is something you take on yourself. That it isn't even your own. But now you own it, you understand? Now it's yours, as much as if you went to Brighton Beach and set it up with Sergei Lukov yourself. And until is paid, I walk up those stairs and shit on living room carpet if that's what I want to do. You understand me? I don't see badge anywhere . . ." Yuri snorted. "Just hockey jersey. So right now, you are simply loan like anyone else. Loan no one is paying."

They stood there for a moment, eye to eye. Yuri was right, the last thing Patrick needed was for people to see him here. Some of the volunteers on the street were cops, firemen. Explaining why this *Vors* from the old country with a sleeve of tattoos up and down his arms was here threatening him would only bring on questions he didn't need to answer.

And the Ukraine was right on something else too. The last thing Patrick wanted was for them to settle the loan in "trade." There was no badge on him right now. The NYPD was a million miles away.

"I hear you loud and clear," Patrick said. "Now I just need you to get back in your car and drive out of here. Please . . ."

The Ukrainian looked at him. There was a spark of softening in his dull, heavy-lidded eyes. But not so much that he probably wouldn't carry out everything he had said he would. He probably already had, as easily as having breakfast.

"You made me almost forget real reason I came. Sergei Lukov has heard that your father has died recently. Is this so?"

Patrick nodded. "Yes."

"He was old man?"

182

"No." Patrick shook his head. "Car accident."

"*Accident*?" Yuri grunted wistfully. "You know saying, death always answers before it is asked? Very common in my work. Anyway, Sergei says no interest charged this week. A man in mourning should not have his mind on someone else's debt."

Patrick looked at Yuri. "Tell Sergei thank you," he said.

Yuri swatted him on the shoulder. It fell with the weight of a diesel.

"You ever stop with the sayings?" Patrick asked as the mobster headed back to his SUV.

"Ha!" Yuri turned at the car door. "Here's one more. Just because you not look at clock, doesn't mean it stop ticking. You know what I mean? Next Thursday, clock starts up again. Tick, tick, tick, tick, tick . . .

"I wish you and your family best." He squeezed into the front seat. "But if I were you," he said, snapping his fingers, "I would make sure those thieves in government work fast, Patrick Kelty."

CHAPTER THIRTY-ONE

I didn't get far.

Just across the Verazzano Bridge and back into Brooklyn, where I took the first exit onto Dahlgren Place and just sat there, at a gas station, not sure what my next step was.

The question kept drumming inside me like a bass drum that wouldn't stop.

Where the hell was I going? I had nowhere to go. After last night I was too scared to take my son home.

Where the hell would I even sleep tonight? In some hotel room, too scared and too uncertain to go back to my home, thinking of what happened to Rollie and my ring? Not just today, but tomorrow. And the day after that. And Brandon . . .? Hide him at Elena's indefinitely? Praying that I hadn't put the person I loved most in the world in danger? Or take him down to Florida and leave him with my folks?

I was pretty certain Patrick knew nothing about the cash his old man had with him in the car. But that didn't mean they wouldn't go after him too. That he wouldn't be the next one on the list who was put in danger. And he wouldn't even know why. Like Rollie. He could have a gun jammed in his mouth and be tied to a chair and he wouldn't have a clue in the world as to what he was dying for.

I couldn't do that.

I sat there for a while, watching people go in and out, mothers running behind their kids. Workmen getting out of their trucks.

Until I came to the conclusion I'd reached earlier this morning when I'd driven down. That I had to give back the money. It was more Patrick's anyway than mine. I'd have to come clean and face the consequences, wherever they led.

Maybe I just wanted a partner in this.

Maybe I just wanted a way I could work this out.

Close to an hour passed before I drove back over the bridge again to Baden Avenue. I stopped at the top of the street and asked myself one last time if I was okay with what I was about to do. Because everything could change. The answer inside me grew firmer and more certain.

I was.

I had to be.

I drove back down to his house and left my car across the street. I stepped up to the porch, and smiled at the teddy bear guarding the top step. "Joe." I knocked on the front door and stepped in the house. Someone in work clothes stuck his head out of the kitchen.

"Patrick here?"

"He's in the back," the workman said above the whine of a power sander. "You can go on in."

I walked through the basically gutted house. There were some new walls being framed, and new windows hammered in. Patrick was on the back deck, nailing down two-by-fours on the newly elevated platform. The sun shone off New York Bay, almost right out the back door. Patrick looked up when he saw me, his eyes brightening. "So you know how to work a chain saw after all?"

"No."

"Okay, how are you with a hammer then? I see you're still wearing the same shoes . . ."

"I need to talk with you, Patrick," I said, my voice slightly cracking.

He stood up and lifted his baseball cap, brushing some sweat off his brow. "Wasn't that just what we just did?"

"I wasn't truthful with you, what I said before. About why I was down here. Is there somewhere we can go?"

"You mean, like, to a place?"

"I mean like anywhere, Patrick, please. Just out of the cold. Away from all the noise."

186

Now I was sure he could see the anxiety in my eyes. "There's Red's. Up on Hylan."

"That'll be fine. Can we go there? It's important. Please."

"Sure." He nodded, placing his hammer on a bench. "I'll just tell the guys."

CHAPTER THIRTY-TWO

Red's wasn't much—a neighborhood bar with a Molson light in the window and a couple of TV screens over the bar. Where a hockey game would feel at home, and on Friday nights the familiar crowd would be knocking back a couple of beers.

Patrick waved to the white-haired guy in a white shirt behind the bar. He also gave a hug to the heavy-set waitress, saying, "Hey, Steph, somewhere quiet, okay . . ."

It felt like he had known her for years.

She took us to a booth near the back and we sat down across from each other. He said, "I've been coming here since I was just past altar boy. On Sundays, my father would sneak us beers for Giants games."

Steph started to rattle off a couple of specials, to

which Patrick told her, "Just some drinks." I asked for an iced tea, though a martini would have felt more like it. Patrick ordered a Diet Coke. We waited until they came. We didn't say much. There was only one other couple in the bar. When the drinks arrived, Patrick kind of leaned his glass forward. "So here we are . . . You said you had something to say."

I nodded, leaning back against the cushioned booth. "I said I hadn't been entirely honest with you," I started in, "about why I came down here. I *was* at the scene when your father went off the road. And I did go down and do my best to help him before Rollie appeared. I could see he was badly hurt. I tried to revive him, but I couldn't get a response. I tried to get him out, but the driver's door was wedged in by a tree, so I ran around to the passenger side. That was when Rollie hollered. I told him to call 911—I'd left my phone in my car. That took a while."

Patrick took a sip of soda and waited for me to go on. "Okay."

"I crawled inside the car and tried to get a response, but I couldn't. I'm sure he was already dead. But there was something on the seat next to him. Not on the seat actually—on the floor. A black leather satchel. Slightly open. It was clearly knocked off the seat in the crash."

"What was in it?" Patrick asked.

I looked at him, knowing the next word out of my mouth was going to change things. *"Money."*

189

The word fell off my lips like a weight, and I could see Patrick, his eyes both confused and surprised, trying to reconcile his dad being up there in the middle of nowhere on some mission he never disclosed, his dad who worked his whole life in the MTA transit tunnels, with a satchel full of cash.

"How much money?"

I didn't say. "Look, here's where I have to tell you some things about myself." My hands edged forward to his side of the table. "I was married. My husband and I have been divorced for four years. I have a son. Brandon. He's a terrific kid, he's just . . . He's just got some developmental issues." I shrugged. "Asperger's . . .

"But there's a very gray line where Asperger's ends and full-out autism begins," I went on, before he could interrupt me. "And that's where Brandon is. He demands a lot of attention. For the past three years I've had him in this special school in Greenwich and he's doing great. It's just . . . It's just very expensive. Almost fifty grand a year. And my ex . . ." I took in a breath and shook my head. "All I can say is, if you met him you'd think he's about the nicest guy in the world, but he's a little short when it comes to the financial responsibility department . . . And a month ago his construction company went belly up."

Patrick leaned back against the booth. "You didn't answer my question. How much money?"

"This is hard," I said, ignoring what was in his mind.

"Just hear me out." I took a sip of iced tea. "The past two years I've paid for everything entirely on my own. I had a job as a divisional comptroller for an advertising agency. It was hard, but I made enough, barely, and when I didn't, I tapped into whatever savings I had. Which is basically gone now. My son's care has taken everything.

"Two Wednesdays ago I got let go. We lost our lead account and the entire division I worked for was shut down. I basically got four weeks' severance and a couple of months on the health plan, which is crucial to me because of Brandon. That was the day before your father's accident."

"Which brings us to the cash," Patrick said, beginning to put it all together. "You took it."

"I took it." I nodded, my throat suddenly dry as parchment. "I heard Rollie making his way down the incline. It was just one of those split-second things. You have to understand, I've never done anything like this before in my life. It was just—" I looked at him and shrugged, with the slightest, self-recriminating smile. "I was just so damn desperate that I didn't see any other way. It was like this gift had fallen into my lap. Your dad was dead. I saw a way to keep my son in school and get out from under some debts that were crippling us.

"So, yes, I zipped the satchel back up and hurled it as far as I could into the woods so no one would find

191

it. Then Rollie made it down. He never knew a thing about it. I guess my plan—such as it was—was to let it sit there until I knew for sure who it belonged to or if anyone was looking for it. Which was why I came to the funeral. I swear I intended to give it back.

"But it didn't seem that anyone *was* . . . looking for it. So I guess I just convinced myself that it was somehow okay. Because how would anyone ever know? No one would know. Except they always know, don't they? And no matter how well you think you handled it, they always find a way. Back to you . . ."

Patrick's tone took on an edge of impatience. "I guess they do . . ."

"I waited over a week before I went back for it. I actually prayed I'd see something like it was your dad's life savings or the proceeds from a business, and I was honestly going to write you and let you know where it was. I swear. I begged my husband to ante up for the school. I did anything I could so I didn't have to go back for it. But he basically just blew me off. He was out in fucking Vail, skiing. His new kids' spring break. All the while he was telling me he was penniless and that his wife was going to have to take a job. My options were to take his ass to court, which would have taken weeks, *if* there was even anything to get. *Or* . . ." I looked at Patrick and it was clear what was in my eyes. "The next day I went back. I swear I didn't want to ever see it again. But it was just *there* . . ." My eyes moistened over with guilt and shame. "I'm sorry."

"How much money?" Patrick asked a last time, fixing on me

I drew in a breath and met his gaze, pushing myself back against the booth. "Half a million dollars."

CHAPTER THIRTY-THREE

Patrick's eyes grew wide, his expression a mix of stupefaction and utter disbelief. "You just said half a million dollars."

"I did."

I could see the gears start to turn. His father was an MTA worker who'd spent a lifetime in the soot and darkness of the New York City transit tunnels. Where would he ever lay his hands on a half-million dollars? He cleared his throat, his voice barely a notch stronger than mine, his eyes tunneling in on me. "*Exact?*"

I nodded. "In bound packs of hundred-dollar bills. Fifty of them."

"In a satchel? On the seat of his car?"

"That's right." I nodded again.

"Jesus son of Mary." He sat back and blew out his cheeks.

194

I said, "I guess it's safe to say I don't think he was up there to see any building supplier, Patrick."

He nodded almost reflexively, then his gaze fell back on me. "You've got a lot of balls, coming in here and telling this to me."

"I realize that," I said. "I'm sorry."

"So where is it all? Now?"

"I'd rather not say exactly where it is, if that's okay. Until I have an idea what you're going to do about it."

"What I'm going to do about it?"

"Don't worry, it's safe. It's more yours than mine. Or someone's—I'm not exactly sure who it belongs to."

"What do you mean, *who* it actually belongs to?"

"Patrick, please, you know it wasn't his. You said at the funeral you didn't even know what he was doing up there."

"I'm trying to make sense of this . . . My father, who spent his whole life repairing tracks; who left a pension of seventy-nine thousand dollars after removing most of it to pay for his wife's medical treatments; and who paid off his mortgage twenty years ago and never had a dollar in debt—somehow had half a million dollars in hundred-dollar bills in his car? And now *you* have it, hidden somewhere?"

"Actually, it's down to four hundred and thirty-seven thousand." I shrugged. "I told you about the school. I also paid my house taxes for half the coming year. And my mortgage. And part of a business note for my parents. I know I'll have to pay it all back."

195

He looked at me without telling me much. The air seemed to go out of his anger.

"Look, I don't know how you want to handle this . . . You want to arrest me, go right ahead. I guess that seems right. It's just that before you do, there's more . . ."

"More *money*?" His eyes grew wide again.

"No. More to the story." I let out a painful breath. "There's Rollie."

"Rollie?"

"Yeah." I swallowed guiltily. "I'm afraid so."

Rollie. The person who, according to all the reports, had been first on the accident scene. And who was now dead. On top of a missing half-million dollars.

I watched Patrick slowly fit the pieces together.

"I told you this was hard. I've no idea if he truly killed himself or not. As much as I could find out, he didn't suffer from depression, he wasn't sick, he was happily married, he didn't have financial problems. I mean, I'm not a detective, but anyone who might be looking into that accident, say, from the point of view of trying to find something that didn't end up on any police report or in the press—say half a million dollars—would discover that Rollie was first on the scene. Before the cops and EMTs even got there. The only one. Not me."

"I think I'm starting to see where this is heading." Patrick exhaled somberly. "And I don't like it."

"I don't like it either. It nearly scared me to death when I first read about it. I'd waited ten days to see if the missing money appeared anywhere. I started to think he was the first one anyone would go to, if the police report didn't mention a satchel of cash being found. Certainly the newspaper never mentioned anything."

"So you're suggesting that this wasn't a suicide? That this guy was *what*, murdered?"

"The people closest to him certainly didn't see it as a suicide. I went on a family grief page and anyone who knew him seemed to be at a loss for words. And nothing's come out since to change that. At first I just thought maybe I'd been watching too many detective shows. I mean, I've been on total edge about this since I took it. Then something else happened. Last night. Something that made me think maybe it wasn't my imagination running away with me after all."

"I'm listening."

"My house got broken into. I don't know if you've heard—why would you?—but there's been a string of them going on up in Westchester. So at first, when I came home, I thought that's all it was. Not *all*, of course—I mean it freaked me out. Brandon and I live there alone. The place looked like a neutron bomb had gone off inside. Things were missing. Drawers rifled through, turned upside down."

"What made you think it wasn't just a normal robbery?"

"I have this ring. My diamond engagement ring. Jim gave it to me. A nice one. Almost four karats. All I could

197

think of was that I'd worn it the day before and never put it away, and I'd left it right out in the open on my dresser. A blind thief would have found it."

"Okay . . ."

"But when I ran up to my room, the place was just as I'd left it. Nothing up there had been touched. I figured we must've come home just as whoever it was had gotten up there, and when they saw us drive up they took off. The door to the deck was open. And I found my ring. Sitting there, right on the dresser. At first I couldn't believe my luck. Then I saw what it was on . . ."

"What *what* was on?" Patrick furrowed his brow.

"The ring. What it was sitting on. Right there on my dresser for me to see."

This time he just sat there, waiting for me to fill in the blank.

And I did.

"It was on a crisp new hundred-dollar bill."

CHAPTER THIRTY-FOUR

"I know it was a warning." I leaned forward, my palms on Patrick's side of the table. "I know the whole robbery thing was just a sham, and what they wanted me to see was that bill. To let me know they knew, or at least suspected. That it was me. Either way, put together with Rollie, someone's looking for that money. Which is why I'm here. I don't know how they could have traced it to me or whether they know for sure—they can't know, only suspect. Otherwise I'd probably be just like Rollie. But I have a son. A son who's the most important thing in my life, and who all of a sudden I'm just a little scared I've put in danger."

"And what exactly were you thinking *I* would do?" Patrick squinted at me. "Clearly, you're aware I work for the New York City police."

"You said that at the funeral. And *I* said that I'm prepared—whatever you have to do, go ahead. I just want him to be safe. But before you do, you might want to hear me out. I'm pretty sure that no one knows this money even exists. No one meaning the police, of course. As far as they would be concerned, so far there's not even been an actual crime that's been committed. Rollie's death was deemed a suicide. Which I suppose there's still one chance in hell it just might be.

"So you can have me arrested. But what happens then? The money gets looked into, and I'm pretty certain it's not going to come back as clean. I can hand it over to you. By rights, I'm guessing it belongs to you more than anyone else. But that isn't going to get these people off my back. Or Brandon's. So I guess there's part of me that hoped, if I came here"—I looked at him, rotating my glass on the table—"there might be a way we could handle this ourselves." I shrugged. "Privately . . ."

"Privately?"

"I need to know where that money came from and who's behind this. If it's someone I have to be afraid of. If they killed Rollie. If someone broke into my house and is after me."

"And if there is . . .?"

"If there is, then I don't know. Maybe the police are the best answer. I surely committed a crime. I don't know what that means for Brandon and me. But I can't put my son at risk. No way."

200

"And if we do . . ."—Patrick waited a beat or two, then looked at me—"handle it privately, as you say. What works in that for me? Other than risking everything I've built my life on."

"Only one thing." I swallowed and held my breath. "Four hundred and thirty-seven thousand dollars."

"Of my father's money," he replied.

"Of someone's money, Patrick. If you want to take the chance on who that someone might be."

He drew in a breath, and for a second I was sure he was going to take out his phone and dial up his superiors on the force right then, right in front of me, and say, *You're not gonna believe the story I just heard.* Instead he just shook his head with a kind of befuddled expression. "You want a drink?"

"A drink?"

"I think I need a shot of something. Tequila, maybe. I'm thinking you probably need one too."

I looked deep into his eyes and smiled. "I'd love a shot of tequila right about now."

"Steph!" He called over the waitress. "Two Don Julio Añejos." He looked back at me. "I think it's fair to say this is going to be it, as far as work is concerned today."

"Trust me, I won't be the one turning you in."

It took just a couple of minutes and the drinks arrived. Patrick raised his glass. "Hell with the salt and limes."

"Right behind you." I lifted mine too.

He downed his in a gulp. I shut my eyes and

swallowed mine too. I blew out my cheeks, feeling my throat on fire, the sharp but pleasurable burning settling into my chest.

For a moment we just looked at each other, Patrick's back against the booth, running his hand across his scalp. Me, not certain if I was about to spend the night in a New York City jail, and potentially a whole lot after.

"So if you were so prepared to hand yourself over," he asked, "why didn't you just take this to the local police up there?"

"I couldn't." I explained how I wasn't completely sure about any of this: The break-in. What happened to Rollie. And if I admitted to the police what I'd done, not just about taking the money, but laundering it as well, I knew I'd definitely be brought up on something, and that scared me, what with Brandon.

All with the possibility, the remote one maybe, that an actual crime hadn't been committed other than mine.

"That's why I needed to know about the money. And even if they let me off," I said, "say on the desperate-single-mother thing and never having committed a crime before, and I agreed to pay it all back, there'd still be this person out there—and I don't have a clue in hell who it even is!—who's already clearly shown what he's willing to do to get back his money. We'd never have a comfortable night again in our lives."

Patrick nodded, tapping his tequila glass against the table. "I guess my next question is, why me?"

"You mean other than I saw you at the funeral, and you seemed like a nice enough guy, and I couldn't *not* tell you, after last night, that your life might be in danger?"

"I appreciate the 911. But, yeah, since you brought it up, other than that, I guess."

I slowly slid my glass on the tabletop, then looked back up at him and shrugged. "Maybe because I couldn't think of anyone else who might have a vested interest in keeping all of this quiet."

Patrick stared. "By 'quiet,'" he said, giving me a wistful smile, "I assume that's another way of saying, 'handle it privately.'"

"Your father got that money from somewhere, Patrick. And I think we both know it's not likely it came out of some secret savings account he'd been keeping from you."

"So you're saying why unnecessarily cast a stain on the reputation of a man everyone loved and looked up to?" It sounded like he was trying to convince himself.

"All I want is to be able to go back to my life and take care of my son. I made a mistake. And I'm prepared to hand the money over and return, over time, every penny I spent, if that's what you want. And the only way I have a chance of achieving this—without an electronic bracelet around my ankle for the next ten years—is if you see it that way as well.

"I know you work for the police. I realize where your obligations lie. But I'm also pretty certain that if that

203

money ends up in police hands, it won't be yours or mine—and there'll be an investigation into where it came from and just why your father had it on him that night. And that won't be pretty."

Patrick smiled, the kind of mirthless smile a chess master might show when his opponent pulls off a completely unpredictable, game-reversing move and corners him. "There's just one thing."

"That you're a cop."

"I work for the department now. In the office of community affairs. And this goes against anything I've ever sworn." He looked at me, continuing to tap his finger. "You're sure you left no trace of yourself at the accident scene?"

"Maybe some prints in the car. But my fingerprints aren't in the system."

"And Rollie . . . . Tell me again what you told him."

"I only gave him my middle name. Jeanine. He asked how to reach me and I said I'd leave my info on his windshield, but I didn't. He made the 911 call to the police. He stayed with your dad's car until they arrived. I was gone by then."

"Still," he said, twisting his mouth, "somehow they found you."

I pressed my back against the booth and shrugged. "Yeah, somehow they did."

Some other customers had come into the café. Patrick waved at one, then turned away.

"I have to think this over. You said you made a bad decision and it may be costing you your life. I don't want to do the same thing."

"Just not too long, okay? I'm kind of hanging out here. Poor choice of words," I said, seeing his face curl into a tight smile. "Sorry, Rollie . . ."

"So where's your son?"

"With my housekeeper. I can keep him there for a couple of nights. I think it's safe."

"Don't go back to your house until we decide what's right."

I nodded. "You don't have to tell me twice."

"Do you have a place to stay?"

"You mean anywhere as cozy as the couch at your father's place? I'll figure something out."

He nodded. "You realize, when they see you're suddenly no longer at your house, if these people weren't sure they had the right person before, this will remove all doubt."

I hadn't. A troubled feeling wormed its way through my stomach. "Thanks."

He took out some cash and set it on the table. "Don't thank me yet. You may well end up in handcuffs by tomorrow."

"I meant for hearing me out. And for the drink."

"You ready to tell me now where you've got the money?"

"Maybe tomorrow. Once we see if I'm in handcuffs or not."

"I'm gonna give you my number. Put it in your phone. Anything happens, anything even slightly suspicious, dial it and keep it on. I'll be able to track your whereabouts."

I looked at him appreciatively.

"I do have a vested interest in keeping you alive."

I smiled, took my bag and made a move to stand up.

He wrapped his hand around my wrist. "Now it's your turn . . . And not like you did with Rollie. You're sitting on a half-million dollars."

"Four hundred thirty-seven five . . ." I smiled, sending him my number.

CHAPTER THIRTY-FIVE

Charles Mirho watched from his car a short way down the block and saw the two of them come out of the café.

"Well, blow me like a horny sailor . . .," he muttered out loud.

They stopped in front of the man's red F-150 and shared a last word. Then the woman walked down the block to her car.

I guess we could put the doubts to rest, Mirho chuckled with satisfaction, over whether he'd found the right woman.

So what are you doing with my half a million dollars, doll?

He knew the guy she was talking to was none other than Joe Kelty's son. What would she be doing here with him? Could the two of them somehow possibly be in this together? Was that accident possibly not as random as everyone might have thought? No, he thought, scratching the mark on his cheek, that was crazy. The police report said a deer had darted in front of Kelty's car. More likely, ol' Hilary here was struck by what might be called a fit of conscience or regret. She hadn't gone in with anything and Mirho hadn't seen an exchange of money. Though it could be in that trunk. He tapped his finger against the steering wheel. So why oh why had she made contact with Kelty's son?

Anyway, this gave him a couple more angles to work on to get back what he wanted.

Not just the money. What he was really after. The money was only part of it.

The money alone wasn't worth what he would have to do.

Kelty waited in his truck until Hilary drove by, giving her a quick wave as she passed.

Mirho pulled out after. He glanced in his rearview mirror as Kelty executed a U-turn and headed back toward his house. He settled in a couple of lengths behind the Acura as it seemed to head back to the Verrazano Bridge.

This was where things were about to get interesting. Where the best of his talents could be put to use. He didn't relish what was going to happen. He had a kid somewhere out there himself, and no one liked leaving one to make his way in this world alone. That had happened to him.

His mother had been killed in a fire with a man other than his dad. He'd been on his own since he was fifteen. The only benefit that ever came from it, he attested, was that since he'd known pain from early on, he also knew how to inflict it as well.

He watched the silver Acura SUV wind around onto the entrance to the bridge.

Mirho knew what had to be done. That was just how it was in this game. How it was with ol' Rollie up there pleading to get down, with a terrified "No!" and those bulging, disbelieving eyes as he kicked the table away. He couldn't have let him down. The trail couldn't be left for anyone to find. It had to be swept over with his boot. And that meant getting his boots dirty.

Every time.

He followed the Acura, knowing the end was getting close. He'd stick to her now like bad credit. The rest . . . The rest would just play out.

Always did.

This ended the rescue part of the operation, Mirho chuckled.

Now the recovery part set in.

CHAPTER THIRTY-SIX

State Senator Frank Landry parked his car in the lot of the posh country club just outside Hartford and stepped inside the clubhouse. He admired the view of the eighteenth green through the large windows in the lobby, the well-known eighteenth hole covered in a layer of fresh white frost. It was a strange place to meet in January. Come April, the place would be alive in manicured, sweet-smelling green. Landry asked a red-vested club employee where the restaurant was and she directed him to the right. A pretty hostess was at a podium.

"Mr. Franzino, please," Landry said.

"He just arrived." The hostess grabbed a menu and led him in. "He's over here."

Landry didn't exactly need her to direct him. There were only two tables with anyone at them in the room, and Landry had been acquainted with the head of the state's Democratic Party for over ten years. Since Landry first contemplated running for office. Steve stood up as he arrived at the table. "Frank, thanks for coming out." He grasped Landry's hand warmly. "I'm sure it seems like a strange place to meet this time of year."

"I was wondering," he said. "Beautiful though, come April."

"They used to have a PGA tourney here every July. All the pros. Anyway, one of the beauties of this time of year is that we can have the place pretty much to ourselves. Which comes in handy, I've found, when you want to escape everyone poking around into your business up in the capital. Sit, please."

Landry took a seat and the hostess left the menu.

Steve said, "Thank you, Jill."

Franzino was a muscular, barrel-chested guy, with bushy gray temples and thick hands, and he looked every bit the part he had played earlier in his career, that of the most intimidating union lobbyist in the state. He was tied into everything. A kingmaker or a career wrecker, depending on where his loyalties fell. A nod from him could do either. Landry asked for coffee. He ordered a fruit plate and a muffin. Franzino ordered a western omelet. They chatted for a while, mostly small talk related to the capital. At a pause Franzino looked at him earnestly. "So how's it going, Frank?"

The question seemed to come with a lot of weight to it.

"Without Kathi," the party chairman clarified. "Such a horrible, horrible thing, what happened down there. To lose her like that, with the family there. You spoke so beautifully at the service."

"It's tough, Steve. I won't say otherwise. The house is empty without her. The kids miss her. I miss her, Steve."

"Of course. Everyone does, Frank. She was a wonderful gal."

Landry smiled. "Thanks." He took a sip of his coffee. "But I know the head of the state Democratic Party didn't ask me all the way down here to hear me talk about that."

"No. No, I didn't, Frank, you're right. And of course, this is the kind of little powwow our colleagues up in Hartford or the local press there didn't have to see. Which was why I asked you here." He pushed back and crossed his legs. "As you know, Governor Taylor is up for reelection next year. And no doubt you've read some things in the press or heard things bantered about the dome . . . But the truth is, one of our state's prestigious Ivy League schools has been interested for some time in his possibly becoming president . . . And Mark's been at this game a long time. I think he's finally ready for a change." Franzino looked at him. "I'm pretty sure he's not going to run again."

"That *is* news." Landry put down his coffee, genuinely surprised.

"Which is gonna leave a big, wide hole in the center of the party, Frank. For someone to fill. Obviously he'd

212

like to ensure that the office stays with the party, so we don't have what happened back in '98."

"I assume Carol and Fazio are at the top of the list," Landry said, referring to the lieutenant governor and the head of the state senate.

"Yes. They are. But as you know, Frank, Carol makes no bones about her sexuality and over the years Tony's put his hands in more shit than a drunk plumber. There's also that hedge fund guy from Greenwich who's always been talking about how he'd like to run . . ."

"Talbot?"

"Yes, that's the one," the state party head said.

"Well, he's certainly got the money."

"He does have the money." Franzino nodded. "But so do we, Frank. If we get the whole apparatus behind someone favorable."

Landry looked him in the eyes. "And who might that person be, Steve, you'd like to get the apparatus fully behind?"

"I was hoping you'd figured that one out by now, Frank. The reason I asked you down here was to explore whether that person might be you."

Landry blinked. A smile of feigned surprise. He put down his coffee. "You took me by surprise with that one, Steve. I'm just a blue-collar guy from Staten Island who's made the most of the opportunities life's presented."

"Oh, come on, let's not pretend to be completely naive on how this process works, Frank. You know how

213

this state runs well as anyone. You've managed the legislature's purse strings for what, six years now? The deficit's down. Jobs are coming back. You're young. You have the right record to run on. Don't take this the wrong way, but you've certainly got the sympathy vote pretty much locked up if you want it. Every woman in the state would feel their heartstrings bend for you."

"No offense taken. It's just too early, Steve."

"It's actually still eighteen months out. And all we want is a signal, Frank. If you'd like to take on more of a role. Or if you simply wanted to spend more time with the kids. Either way, of course, anyone would understand."

Landry felt his blood rush. He pushed around a slice of grapefruit, barely able to hide the thumping of his heart.

How long could he even pretend this had never been on his mind?

"I'll have to think about it, of course. Run it by the kids. They'd have to be partners."

"Of course."

"But I think I could assure you, Steve," Landry said, piercing the grapefruit with his fork "if you really thought *I* was a person you could rally around, I'd be happy to take on whatever role you saw fit."

CHAPTER THIRTY-SEVEN

After meeting with Patrick, I didn't know where to go or where to spend the night.

The last place I wanted to go was home. I had Brandon with Elena, which I could do for a day or two; her daughter Sarah was fifteen and happy to help out. And they always liked having Remi around. I didn't want to create a sense of alarm.

It dawned on me that the safest place for me to go was to my father's boatyard on Long Beach Island.

The island was a tiny five-block-wide strip of land that separated the borough of Queens from the Atlantic Ocean. The yard was kind of a mom-and-pop type of operation; my dad had bought it ten years ago after he retired from teaching biology for thirty years, and when my mother, a math teacher, retired two years later, she worked there too. It was situated on the northern shore of the islet that looked out at Island Park, Queens, which explained why they suffered only minimal damage from the storm, while much of the rest of the narrow island was underwater. There was a room in the back of the office where my dad had spent many a night. Riding out storms. Catching naps in the spring and summer when the business was 24/7. He'd been trying to sell the place for two years. The boat business had fallen apart and the thing had eaten up most of their pensions, the part that I hadn't eaten up already.

I drove there after dark. My folks were in Sarasota, where they had a condo and spent the winter, even though this year they remained up north into January, after Sandy, getting the place back together. They did have a yard manager, Artie, who even in winter still came in most days. But the place was usually deserted after dark.

No one knew about it. No one would connect me to here. I figured this had to be the safest place for me to be.

I took Atlantic Avenue from the Belt and crossed over on Long Beach Avenue. Just to be sure, I made sure no one was following me. After Sandy, I'd pitched in as much as time would allow, bringing Brandon down on weekends, helping to clear away the fallen trees and a thousand branches, sifting through scattered tools and supplies, and raising machines that were under a foot of water. The houses along the beach were still a mangled mess. Four months later, the building department still hadn't determined by how much more they needed to be raised, so construction was at a standstill. There were only a few lights on anywhere near the yard.

The yard was blocked off by a wire gate that opened with a security code, 6-15-75, my parents' wedding day. My aunt and uncle actually. There was no one around; only the sallow light from a single streetlamp barely illuminated the old sign, PARADISE MARINA AND SALES. I drove my car through and the gates automatically closed behind me. I felt I'd left all bad things outside when I heard the wire gate close.

The place was dark. The pavement was a little rutted and in need of repair. Everything here was. What little light there was came from a couple of time-set spots that went on at dark, one of which blinked intermittently. I drove up to the office, a shingled cabin with a front porch that abutted a large maintenance shed that housed our supplies, spare engine parts, forklifts, with a couple of bays where they could put boats they were working on up on blocks. Eight or ten of the larger boats had been shrink-wrapped against the elements and were up on blocks outside.

I parked on the side of the office and went up the steps. I knew where we always kept a spare key, in a jar underneath a loose floorboard at the end of the porch. It was there. Thank God, because it was freezing. I took it out of the jar and shivered as I shoved it in the lock. The front door opened.

Brrrr . . . It was cold as shit inside too. I flicked on the light. There were a bunch of files and boat catalogues piled on my father's desk. A computer on my mom's desk, where she handled the books. They'd always sold a few boats each spring. Not large ones—this was Queens, not the Hamptons. But the business had changed, like every other, to lower-cost online sales and Dad had gotten stuck with a couple of thirty-five-foot Hatterases whose finance charges were larger than his house payments. And if the economy's falling apart and the shifting state of the boat business hadn't made him question his decision to get into this line of work, their declining finances did. It made me feel good, looking at the hardscrabble way they lived and conducted business, to know I'd made them current on their notes.

I put on some heat and opened the door to the maintenance shed and flicked on the overhead halogen lights. There was one boat up on blocks—a wood-hulled trawler which it looked like Artie was in the midst of painting. I breathed in the familiar marine smell, which is somewhere between gasoline, the bay, and paint. It was cold as shit in here as well. I shut off the lights and went into the room in back of the main office, where there was a cot and a small kitchen, and a bathroom off it. I found an electric space heater and plugged it in. I immediately felt some warmth. I put on some coffee and turned on the radio to 1010 WINS.

I sat on the squeaky single spring bed. *Welcome to Paradise*, I thought.

I took out my phone and called Brandon at Elena's. "How's he doing?" I asked when she picked up.

"Heez doing fine, missus. Heez playing with Sarah. Heez almost ready for bed. You want to talk to heem now?"

"Yes. Thanks, Elena. Thanks so much for doing this. And listen, you know where Dr. Goodwin is?" Brandon's neurologist. "In White Plains . . ."

"Yes, Miz B. I know."

"He has an appointment tomorrow at four. After school."

"No problem, missus. I will take him there."

"I really appreciate this, Elena." I hadn't told her why, or where I was, of course. Only that I had to stay in the city for a night. Maybe two. And for her not to go back to the house. I didn't want to alarm her, so I told her there was some work being done there. I gave her the next two days off.

Brandon came on. He didn't exactly sound enthused to hear from me.

"Hullo."

"Hey, tiger!" I tried to sound upbeat. "How you doing there?"

"Fine, Mommy. Where are you?"

219

"I'm just away for a night. Maybe two. On business. You like staying with Elena, don't you? And Sarah."

"I thought you weren't in business anymore."

"Well, I'm trying to get back in. You know that. Someone needs to pay the bills. Unless you want to. So how was school today?'

"I can't play FLOW," he said. "I left my iPad at the house. Elena wouldn't go back and get it."

"I think we should leave it for a while, Brandon. You'll be fine. It's almost time for bed anyway. How's Remi doing?"

"Are we going to go back home tomorrow, Mommy?"

"I don't know, Brandon. Soon. Go to bed, okay? I love you, sport. And listen to Elena . . ."

"I want my iPad, Mommy . . ."

"Play on Sarah's computer. I'll talk to you tomorrow, honey. Bye."

"Bye."

He hung up and I sat there on the cot with the phone to my ear, feeling like there was something I needed to say to him, about how much I loved him, and what I was doing for him, wondering how someone whose trajectory in life had always gone upward, me, was sitting alone in the cold, sparse room, believing against all that I knew to be true that I was safe.

CHAPTER THIRTY-EIGHT

Mirho left his car on the shoulder off the dark street. There was no traffic this time of night. Going on midnight. No one anywhere. He smelled the ocean nearby. Most of the lights from the apartment high-rises along the water had been dimmed. He screwed in the sound suppressor on his HK 9 millimeter and stuffed the gun under his leather jacket into his belt. He took out the wire cutters.

He turned off the electronic tracker that had led him here.

Shutting the door, he made his way over to the wire fence and ran his hand along the links until he found a spot with some give. Here it would be easier to cut. Using two hands, one by one he snapped the metal links in a straight line down to the ground. Around

221

twenty. Until he was able to pull a seam back in the fence—wide enough for him to wedge himself through and squeeze inside the yard. He planned not to have the same worries a little bit later when it was time to leave.

A few lights marked the way and he headed toward the water, his heels crunching on the compacted earth and snow. The cold coming off the water stung his cheeks. He moved his fingers to keep them warm. He could almost taste the fear he was about to cause.

As he got within a few yards of the office, he stopped. Across the narrow bay, lights flickered in Queens. He saw the hulking silhouette of boats up on blocks, plastic glinting off the intermittent spots, one of them blinking. A five-foot wooden boathook leaned against one of the boat blocks. He stepped more carefully now, removing the gun from his belt. A gull honked out on the water. That was the only sound. There was a large warehouse kind of structure with a retractable aluminum-sided door. And a small, shingled cabin with a wood porch adjoining it.

He decided that was where she had to be.

He blew out a frosty breath.

He looked inside the windows. The interior was dark. He stopped. He didn't hear anything from within. Or sense any movement. *Here's where the fun starts, partner . . .*

He put the gun to his side and stepped onto the porch.

CHAPTER THIRTY-NINE

I woke.

I didn't know if it was due to the temperature, which had suddenly gone through the roof as the space heater had kicked in full bore. Or that damn light that was flickering outside.

I reached over and checked the time on my cell phone: 11:51. I threw off the blanket and lay there, feeling like a hundred degrees. I got up, turned down the heater, and cracked the window a couple of inches to let air in the room. I lay back on the bed and shut my eyes and tried to push everything away again. Last night's break-in. Patrick. Whether someone was really after me. I was safe here, hearing nothing but the sizzle of the flickering spot outside, the occasional sound of a gull honking on the bay.

That's when I heard it. At first, just the sound of crunching snow.

What was that?

I listened. It could well be nothing. No one knew I was here. I didn't hear anything again for a long time. I blew out a breath and closed my eyes to sleep.

Then I heard it again. Like a branch cracking on the ground. Or footsteps. My eyes bolted open and my heart immediately came to a stop and stayed there. Totally immobile.

This time there was no mistaking it.

Something *was* outside.

I froze. It could easily be an animal, I told myself. A raccoon. In winter, they liked to crawl under the shrink-wrap for warmth. Or a wharf rat. Big, ugly suckers—the size of a cat. Every yard had them. Then I heard it again. Not a fleeting, scurrying sound, but something flat. Crunching. Going along the side of the house.

Footsteps.

I pushed up to my elbows, ice now running through my veins. I listened so closely I heard the brush of the window shade against the glass, the dust blowing across the floor.

There it was again. *Oh God!* This time it seemed to be moving away from me. Toward the front of the house.

My heart was pounding crazily. *Shit, Hilary, what the hell are you gonna do . . .*

I got to my feet, careful not to make a sound. I'd fallen asleep in my clothes, so all I had to do was slip on my shoes. I picked up my car keys and cell phone off the table. Patrick had told me to call at the first sign of anything suspicious. But before I did, I at least wanted to be sure. And anyway, what could he do? He was in Staten Island. An hour away. Call the cops?

Then everything was over.

Silently, I tiptoed to the door to the main office. I stood, every cell in my body rigid, afraid to make a single sound.

I scrolled to his number in my cell phone.

For a long time there was only silence. I prayed that it was all somehow just the wind or an animal. A false alarm. I stood there, thinking how I could make it to my car. Trying to recall if I'd locked the front door to the office behind me. How could someone even get in here?

Then I heard the creaking of a floorboard. Whoever it was had stepped up on the front porch.

My God, he was coming in . . .

My heart climbed up in my throat. I had to get out of here now.

I ran to the maintenance shed door and flung it open. By now, my footsteps probably sounded like loud banging on the floorboards, likely giving myself away. Whoever it was clearly heard me and ran up to the door. They twisted the knob, trying to open it. They pushed on the doorframe, rattling it forcefully. It would hold for only so long.

What the hell do I do? I could try to wedge myself out the windows in back, but I'd have to push the glass up and kick out the screens. By that time he could be all over me. I heard the sound of glass shattering. A man's hand snaked through a windowpane, trying to get to the lock.

Panic took hold of me.

The shed was my only way out.

CHAPTER FORTY

We called it a shed, but it was more like an airplane hangar, maybe eighty feet long, two stories high. It was pitch-dark and it felt as cold as a meat locker in there. The boats that were lined up in dry dock on blocks in long rows, the forklifts and other heavy machinery were only large, hulking shadows to me.

I shut the door behind me. I could lock it from the inside, but that would only lock me in, anyway, so what good was that to me? There was a fuse box on the wall next to the door and I wildly switched six or seven fuses on one panel trying to disable the lights. Inside, I heard the front door finally crash open and whoever was there go in.

He couldn't be sure exactly where I'd headed. I figured his first move would be to go through the office, searching the back rooms. There could well be a rear door that I'd run out of.

Then he'd come in here.

I ran down the steps and onto the concrete floor, determined not to make a sound. My first thought was to make a run for the outside door. Actually, there were two doors. The large aluminum retractable one the boats went through, which took forever to go up and clattered like a noisy elevator. Which would immediately give me away.

And a regular pedestrian door to the side. But they were sixty or seventy feet away. I stood there, unable to fully summon the courage, petrified that he'd hear me and I would never make it to the car.

Which was where I had to get to.

I weaved through the blocks where some of the smaller boats were stored to the far end of the shed where Artie had been painting the wooden-hulled boat. I heard footsteps inside the office and knew this was my chance. There were shelves everywhere, crammed with boxes of engine parts, oil, paints, waterproofing material, and I snaked in and out of a maze of boxes and equipment to get to that door.

Then the shed door flung open.

He came in.

I froze, crouched behind a canvas boat cover. I begged every cell in my body to stay completely still. Especially my heart, which was going off like a panic alarm to me.

228

"There's nowhere for you to go," I heard the man call out. I shuddered. He was clicking switches one by one, trying to turn on the lights. But they didn't go on. Thank God!

"I know you're in here." I heard him come down the steps. "We both know I'm going to catch you. And then it won't be pretty. The longer you resist is only going to make me madder and I reckon you've already seen what that results in. *Right?*"

I ducked behind the forklift.

"How about I make you a deal?" His voice started getting closer, his words bouncing into me like bullets. "You show me where the money is . . . I won't hurt your son. How's that? *Sound good . . .?*" I heard him stepping in between the boats, looking behind the equipment shelves to see if I was there. "You knew that was always a possibility, right? You're a good mom. Why would you want to put that nice-looking boy of yours at risk? I saw him the other day. At your home . . ."

His voice grew louder, penetrating through me like a knife. Making me shiver at the thought of him staying around and watching us after we arrived home. I glanced to the door. It was maybe forty feet away. No way I could make it there, get it open, and get to my car. *Alive.* I felt my heart going crazy. *You've got to do something, Hilary . . .* I was so scared I wanted to cry, but I thought of Brandon. Of him without me. Possibly never even knowing what would happen to me. I pushed the fear back.

229

You have to be strong.

"You know I was in there, right?" I heard his footsteps on the other side of the shed, kicking over boxes, pushing paint canisters on the concrete floor, making a sandpapery sound that raised the hairs on my arms. "You saw what I left for you? In your closet. Pretty good, you have to admit. Bet I gave you a jolt on that one! That's why you went to Kelty's son, right? Because you knew I'd found you and you wanted to give the money back. Am I right . . .?"

His voice knifed through me. It was as if he was waiting for me to panic, knowing how scared I was, and just blurt something out.

And I almost did.

A sheen of sweat rose up, completely covering my skin.

"Of course, it's not just about the money." I stood there, listening to him come closer. "The money's only part of it."

What did he mean?

"Which is why your boyfriend has got to be next. Did you find what I'm talking about? Those pages? Kelty kept it. A diary, maybe a photocopy of one. Maybe he had it in the car. Perhaps you saw it . . ." He came to a stop. Maybe twenty feet from me. My heart stood still.

"So here we are . . . you and me, Jeanine, just us . . . And now it's time to get down to business."

I eyed the door and knew I had to run for it. I also knew I'd never make it. Even if I got there, he'd overpower me before I ever started up my car.

"The longer you hold out, you know that's only going to make me madder."

I looked up and my eyes landed on the hydraulic hoist that was suspended over the boat Artie had up on the blocks. They used it to pull out the engines to work on them. He was nearby. Kicking over boxes. Coming closer. The power station and maneuvering arm were on the wall just behind me.

I looked at the forklift and something crazy went through my brain.

The lift was one of two we kept. A large one that lifted the boats, with an enclosed driver's cabin. And the one I was crouched behind, much smaller, for lifting heavy boxes and supplies. With an open operator's seat. I spotted the key in a dish on the console. I heard the man coming around near the boat. I reached out and took the key and guided it into the ignition. I closed my eyes for a second and held my breath. *Just work. Please.* My life depended on this.

I twisted it and heard the soft click. The yellow power light went on.

Thank God!

The guy was now directly beneath the boat Artie had up on the blocks. He was just a darkened figure, but I saw him kneel, looking underneath it. For the first time

231

I could see he had a gun. That sent my heart rate galloping.

Then he looked up at the boat above him.

"Mirror, mirror on the wall . . . Who's the craftiest sonovabitch of them all? I wonder . . ."

The boat might well be a place to hide. That guy Tsarnaev had done it, up in Boston, the marathon suspect. There was a ladder leaning against the hull. What Artie would have used to get up there. The man took one or two steps up.

"I know how it goes," he said. "You probably never expected anything like this when you took that money. How could you? But you know, maybe you should have thought of that, right? When you did." He raised up and peered into the boat. "Now look what it's come down to. You see the consequences of it. Stuff just happens, right?"

I drew a bolstering breath deep into my lungs.

Right.

I slapped the power switch to the hoist on the wall and the large hydraulic arm loudly came to life.

The guy's eyes shot above him, startled.

I jumped behind the wheel of the forklift and started it up. The guy probably didn't know which way to look or what was happening. I jammed it in gear, forward, and headed toward him, concealed by the darkness at first, and by the noise from the hoist. The whole shed seemed to be shaking.

By the time he saw which noise was the one to pay attention to, it was too late.

He leaped off the ladder, training his gun on the advancing lift, and fired. I screamed, seeing a flash that could end my life and hearing the bullet ricochet off the lift.

I barreled into the ladder, which fell back over him, the side of my lift careening into the wooden blocks holding up the boat, knocking into one of the stanchions. The boat teetered for a second; then the whole structure collapsed, rolling over the forklift and toppling over me with a loud crash.

I screamed, wooden tiers and a three-thousand-pound boat coming down around me.

For a moment I was sure I was dead. The wood-hulled boat toppled over both of us. But the safety bars on the forklift held and the craft rolled, crashing into a ten-foot aluminum shelf filled with paint cans, oil canisters, and engine parts.

Like an entire building imploding.

It took a second for me to realize that I was all right. Dazed, I pulled myself out of the lift. I heard the guy with the gun, buried under the debris, groaning, "Shit. Fuck." I spotted his gun. It must have fallen free in the crash. I ran over and grabbed it, the guy slowly trying to unpin himself. I'd never even held a gun before.

My first thought was, did I just hold him there at gunpoint and call the police? Turn everything over now.

Or call Patrick, who was at least an hour away. I surely knew I couldn't just hold him that long. Truth was, I didn't know if I could shoot. So I ran. I took his gun and sprinted toward the front of the shed, hurling myself into the door. Twisting the knob.

It didn't budge.

God, no! It was locked. I looked behind me. The guy was climbing out from under the rubble. Frantically I twisted the knob as hard as I could. *Open, open . . .*

Please. Now!

It must have been locked from the outside. I jammed my hand on the button for the big retractable door. Noisily it sprang to life and started to slowly climb. It got as far as my knees, my waist, rattling and clanking at a snail's pace. I looked back and saw the guy get to his feet, searching around for his gun.

Then he must've just said the hell with it and started coming after me.

My heart climbed up my throat in panic.

I ducked under the retracting door and ran as hard as I could around the bend to where I'd left my car. I reached into my pocket for my keys and took them, dropping them on the ground, then grabbing them and yanking open the car door and jamming the key into the ignition just as I saw the guy come out of the shed, looking around, and as soon as he heard the car go on, head toward me.

I jammed it into reverse and hit the gas, doing a half

U-turn, my heart slamming in my chest. I pressed the door-lock button and heard the click just as he reached me. He grabbed on the door handle, futilely pulling on it, then slamming his fist against the window in fury. I screamed, jumping out of my seat. Then I hit the gas again, gunning the vehicle as hard as I could, the Acura lurching forward and pulling out of his grasp, barely missing a tree as I went by and headed for the front gate.

It was maybe fifty yards in front of me.

Which was the moment when I realized that it was locked! The gate was a heavy chain link. No way I could just ram through it. *Oh God . . .* I had to wait for it to open on an automatic sensor.

I looked behind and suddenly couldn't find any sight of him. He was probably going for his car, wherever it was. I got within a few yards of the gate and braked, my heart doing its best imitation of a chain saw trying to slice through my chest. *"Where the hell are you?"* I yelled, panicked. *"Where?"*

In front of me, the gates slowly began to open. I suddenly had the sensation that I was going to make it. Three or four seconds and there would be enough space for me to bolt through. I pulled forward, ready to gun the engine.

Then everything just imploded.

The car shook. Glass splintering all around me.

I never saw him—only felt the force of something

heavy crash through the window and a rain of shattered glass in my lap.

I screamed.

Like some animal, he charged at me on the passenger side, the wooden six-foot boathook I'd seen against the office now like a lance jammed through the car. It had missed my head by a millimeter.

The man jammed his hand through the caved-in window, trying to wrestle the door open.

Oh God!

I gunned the car, pulling away from him, tearing through the open gate, the hook still sticking through the car. I skidded onto Harbor, making a sharp turn.

I looked behind and saw a figure come out into the street, futilely watching me.

My body was shuddering. My face was mashed with tears.

"You're okay, you're okay, you're okay!" I shouted to myself. Half crying, half convulsing, craning my head around to be sure no one was following.

I drove until I made it back over the bridge and into Queens. I drove on Long Beach Road for blocks and then made a left onto Atlantic Avenue into a darkened gas station. I pulled around to the back and turned off my lights.

My hands were still shaking as I took out my phone and pressed Patrick's number.

CHAPTER FORTY-ONE

"*What's happened?*" Patrick said, picking up on the third ring. It was twenty minutes after midnight. *Why else would I be calling?* I was sure he could hear the panic in my voice.

"Patrick, they found me!" I said, my heart pumping as furiously as when I'd driven away from the boatyard only minutes before. "I was at my father's boatyard on Long Beach Island, and this man . . . He must have followed me there somehow and gotten in. He was trying to kill me, Patrick." I held my phone with both hands, trying to keep it from shaking. "He chased me. I can't believe what I had to do. I can't believe I was able to get away."

"*Who?*" he asked me, his voice suddenly completely alert and ready.

"I don't know!" I tried to catch my breath. "I only know I was lucky I woke up and heard him outside or I would probably be dead."

"I want you to tell me everything, Hilary. But right now where are you?"

I looked around. "At a gas station somewhere in Queens. I can't believe what I just had to do. He had a gun and I couldn't make a run for the door. I had to—"

"Hilary, listen, you can tell me all about it when we're together. In the meantime, are you sure that you're safe where you're calling from now?"

"Yes. Yes. I'm in my car. I left him back at the yard."

"You're absolutely positive of that? There's no way he could have followed you?"

"No. My lights are off. The station's closed. There's no one around. But there's a boathook through my window where the guy tried to stop me. Glass everywhere!"

"Hilary, listen . . ." His voice was steady and comforting. "Here's what we're going to do. I'm going to give you an address. In Brooklyn. It's my house. But I don't want you to drive there yourself. I want you to leave your car on the street and find a cab. Are you in a position to do that?"

"Why?"

"You said this guy found you at the boatyard. You don't think you were followed there?"

"No, no. I thought of that when I left you. I did my best to make sure I wasn't."

"I'm thinking there might be a tracking device attached to your car somewhere. So just leave it on the street and find a cab. Are you up to that? Or else you can sit where you are and I'll come get you? But that'll take some time."

"No, I can do it," I said, sucking in a breath. "A tracking device?"

"I don't know. But I just want to make sure he doesn't follow you anymore. Do you know Brooklyn? The address I'm going to give you is in Bensonhurst."

"I'll write it down."

He told me the address: 3371-60 Crescent Avenue. I scrawled it on a grocery receipt I found on the dashboard. "You said that you're in Queens?"

"Yes. Near the Rockaways. On Atlantic Avenue."

"Good. That's only about fifteen minutes away. Now, listen, do what I told you, quick. Get away from your car. And you have to make absolutely certain before leaving that this guy's not around, waiting for you to make a move."

"No, I'm positive. I made several turns. The streets are empty. He's not here."

"Okay, then go. But keep your phone on. You can talk to me. Wait in the driveway on the side of the house. I'm at my dad's house in Staten Island. I'll be there in about half an hour."

"What about my car?"

"Don't worry about your car. I'll take care of it tomorrow."

"Thank you, Patrick." I was trembling. "I was just so scared and I didn't have anywhere else to turn."

"It was right that you called me. But, listen . . . you said there's a boathook sticking out of your car?"

"That's right. The window's shattered. He smashed it through and it missed my head by inches."

He paused. "What do you say you give some serious thought to maybe taking it out before you put it back on the street?"

He gave me a bolstering chuckle.

"Yes. Yes, I will. Of course!" I said. I actually laughed myself. "It was terrifying, Patrick! And you have no idea how close it came."

"You can tell me about it soon. I'm on my way. And, Hilary, if you feel even the slightest nerves or danger, you holler in that phone, okay? I'll be there."

"Okay, I will. Thank you, Patrick. I don't know what to say."

"You don't have to say anything. I'll see you soon."

We hung up. In the dark of the station I pulled out the hook and left it next to the garage. I looked around and parked the Acura along the darkened street. There were a few cars left out there. It seemed safe.

Then I spotted a cab coming down Atlantic Avenue. I ran out after it and flagged it down. It pulled over and I blurted out Patrick's address. The cabbie pulled away and I looked behind me. I didn't see anyone following us.

Only then did I start to breathe easier.

We headed west on Atlantic, toward Brooklyn, putting a lot of distance between me and whoever was after me. Shaken, I pressed my face against the window. I couldn't believe what I'd just done. I couldn't believe what had happened.

Then something wormed into my mind.

About the conversation I'd just had. I stared at my phone.

I'd just told Patrick that someone had tried to kill me and he said he would come get me if I was in danger. He worked for the NYPD.

Never once did he mention a thing about calling in the police.

CHAPTER FORTY-TWO

I got to his place first. The house was a typical two-family home on a darkened, residential street in a part of Brooklyn I didn't know at all. Patrick was right—it was about a fifteen-minute cab ride from where I'd been. On the way, I must have glanced behind about a hundred times, checking to see if anyone was following. The streets were quiet. I was pretty sure we were alone. But I had the cabbie make a few random turns and double back until I was absolutely positive.

He let me off and I waited in the driveway.

I knew I'd have to own up to what had happened back at the boatyard. I couldn't have Artie or my dad call the police. That would blow everything up. I'd have to make up some kind of story. In the meantime, I knew I was lucky to even be alive. Lucky that that man wasn't in the backseat of my Accura with a gun to my head as we drove back to Armonk to get the money.

Around one, I saw a headlight come down the street and Patrick's truck pull up at the house. He rolled down his window and motioned for me to follow him in.

He got out and held me by the shoulders. "You're okay? No problems on the way?"

"No. No one was following us. Look, I can't thank you enough for letting me—"

I know I looked as if I'd just stepped off the most harrowing roller coaster ever. My legs were wobbly and my face was probably just as gray as when I'd called him, even in no light. He just opened his arms and I kind of melted into them. I'm not sure I've ever needed a hug more. I stayed, my head buried in his chest, tears welling, not wanting to lift my face. I couldn't even remember the last time I'd been in someone's arms.

"You're safe now," he said, patting me. "Come on inside. I want you to go through everything that happened. I'll put on a cup of tea."

"That would be great." I exhaled and my whole body seemed to ease.

We went in through the kitchen door. It was a modest place, but cute. Nicely done. The wooden cabinetry looked new. I guessed Patrick had done a lot of the work. "I thought you lived on Staten Island?"

"I grew up there. That was my family house where you saw me today. I, uh, actually am of age. I moved out a long time ago. I'll make you some tea. Or I can pour you another tequila if that's not strong enough."

"No. Tea is perfect." I laughed, relieved.

I sat down at the small kitchen table while he put on some water. There was a wooden door that led to a small yard and a cute eating alcove in an arched portico. He had a bunch of old copper and antique kitchen tools on the walls. It all looked tasteful and nice.

"Sleepytime," he said. "It'll calm your nerves." He brought it over with a napkin and even sliced a lemon. I took a sip and everything started to feel better. "All right, let me hear it." He sat down across from me. "From the time you left me today. Don't leave anything out."

I went through it. From calling Elena to make sure Brandon was okay, to driving out to my dad's yard and figuring it was the safest place I could be. I even mentioned how they had bought the yard after he retired from teaching.

"What did he teach?" Patrick asked.

"Biology and chemistry. At Hunter College High School. My mom taught math."

"My mom worked in a school too. She was a secretary in the guidance office. New Dorp High School on Staten Island."

"I guess we're kindred souls."

The rest I tried to put together as best I could, although

it all came back to me jumbled and rambling, as if I was recalling a dream.

A nightmare.

I told him how I'd run into the shed and knew I couldn't make it to the car, and had to do something when the guy came in. How I'd started up the hoist and rammed him with the forklift when his attention went up to the boat on blocks. Patrick's eyes widened. How the outside door wouldn't open and how he came after me and crashed the hook through the car.

"Jeez, Angelina Jolie's got nothing on you," he said, giving me a crooked grin, but one that was lit with admiration. "You're lucky to be alive."

"I know. He killed Rollie, Patrick. He basically admitted it coming after me in the shed. He mentioned Brandon too. He said he was watching us the night of the break-in. He must've followed me out there; there's no other way he would have known."

"Unless he attached a GPS the night he broke in. We'll find out. Both of which mean, however, he likely knows about me as well."

"He does know about you, Patrick. He said something weird, that all this wasn't just about the money. I forget how he put it—it's all so jumbled in my head and I was so scared."

"Don't worry," Patrick said, reassuring me. "Slow down."

I took another sip of tea. "He said the money was

only part of what they were looking for. That there was something else your father had. A page. From a diary or something . . ."

"*Diary?*"

"That's why he brought your name up. He said, 'Your boyfriend's gonna be next, you know. . . .' That the money was only part of it. That 'ol' Joe had something else with him.' And I was gonna take him to it. Or else. What did he mean by that?"

"I'm not sure what my father managed to get himself wrapped up in," Patrick said.

"Patrick, I'm sorry to have to say this . . ." I looked at him. "But it's sure starting to sound a lot like some kind of blackmail to me."

His nod was somber and filled with resignation. "I know."

I put down my tea. "Patrick, look, this has all just gotten a little crazy for me. Rollie was murdered. He was killed to get to me. I'm sure of that now. And this guy also knows about Brandon. I'm prepared to turn myself in. Whatever happens, happens . . . But I can't live with the risk. Not anymore."

He nodded sympathetically. "Did you happen to get a look at the guy?"

"Not a good one. It was dark. Short hair. Maybe light complexion. Medium build. He was all bloodied when he came at my car. I wouldn't want to have to pick him out of a lineup. I just don't want to think that he's still out there. That this could happen again. I know what I said earlier, about handling this between us. But not anymore. I can't take the risk. Not with Brandon."

Patrick nodded and stood up. He went over and leaned against the counter.

My heart grew fitful. "That's the second time I've said that to you and you haven't come back with what I expected."

"What were you expecting?" He stood there looking at me.

"I've just had someone try to kill me, Patrick. I expected you to say that we're going to hand this over to the police. The money. Everything. You're part of the NYPD. I said I was prepared. That you would make the call."

"We're not going to take this to the police, Hilary," he said back to me.

"*What*?" I squinted my eyes as if I hadn't heard correctly. His answer hit me like a meteor falling out of the sky.

"We're not going to go to the police," he said again. He took in a breath. "I can't." He just kept looking at me as if the situation had now changed. And there wasn't even the slightest blink in his eyes.

"Look, I'm sorry about your father," I said. "I know it's clear he was into something that you don't want to come out. I get that. But people are dead. This guy knows who I am. You are a cop, aren't you? Or at least you work with the fucking department. We don't have a choice anymore. We have to turn it in."

"It's not about my father." Patrick looked at me. "At least, not anymore."

I put down my tea and stared back. "You're starting to scare me a little. I'm not sure I understand."

I guess I'd sensed it, when I was back at the gas station and he said he would come and get me. That I could go to him, but never once mentioning the police. Which was the logical response. Given that the guy had tried to kill me. My heart rate started to pick up. "What do you mean, this isn't about your father?"

"You're right." He came back over and sat across from me. "I am a cop. Maybe not exactly a cop so much these days. A lieutenant, though I'm no longer in a uniform. But I do work for the NYPD. And the oaths I swore still apply . . ."

"I'm not sure where we're going with this, Patrick . . . Someone tried to kill me tonight."

"I understand. But the police can't know about this. In spite of everything I just said. And when I said it wasn't about what my father has done, it's not. Or some loyal son's attempt to protect him. It's for my sister."

"*Sister?*" I blinked with total surprise. "Patrick, I don't know what the hell you're talking about."

"She lives in Tottenville. That's all the way down at the southern tip of Staten Island. You might have seen her at the funeral."

I thought back to the pretty woman I'd seen walking down the aisle ahead of him and sitting in the first row. "She has two kids, right?"

Patrick nodded. "Chris and Alec. Good kids. Annette and her husband are separated these days. He used to work as a field inspector for New Jersey Power and Light, but got laid off. Part of the sequester cuts. Bills were mounting. Kids in a Catholic academy. They had a summer place in the Poconos. Two mortgages to pay. Like a lot of people, maybe living a bit over what they could afford. I think you know the scenario, right?"

I nodded. But I had no idea where this was heading.

"Then Sandy came. A lot of homes around them were hit hard. Just like we were. Two people in her neighborhood even died. They . . ." He paused and wet his lips, tapping his index finger gently on the chair arm. ". . . Maybe they did some things that weren't a hundred percent right." He hesitated again. "When it came to the insurance claims. Let's just say they were desperate . . . I think you can understand what it's like to feel desperate, Hilary, right?"

"Yes. But I still don't see what any of this has to do with me . . ."

"Let's just say they put in for claims on their house that weren't exactly by the book. And then made them look that way. A flooded basement. Some things of value that might have ended up down there. Some roof damage that might not have been directly related to the storm. There were a thousand claims being filed all around them. They figured, who would know? But one of their contractors got suspicious and turned them in . . ."

"I'm sorry, Patrick. You're right. I know how when you lose a job and you have a family to support it can make you do certain things . . ."

"Ryan's not a bad guy." He shrugged. "In fact, he's as honest as they come." He tapped his thumb against the table one more time. "The thing I'm saying is, he wasn't the one who filed the claim."

"*Oh*." It suddenly sank in exactly why he was telling all this to me. Our eyes met.

His sister had.

"What happened?"

"I got them a lawyer and we were able to negotiate with the insurer to avoid it going any further. As long as she paid back whatever they'd given her. Which in light of all the Sandy victims who hadn't gotten a thing at that point, would be doubly bad. I didn't want my father to know. Hell, he had barely enough socked away to keep himself afloat. Plus he didn't need to know at his stage—did it ever come out that he had advanced prostate cancer?—that his daughter might be spending his last months on earth awaiting trial on insurance fraud. We had our own claims coming in on the house in Midland Beach. So I just kind of . . . took it over."

"Took *what* over?" I asked. "I don't understand."

"Her debt. To the insurance company. I just paid it."

"How much are we talking about?" I still didn't see how this connected to the half-million dollars I'd taken.

He let out a breath. "Give or take, seventy thousand or so."

"Shit." I felt my stomach fall off a ledge. "That really stinks. And that makes you an awfully nice brother, Patrick, but I'm still not seeing what any of this has to do with you not being able to go to the police."

"I didn't have seventy thousand dollars," he said, continuing to hold his gaze on me.

He got up and went to the fridge and came back with a can of beer. He cracked it open and took a swig. Sat back down. "So I kind of borrowed it," he said. "To me it was only a matter of time until the FEMA claims on this house came through and I'd be able to pay it back. In the meantime I did a lot of the work on our house myself that would make up the difference. The department gave me the time."

"You borrowed it?" I asked, looking up at him. "From whom? A bank?"

Patrick chuckled. Then he smiled kind of grimly. "Unless you call it the National Bank of Kiev. Brooklyn branch."

My eyes widened. "The Russian mob? You took a loan from the Russian mob to pay your sister's debt."

"*Ukrainian*," Patrick said with a chortle, "or so they keep reminding me. This sort of loan, the interest keeps escalating daily."

251

"How much is it up to?" I had no idea what the street rate for that kind of transaction was. Maybe as high as 20 percent a week.

He shrugged. "A little over a hundred thousand dollars and climbing."

"Oh my God!" I saw the whole thing now.

"At first I tried to re-fi this place, but that's a three-month process. And I never thought the FEMA claims would drag on as long as they have. But it's not just the money . . . It's the collateral. It's the security they demanded on the loan that's become the real problem for me."

"*Collateral?*"

He pushed himself back in his chair and said resignedly, "My job."

"You mean they'd own you?" I saw what he was saying and the situation he was in. "You'd basically be working for the Russian mob."

"*Ukrainian,*" he said with a rueful smile. "And they'd be delighted if they got to take it back that way. They'd get ten times the value. Their hooks in someone who goes between the NYPD and the mayor's administration.

"Hilary, look, I don't know what kind of crap my father got mixed up in. Whatever he found that these people seem to value so much. That's worth killing for. All I know is that half a million dollars is a way out for me, as much as it was for you. I'm sorry. Maybe it's not the story you were expecting to hear. But I can't let the police get involved. I can't let this pass by. I can't."

He looked at me, his cheeks blown out, an expression somewhere between guilt and disappointment.

"So what are you suggesting we do?"

He shrugged. "I'm suggesting we find a way to keep the money."

I stared blankly at him. Going to the police and possibly facing charges and maybe even going to jail wasn't exactly at the top of my top ten list. "You know if we do that, Patrick, once you let this chance go by, you'll never be able to turn yourself back in. If it ever comes out, you won't even have a job to go back to."

He nodded. "I'd rather risk it doing something to protect my family than put it at risk every day doing favors for people I took an oath to put away. You're right, it is sounding like blackmail. And I want to find out what the hell my father got himself into. Before someone else does."

I shook my head. "I'm sorry, Patrick, but I just can't put my son at risk."

"That's task number one. First thing in the A.M. I can reach out for a favor to the local police up there and make sure that wherever he's staying has a patrol car on watch for a while."

"He's safe for the time being. He's with my house-keeper. No one would know about her. But thanks." I nodded appreciatively. "So what's task number two?"

"Task number two is that *we* find out just who the

253

hell is behind this and exactly what it is they're trying to protect that's worth paying five hundred thousand dollars for."

"I think I'm stepping a little out of my league," I said, a beat of trepidation rising up.

"I thought you were the one who came to me and said you wanted to handle this privately . . ."

I smiled. But a smile with the same enthusiasm as if I'd just swallowed a mouthful of calf's brains, sorting through my options. I could say no and still go to the police on my own. It might mean jail. It might even mean losing my son. At least for a while. Brandon's life would be turned upside down, that was for sure. And there would still be those people out there. Behind this. I didn't have a clue who they even were. Would they just let me off the hook for what I'd done? The commitment of the man who tried to get me at the boatyard didn't convince me they would. And the stakes had been raised. By whatever he meant when he said that there was more. *The diary.* Patrick's father was clearly blackmailing someone. Who? Not to mention, if I did turn this over to the authorities now, I'd clearly be hanging Patrick out to dry.

But there was also something new to factor in, which was making me feel a whole lot more secure.

I had him.

I said, "You realize how scary this is? Not just for me. But for Brandon."

He nodded. "I guess I'll take that as a yes?"

"It's a yes." I nodded, but slowly, halfheartedly. "At least, kind of."

He reached across the table and put out his hand. "So I guess that makes us kind of partners. Just one more thing . . ."

"What's that?"

"It's almost two in the morning. This might be the best chance we'll ever have . . ."

"The best chance for what?" I asked. His hand was still out.

"For getting that money," he said.

"You mean tonight? Go back home?"

"If you did to him what you said you did, then there might never be a better time."

I felt my heart pick up with nerves. I looked at him measuringly. "You're not married or anything, are you?"

He shook his head. "I was. Not anymore. Why?"

"No reason." I finally shook his hand. "My car's a little beaten up. I think you're driving."

CHAPTER FORTY-THREE

Mirho's phone rang. It was one in the morning. He didn't have to look to see who it was. The boss didn't like failure, and so far, all he'd gotten was a busted rib and a broken nose. He pulled the car over. He didn't want to answer. He just cleared his throat.

"I'm here."

"I was supposed to hear from you. Do we have it? You seemed to feel you had it in the bag earlier. I didn't hear back."

Mirho dabbed away some blood from a cut on his face. "Maybe I was a little premature."

The pause on the other end was like a blade thrust in him. "I don't have to remind you that we don't have time. There are things happening, and I can't have this out there like that. Not to mention it doesn't exactly sit well with me that someone's spreading around my money."

"Nothing's changed," Mirho said. "I just have to find another way in."

"What other way . . .?"

"You don't have to know the details. You just want your peace of mind back. Let me handle the rest. I haven't let you down yet, have I?"

"You know, if I didn't know better . . ." His boss chuckled. "It might seem as if this woman's got the better of you. Maybe I should have gone out and hired her."

"Trust me, she's going to regret it," Mirho said. He took in a breath and winced. Probably a fractured rib or two from the boat that fell on him. "So much for Mister Nice Guy. I know exactly how I'm going to handle it next."

MRS. O'B

CHAPTER FORTY-FOUR

Six weeks earlier.

Sheila O'Byrne sorted through what was left of her husband Tom's belongings, the first time she'd been able to face it since the storm.

The navy suit he wore to Rich's wedding; Rich was now a fireman down in Delaware. Tom's favorite Hawaiian shirt that he always wore at the grill for his famous summer barbecues. The old Yankees cap with a Yogi Berra autograph on the bill that his father had given him. Everything she held brought back an important memory for her. Memories she struggled to have to relive right now. Their lives. He had been gone only two months. It was still too soon. Too raw. She ought to do this some other time, she began to feel. Or with her sister, when she came back from Ohio.

This was the second time that the person who meant the most in the world to her had been stolen.

The first, it took months just for her to be able to go out again or do her chores. But that was twenty years ago. She never thought she'd have to go through it all over again.

Go through it all again, she thought, and alone.

Two months out, the house was still mostly rotted roofing and drywall, and covered with debris. It was still laid open where the elm had gone right through their roof and the bay had rushed in, her only protection a weatherproof tarp and some temporary insulation to bar the cold. Everyone promised help; so far none had come. Other than Joe's son, Patrick, who had come back to help his dad rebuild. Volunteers were everywhere; but volunteers could only help clear the mess and bring them food and blankets. They couldn't rebuild their homes. They couldn't give her back her memories.

Sheila took out the white dress shirt with his initials monogrammed on the sleeve that Tom had worn to Rich's graduation from the academy.

T. L. O'B

The tears rushed in again. Like the storm. She put her hand in front of her face and began to cry.

That was when she heard a knock coming from

downstairs, and a voice from the front porch. *"Hello. Anyone here?"* The stairs were about all that was structurally left of their old place; everything else was still all gutted and open to the world. And to the biting wind and the cold. And now the snow. For a few weeks Sheila had gone to her son's place in Delaware, but they didn't have much room. And then to a cousin's in Ridgewood. Finally she just thought, *Tom would want me back here.* There were all their memories to protect. And a house to rebuild. Their house. That was all she had now.

Sheila went downstairs to see who it was. A young couple was at the front door, visible through the glass. They looked in their thirties maybe. Sheila opened the door. The woman was pretty in a quilted down jacket, carrying a shopping bag. The man was tall and thin, and wore glasses. He looked professional. They were probably from a church group with some food or a prayer to deliver.

Food helped these days.

"Mrs. O'Byrne?"

"Yes." Sheila pointed to the mess. "Sorry not to invite you in. In or out, I guess it's all the same now," she said with a smile.

"That's okay . . ." The woman smiled back. "We won't stay. We just . . ." She glanced at her husband as if searching for the right words. "We think we have something that might belong to you."

"To me . . .?" Sheila looked back at her with surprise.

"Yes. We're the Richmans," the husband said, introducing them. "Alan and Nina. We have a beach house in Deal, on the Jersey shore. We were pretty battered too. But we were out on the beach the other day looking at the erosion there and we saw that this had washed up. There was a name inside it . . ." She opened the bag and took out the hand-painted lacquer box that was inside. "Deirdre Annemarie O'Byrne. It said Midland Beach. Is this yours . . .?"

Sheila's breath went out of her. She stared. At first it was like her heart just stopped, like someone pulled the plug in an instant. And then it kicked right up again, not in worry this time, but in giddiness, joy, something she hadn't felt in a long time. She took the box in her hands, let her fingers wrap around it. Lovingly. "Oh good Lord . . ."

She felt as if her legs were about to give out.

"Are you all right?" the husband asked. "I hope we didn't upset you. Maybe you ought to sit down."

"Please." Sheila nodded, a little wobbly. They helped her over to a chair in what used to be her living room.

The wife came over to her. "Can I get you some water?"

"No, I'm fine. I'm fine. It's just that . . ." She looked up at them. "This was my daughter's."

She opened the box's clasp and peered inside. The bound leather diary was still there, amazingly intact. And the little box containing Deirdre's baby teeth, along with a cutting of her hair. "She's not with us any longer.

264

This is all we had left of her. I was sure it was gone. We lost it in the storm."

"I'm so sorry," the wife said. "It's amazing, it doesn't even seem so badly damaged. It must have been carried by the tide."

"Yes. All the way down to Deal," Sheila said, her eyes glistening. She took out a couple of the waterlogged pictures. And Deirdre's journal. Miraculously, it seemed like most of the handwritten pages—pages she had written right up to the day she disappeared, the day, they found out later, she had died—still seemed legible. "She was headed to college. Up in Buffalo. She was killed. August 21, 1992. We never even found her body. For over ten years . . . until they dug up the ground in the area over by the Goethals Bridge to make some new apartment complex. We never knew what she was even doing over there. Or if that's just where they dumped her . . . She had some boyfriend we never knew . . ."

"I'm so sorry," the woman said. She looked at her husband. "I wish there was something we could do."

"Oh, you have. You already have!" Sheila O'Byrne looked up at them. "The storm took everything from me. *Everything*. But this . . . This is almost like you gave me something back. Thank you," she said, and stood up and hugged them both. "You can't know how much it means."

Later, in the kitchen, warmed by a blanket and a space heater, she ate the Chinese meal that Patrick had brought

265

her and brewed herself a cup of tea. She knew she should have called Rich and told him what had turned up today. What she was holding in her hand.

But just for a few minutes, Sheila wanted this moment to herself.

She opened Deirdre's journal. Many of the pages had the crisp, dried-out feel of antique parchment; on others the twenty-year-old ink had run. Over the years, she'd read through it so many times. Maybe a hundred since Deirdre had never come back that day. She knew the musicians her daughter had liked by heart: Cyndi Lauper, Madonna, Michael Jackson. The boys she had an eye on then. Her inner dreams and ambitions. She said she wanted to study veterinary medicine.

And this one boy . . .

She had never had much to say about him. She never even wrote his full name, only some nickname. He was a year younger and came from a different school. He was poor. How they met at a summer street fair.

What was the point? Sheila shut the book tight. All it brought back was pain that was twenty years old. And now, with Tom gone, the tide of it felt as strong and wounding as if it had all happened yesterday.

It had taken twelve years to even find her. And then it was just by matching up her DNA; what was left of her was too far gone. The first year or two she and Tom still held out hope that one day she'd come running back through the door. But in their hearts they knew.

They always knew. Deirdre would call if she was going to be home an hour late from school.

They knew.

One of her girlfriends confirmed for them that she'd recently met this guy. He didn't have much; Deirdre was always a rescuer. Some stray cat, a dog, a homeless person. She was there for any cause. No one knew his name or how to locate him. They tried, of course. Even just to see if he knew where she was that night. What time she might have left him. She was leaving for college in a week. The pain came back. She was just eighteen . . .

Why? Sheila sat there with the journal and asked herself. *Why play this old record all over again and again . . .?*

She opened it once more. Like she had so many times. To the same, familiar spot. Near the end.

"It makes it all the more fun," her daughter had written, "if we keep everything shrouded in mystery. As if we were at some kind of masked ball, like in *The Count of Monte Cristo*. There's no hope of it lasting, of course. I'm leaving on the twenty-fourth for college and he'll be going back to school. So we decided not to even call each other by our real names. He only calls me Cordelia. What a beautiful name. From *King Lear*. The most beautiful and the most loyal.

"And I call him by this name his family had given him . . ."

Sheila paged to the last entry: August 22.

They never knew if it was him or someone else. They

267

could never locate him. But reading the name again brought everything back. As if it had all happened yesterday. As if it was happening all over again.

His name, like a knife piercing her heart, the name of the person who had cost her everything.

"Streak," her daughter had written in that graceful, familiar script of hers.

That's what she called him.

She wrote, *"We'll see how it goes. I'm going to meet Streak one last time."*

CHAPTER FORTY-FIVE

Patrick and I rushed back to my house in Armonk at two thirty in the morning. It took only forty minutes; there was barely another car on the road. Turning up my cul-de-sac, I kept my eyes peeled for any suspicious cars around.

I didn't see any.

"Whoa!" Patrick ogled, his eyes widening as we drove into the driveway. The place did look impressive with its second-floor dormers, mullioned windows, the three-car garage, and the outside lights turned on.

"Make me an offer." I grinned. "We can start with your share of the cash."

"Sorry." He pulled the car up in front of the garage. "Just a shade out of my league."

"I hope you don't mind if we dispense with the tour.

I'll be back in a minute." I ran in through the garage and hurriedly threw together a change of clothes and a few toiletries as Patrick stayed in front and stood guard.

Then I went around the back.

It was a bit eerie going under the deck, my feet crunching on a crusty layer of snow, no light but the moon. I crawled over to the cooler and breathed a sigh of relief to find the ski bag where I'd left it. I was even more relieved when I opened it and saw the money still there. I zipped the case up and went back upstairs.

Barely five minutes had passed and I was back in the car.

"Let's just get out of here," I said.

"Mind if I take a peek?" Patrick asked, and zipped open the nylon case. His eyes grew wide. "Always wondered what half a million dollars looked like."

"Four hundred and thirty-seven five," I reminded him. "Now can we please get the hell out of here?"

It took even less time to make it back to his house in Bensonhurst. The late hour, along with the intensity of everything I'd been through tonight, began to take its toll. I even closed my eyes and dozed on the way back.

Back at his house, Patrick insisted I take the bedroom and threw a sheet and a quilt over the couch for himself. He threw the money in a storage nook in the basement. In about thirty seconds I was dead to the world. The next thing I knew I was opening my eyes and it was light. The smell of bacon was coming from the kitchen. I threw a T-shirt on over my jeans and stepped out.

I couldn't believe it was almost noon.

"I don't think I've slept this late since college." I gave Patrick a sleepy wave at the stove.

He was in a cut-off sweatshirt and jeans. "Breakfast's almost ready. You mind green salsa in your eggs?"

"You mean lunch, right? And sure, I love salsa."

"Grab a seat." The table we sat at last night was already set. "It's not much—I found whatever I could in the fridge. Turkey bacon, scrambled eggs and cheese over a tortilla. Help yourself to some coffee. There's milk in the fridge."

"Not much? This is great! Any chance for some tea?"

"It's usually extra, but in your case, you did put up a larger deposit than usual." He pointed to the counter. "There ought to be some in that jar over there."

I found a tin and some English Breakfast inside. Next to it, I noticed a framed photo I hadn't seen last night. A young boy, seemingly around eight. Bangs of light brown hair down to his eyes. An adorable smile.

The boy I'd noticed with him the day of the funeral.

"That's Matt," Patrick said. "His mother moved out west and remarried a guy who lives in Phoenix. He adored his grandpa." He scooped the eggs out of the pan onto two plates and added a couple of strips of bacon.

271

"I bet he did," I said. "He's adorable."

"*You kidding . . .?*" Patrick grinned, putting a plate in front of me. "The kid's a rock star. Takes after his mother, fortunately. Here . . ."

"Thanks." I took the plate and looked up at him. "*Really.* For everything, Patrick."

"C'mon. Eggs are getting cold."

They were delicious. Scrambled eggs over a tortilla with a spicy green salsa and cheese. "You were obviously a short-order cook before you became a cop."

He shrugged. "Remnants of a hospitality major for a while when I was in college."

He read my look, which was kind of like, how the hell did a hospitality major end up working for the police?

"Switched to government in my junior year," he volunteered without my asking.

"Where?" I asked, scooping a forkful of eggs onto a tortilla.

"Upstate New York. Cornell."

"Jeez," I said, "you're also some kind of brain on top of everything else?"

He sniffed, shaking his head. "Hockey. I got recruited there, but by my junior year I'd banged up my knee and didn't even play."

"Well, these are good. At least that hospitality major didn't go to waste. How'd that wife of yours ever let you go?"

"Didn't. She left me. Long tale."

"They all are," I said. "And we all have one."

"Anyway, after nine-eleven I had a change of heart. I decided to go into police work. And you?"

"You mean how I became a cop?"

"I was thinking more how you became single."

I gave him the sixty-second version. Jim. My days in magazines, then my time at the agency. The Cesta debacle. I'd already talked about the divorce and Brandon.

"So he's okay?" Patrick asked. He clearly meant Brandon. "Where he's staying now?"

I nodded. "He and Remi stayed with Elena whenever I had to travel and my folks weren't around. No one would know that. I had her pick him up from school yesterday afternoon. Speaking of which, he's got a doctor's appointment today with his neurologist. I have to remind Elena."

"Who's Remi?" he asked.

"Remi's the dog."

"It must be very tough." He broke off a piece of tortilla and dipped it in the salsa. "Dealing with all this on your own. And I don't mean taking the money."

"It's tough . . ." I nodded. "Not like there's a choice in the matter . . . But these past two years, with Brandon at Milton Farms, watching him evolve, it's strangely also become the most rewarding time of my life. One I don't want to let go of. Sorry, but in my book he's kind of a rock star too.."

Patrick smiled. "I bet he is."

"So I guess that brings us to present time . . ." I pushed my plate aside. It was pretty clean. "You have a next step?"

"I've been thinking . . . My dad had a GPS with him in his Honda. I'd thought about tracking down where he went that night, but until all this came up, it wasn't exactly a mystery that needed to be solved. You know what I mean? But there'll be a record in there of where he went. Maybe someone might know who he was there to see."

I nodded. "Seems a start," I said.

"A start?" he said, stacking my plate and putting it on the counter near the sink.

"Look, there's something else I didn't tell you." I stood up.

"The mike's all yours . . ." he said, and leaned with his palms against the counter.

"I found your father's cell phone on the floor mat when I went into his car. Something made me take a look. I'm not sure why. There was a text message in there he had written."

"Wasn't his. My dad didn't text message," he said, shrugging.

"Well, I'm sorry, but he did that night. I even noticed the time of it. It was almost exactly when he went off the road. I can't remember who it was to, but he

274

was telling someone that he was on his way back, just as that deer ran in front of him. The police never mentioned that?"

"No. They didn't." He shook his head with surprise.

"I'm trying to recall who it was to. It was a woman. With a P. Patty, maybe . . .?"

"Paula?" Patrick suggested, wrinkling his brow.

"Paula. That's it. I remember now. Who is she?"

"Paula was my mom. But she's been dead a couple of years. Why the hell would he be texting her? You're sure? What did it say?"

"That he was heading home. Then just a 'w,' which I assumed meant *with* . . . That he was heading home *with*—"

"With *what* . . .? The money?"

I shrugged. "That would be my guess, Patrick."

"He could just have been letting let me know he was on his way back and hit the wrong key. My mother's name would've come right after mine."

"I thought you just said your father didn't text? And anyway, what else could he have meant but 'with the money'? Which wouldn't have meant anything to you. It wouldn't have ever meant anything to anyone, even the police, because no one knew it was in there. But it damn well did to someone."

"So you're saying *what*?" Patrick scratched his head. "He was letting someone know?"

"He may have hit the wrong key, Patrick; I don't have a clue. But he was definitely telling someone he had that money. So who would that be? I'm not the detective here, you are. That said"—I smiled— "I'm kind of thinking it wouldn't be such a bad idea to get your hands on that phone."

CHAPTER FORTY-SIX

An hour later, Patrick was back on Baden Avenue. He pulled his truck up in front of his father's house.

It was after two P.M. He hadn't assigned any work crew for today. Patrick went in through the kitchen and checked out what they'd done. A whole wall of new drywall had gone up yesterday. The kitchen island would be new, as well as a new fridge and the stove. And he'd also put new wood facings on the cabinets, which were probably from before the war. He pulled out a utility drawer in the counter where his folks kept loose things they used around the house: calculators, picture hooks, thumbtacks for the bulletin board. The ferry schedule.

He had to find his dad's GPS. But this was also where they threw their old cell phones.

The more he thought about it, the more he knew

Hilary had to be right. His dad was contacting someone. He was trying to tell someone what he had.

He rummaged through the drawer. When the police in Westchester returned his father's belongings, the phone was in the box, along with his wedding ring, his Longines watch, and his wallet—all of which Patrick had given to his sister as keepsakes.

All except the phone, which they had no use for, and which Patrick was pretty sure they had tossed in here.

His mom and dad weren't exactly tech savvy—they honestly didn't even know how to get on a computer—but you could literally trace the evolution of cell phone evolution by pawing through the kitchen drawer. There were a bunch of them in there, all sizes and weights. He searched around for the BlackBerry his dad had had with him that night. It had been a Christmas gift from him and Annette a couple of years back, and while his dad first claimed he had zero use for all this new technology crap, as he called it, within a month, he was looking up the weather anyplace Patrick or one of the grandkids would go, as well as pointing out constant weather reports on some app along with all the cheap garages wherever he went.

Where the hell was it? Patrick said to himself, sifting through the drawer. It had to be in here. They'd just thrown it in a week before.

He turned over a calendar and there it was.

He took it over to an electrical outlet and plugged

it in. It took a few minutes for the phone to come to life.

The first thing he did was look for the text message Hilary said that his dad had sent from the car.

He found it. To Paula. Just as Hilary had said. *To his mom?*

I'm on my way it read. He'd probably been writing it just as the deer bolted out. Maybe his attention had been diverted. It probably killed him. And Hilary was also likely right about what he was saying:

I'm on my way with the money.

So who could he possibly have been telling? Patrick leaned against the counter. His mom had been dead for two years.

Paula.

He pushed the button on the upper-left-hand corner of the keyboard. It displayed the history of recent calls and texts.

He saw three or four calls that were to him, going back maybe a week. And there were a couple to Annette, his sister, two days before the accident, and one to Chris, his grandson. Probably to discuss the Knicks, Patrick smiled.

Then something took him by surprise.

He counted them: five alone over the three days leading up to the accident. Five calls from his mother's old cell phone number.

That phone had been inactive for almost two years.

279

It didn't make sense.

Who the hell could be calling him from there? And why?

He put his father's phone down and dug through the utility drawer again, looking for his mom's old Nokia, which he knew was in here somewhere too. Joe would never throw it away or close down the number. For sentimental reasons. It was a memento for him. Patrick could visualize the damn thing. They didn't throw out anything. This was definitely where it had to be.

One by one he removed each old phone from the drawer and placed it on the counter.

It wasn't there.

A numbing feeling rose up in Patrick's gut as he stood there staring at the counter full of phones.

Either his father was calling a ghost to say he was on his way back with a half million dollars.

Or he'd given the phone out. And he was in this, this scheme that had gotten him killed, with someone else.

CHAPTER FORTY-SEVEN

Patrick came back that afternoon, and around five we drove over the Whitestone Bridge, retracing his father's route.

We found the address in his GPS device under "Recent Destinations": 110 Main Street in Banksville, New York. I Googled it on my phone and it came back it was something called the Stateline Diner.

"You know the place?" Patrick asked.

I shook my head. "I've probably passed it a dozen times. Banksville is the size of a postage stamp on the New York–Connecticut border. There's not much there beyond a food market, a pharmacy and a post office. And this fancy French restaurant Jim took me to a couple of times, Le Cremaillaie."

Patrick shrugged. "Well, I'd bet you a buck to a dime that my father damn well didn't know it."

"Maybe. But I'd take that bet that he was meeting someone who did."

It took about an hour for us to get up there. Patrick told me about the missing phone and the calls back and forth between his father and whoever he'd given it to. He had no idea who that could be. We didn't need to follow his dad's exact route, as Patrick had already gone up there to reclaim his father's belongings and visited the accident site. "He must have come up through New Jersey and over the Tappan Zee to avoid the BQE. That's why he was on that back road."

"You're probably right," I agreed. I called Elena, thinking of how his father's choice of routes had probably cost him his life. Brandon had a doctor's appointment at four.

I got her voice mail in Spanish.

They were probably in there now.

We took the Merritt up to Greenwich and then all the way out on North Street to the New York state line. We wound past some of the huge estates—sprawling gated properties hiding Loire-like chateaux set back from the road. It was enough to impress anyone, but these were clearly not the kind of places Patrick saw on a regular basis on Staten Island and in Bensonhurst.

"Kinda reminds me of your place." He chuckled as we drove by a particularly impressive one.

"My place would be the garage for some of these homes," I said. "And trust me, they can fill it!"

We slowed when the GPS announced we were a quarter mile from Banksville. The Stateline Diner was on Main Street, a cozy, shingled white house, and if you didn't stop quickly, you'd pass through the town. About four or five cars were parked in the lot. We were talking about as out of the way as one could get here. If you were meeting someone and you didn't want anyone else in the world to see, you came to the right place.

We parked, went up the porch steps, and stepped inside. The early dinner crowd seemed pretty local. Three or four tables were filled, a handful of stragglers at the counter. FOX News was on the screen with the sound muted.

A middle-aged hostess told us to take a seat. We found an empty table in the corner. A waitress came over, a girl with frizzy red hair and multiple earrings who seemed in her early twenties and who said her name was Amy. She pointed to a board on the wall that listed the specials. I was dying for a glass of wine, but I went for a Diet Coke instead. Patrick asked for a light beer. A few minutes later when Amy brought them back, Patrick asked her if we could show her something.

"My father was in here," he said, "a couple of weeks ago." He took out a photo. His dad smiling proudly with

Patrick's son. "It was a Thursday. Maybe an hour or so later than now. I wonder if anyone here might recognize him?"

"I'm not in on Thursdays," the waitress said. "Lorraine might remember." She indicated the hostess. "I'll have her come by."

A couple of minutes later the hostess came over. Patrick showed her the photo and asked if she recalled him from the week before.

At first she just stared. "He looks familiar . . ."

"Maybe you heard," Patrick said. "He was killed in a car accident on his way home."

"Oh my, yes, of course we heard!" the hostess said with an empathetic sigh. "Dina read about it in the local papers. Such sad, sad news. That was your father? I'm so, so sorry, dear . . ."

"Thank you," Patrick said. "Appreciate it. We're trying to reconstruct what brought him up here, and who he might have been meeting with. The truth is, we don't have a clue."

"Well, I don't know," The hostess shook her head. "I know I served him coffee. It was just before dinnertime if I recall."

"He was here with someone?"

Lorraine put a hand to her curly blond hair as if trying to jog her memory. "Not when he came in, if I recall. But yes, someone did sit down with him a while later. They didn't stay very long. They both got up and continued their conversation outside. I remember because I ran to take some leftovers out to a customer who had left them on the table and saw them over by a car . . ." She pointed. "Over there."

Out in the dark parking lot.

"Any chance you know who this person was?" Patrick asked. "It's really important."

"I don't, hon. Sorry. But Deena might. I've seen the man in here from time to time. I think she's waited on him before. *Deen . . .*"

She called over a pretty waitress who looked to be in her forties with her dark, long hair in a ponytail. "You remember that guy you read about who was killed after he was in here? The one who got into that accident . . ."

" 'Course . . . Wasn't I the one who brought the newspaper in?"

"Well, this is his son. You remember the guy he was in here with that night? Stocky, short lightish hair. He's got a mark on his face . . ." She touched her cheek. "Here. I know you've waited on him before."

"You mean Charlie," Deena the waitress said.

Charlie.

Patrick glanced at me, a rush in his eyes, as if we were finally getting somewhere. "Charlie *who*? Do you happen to know a last name? Or where he's from?"

"Sorry. To me, he's just Charlie. He comes in here maybe once a month. Mostly lunch or breakfast."

"There must be something you can tell me about him?" Patrick asked. "Anything would be helpful."

Deena shrugged, kind of blankly. Then, "Maybe one thing," she said. "He works up in Hartford, I'm pretty sure."

"Hartford?"

"In the state capital. Always bragging how he's such a VIP. Acts like he's God's gift to women, which I assure you he ain't." Deena rolled her eyes.

"You think he works for a lawyer up there?" Patrick asked. "Or in law enforcement?"

"No." Deena shook her head. "I think he works for some big-shot representative. Someone high up, he likes to brag. In the state government up there."

CHAPTER FORTY-EIGHT

The army changed me.

Maybe it was what it took to make it through. The discipline. Or how they broke you down, completely down, until there was virtually nothing of who you were before, which helped me put the past behind.

Maybe it was being at war. Or for the first time having people who relied on me. Who didn't know me. And me them.

I've read it happens like that sometimes. To people with my kind of nature.

Sometimes it just does.

We moved one last time, shortly after what happened with Deirdre. This time we went away from Staten Island completely, to Waterbury, Connecticut, to live with my uncle. I did my senior year up there and used my middle name, Frank, instead of John, and I just kind of continued it, even after I graduated and enlisted.

Frank Landry. It just stuck.

John simply disappeared.

And I never heard a thing again about what had happened back on Staten Island under the bridge that night. They likely never even found her. Probably for years. Those holes out there near the old soap factory led into tunnels that went on forever. I stuffed her in an empty oil drum and rolled her to one deep in the brush. I dragged a bush over there and kicked and scraped in gravel to cover the smell. Maybe the animals got to her. Or rats. They had large ones there. No one knew of me. We'd gone to different schools. Lived different lives. I'm not even sure she ever knew my last name. Just Streak. No one would ever even connect us. One night she went out on a hot summer eve to meet a friend and never came back.

I wanted to put the past behind. The army made that easy. Soon it was like none of it ever even happened. Like some event in your past that you couldn't even remember whether you'd actually done it or thought you had done it, kind of just made up, and from then on it's part of who you are. We all have something like that. Of all the things I'd done, that was the one that I truly regretted. That when I did think of it, feeling her heart beating next to me, touching her body, truly made me feel bad. She was the one person I knew who saw the good in me. I never went back there, to Staten Island. Never set foot on it again.

I truly loved her.

It was during Desert Storm, and I was trained as a tank gunner. I saw a bunch of combat in Kuwait and Iraq. The real stuff. I bet I killed fifteen to twenty of Saddam's infantry. Pow, pow, pow, pow. Whether they had their hands in the air or were running away didn't matter. They were just like target practice to me. A video game.

Pow, pow, pow.

I was even awarded a Bronze Star. For going back in and pulling out two of my crew when our tank got hit by an RPG. I wasn't brave. It all just happened in kind of a daze. Left a bad burn on my face and arm. I never felt that way before. A hero. And that's when it happened. That I no longer thought of myself as John anymore. The silent kid always at war with his inner voices and urges. Whose father ran out on the family because of him.

Instead, I began to see myself as Billy, my older brother who died in that helicopter crash at Camp Lejeune. I began to ask myself, how would Billy handle a certain situation? What would Billy do? And I learned I had something in me. Something buried deep beneath all those other things. That I worked hard to now control. And as Frank I could do it. I could distance myself from my past. From John's past. The awful things he had done.

With that medal pinned on my chest, I began to think there was something important being saved for me. That fate had spared me to achieve. I remember my mother, seeing me in my crisp green fatigues, that fancy medal, and it was like she saw me as something new. Something

*scrubbed fresh and clean. All those bad things, washed
away.*

Gone. Forever.

The army cured me, I remember thinking.

At least for a while.

Her name was April. A-prille, she used to say it.

Like she was in Paris, France, or something, not Paris
fucking Island, and that she was a fashion designer with that
fancy air and not some filthy whore.

She was a little chubby with streaky red hair and too much
makeup. I saw her a couple of times in the town in the months
after I came back from my deployment.

I'd only been with one girl before.

She asked me about my burns, and when I told her how
they'd come about she said she didn't mind. She even asked
me to wear my medal. She said she'd been with burn victims
and amputees, no matter. She'd even done it with some guy
who'd come back with his dick blown off, which made me
curious how that was done.

I found myself telling her things. About my family. Billy at
Camp Lejeune. About ol' Jerry the dog and what I'd done,
which seemed pretty funny now on half a bottle of Jack. "Hey,
pooch." I sniffed around the bed like a horny bloodhound.
"Here, poochie, poochie." I told her about some of the other
things I'd done. She said violence kind of turned her on.

"You have anyone to go back to?" she asked me one night
after we did it. She even stroked my face.

"No. I don't."

So I guess I started thinking, why not her?

Next time I saw her I brought her this foxy red dress. I picked it out special for her. I thought it matched her hair. She took it out of the plastic and put it on "You brought me this?" All excited. Danced around in it and struck a sexy pose. "So, Frankie boy," she said, climbing onto me and finding me hard. "What is it you'd like me to do?"

I started to think she reminded me of someone. How she made me feel. I started to tell her something. "Back home there was this girl . . ."

"What girl, Frank . . .?" She lifted that dress up and climbed on top of me. "What girl . . .?"

"I did something bad."

I had trouble doing it this time. "Time's up, darling," she said after a while. "There's more business to be done." She sat up and unzipped the back of the dress. "You don't think you're the only rooster in the barn, do you? Here . . ." She pulled it over her head. "Maybe you want to give this to someone else." Like the whole thing had been an act.

I looked at her brushing her hair. "It was yours."

I can't even tell you what went through me. It wasn't hatred. I actually liked her. At least up until that moment I did. And it wasn't even anger. It was like I was just watching her brush her hair and I realized she wasn't the person I thought she was and I had told her those things. Like everyone else, none of them really cared.

"And don't go thinking this goes toward what you owe me." She brushed out her curly red hair.

I crawled over on the bed behind her. I cupped my hands over her breasts and brought her close and whispered in her ear, "I promise I won't."

I took the plastic off the floor and wrapped it tightly over her face. She turned, surprised. At first, like it was part of the game. Then I kept wrapping it and wrapping it around her, so tightly her face looked like a steak in the meat department. Her fat nose pressed flat, her eyes bulging. Then her arms suddenly thrashing at me. She made a couple of frantic, garbled sounds and movements, trying to fend me off.

I just kept twisting and twisting, forcing her onto the bed, the weight of my body pressing against her.

"It was a present, you stupid bitch." I glared into her desperate eyes. "You could've just fucking worn it."

It took about two minutes until she finally went limp. The whole thing had happened with a lot of grunting and writhing. But she barely made a sound. My own breaths were the loudest noise. I unwrapped her. Her eyes were white and wide and her face grotesquely twisted. I stared at her awhile and couldn't remember what it was I'd ever found attractive. I gathered up my uniform and left her on the bed, one leg hanging off it, one arm crooked above her head. I took the dress and crumpled it into a garbage bag that I tossed into the river.

I looked down in my shorts and noticed I'd come.

When I got out I, enrolled in Southern Connecticut State College and studied health administration. I worked in hospitals in Bridgeport and New Haven, starting in administration *and then moving into claims management under my new name. A partner and I opened a private health clinic in a rundown section of Bridgeport. Then another up in Hamden. We expanded it into a small health care network. Which we sold to a larger one. I met Kathi, who was a nurse, who saw me as a person with the right qualities and the right amount of drive. She didn't know anything about the things I'd done. We got married. Had Erin and Taylor. People started seeing me as someone who was doing good in the community, and when a state assembly seat opened and there was no one to fill it, the Democratic Party asked me to consider running. So I did and I won. I began to see that anything I wanted was suddenly open to me. I got on the appropriations committee; ten years and four elections later, I became the majority chair. I had sway over who got what, and what projects were funded. And in whose district. People actually kowtowed to me.*

Maybe I grew to feel a little invincible. Like I could do anything, reinvent myself any way. Like the laws didn't quite apply to me. And maybe I did write my own rules. Maybe I did deserve those names they called me. The Fist. The Scythe.

After all, I knew how to hurt people.

And that was all it took, right? The more I buried all those urges, the more power seemed to come to me.

For years they didn't visit me again.

There was this pretty intern once . . . She was from the Midwest and wanted to get into politics. We went out to dinner and I listened to her tell me about boyfriends and college, and

I thought, as I stared at her, what it would be like to fuck her and then kill her. Who would ever know?

Then her boyfriend called and the whole thing was gone.

Yes, the army cured me. It washed the sand over my past, buried all those things I'd done. Deirdre. April. Buried them deep into my past.

John was history.

And for almost twenty years I believed that was true.

CHAPTER FORTY-NINE

Things were fitting together.

We finally had a name, at least a first name, and that he worked for someone high up in the capital in Hartford. Someone in the government. Patrick always felt that the guy who came after me was simply the muscle for someone else.

Someone Patrick's father was clearly blackmailing.

I'm on my way back wi—

The exchange of money probably took place in the lot of the Stateline Diner.

"You know it's not just about the money," this Charlie had said as he stalked me at the boatyard. "The money's only the tip of it."

The tip of what?

"We want those pages," he said. A diary. A journal.

Whose diary? And describing what? What had Patrick's father found?

We also knew he was tied in with a partner in this. He'd given his cell phone out to someone.

"Who the hell doesn't have a cell phone today?" I asked Patrick while he drove back home.

For a lot of the ride he seemed lost in thought. As if coming to grips with the fact that the man he respected so much had gotten involved in something ugly. Remembering how he was described at the funeral—"salt of the earth"; a guy "who gave his word and kept it"; who "didn't start out with much and didn't leave with much either." I tried to reconcile how these things fit into a person who was blackmailing someone. Maybe someone high up in the state government.

When we finally made it back to Bensonhurst, Patrick drove up to the driveway and stopped.

I opened the door. He didn't move. "You're not coming in?" I asked.

"Not right now."

"Why?"

"I have to see someone. I think I may have an idea who my father was working with."

"Where're you going?" I asked. Though I didn't have to. I knew. I could read it in his eyes.

"Back to Staten Island," he said.

CHAPTER FIFTY

I tried Elena again as soon as I got upstairs, and again there was no answer. Which was really starting to worry me now.

It was after six P.M. Brandon's doctor's appointment was for five o clock and they should have been out by now. Unless Goodwin was running late. Which sometimes happened, of course. But never this late.

This time I left her a message: "Elena, it's Mrs. Cantor. I just wanted to make sure Brandon got to Dr. Goodwin's on time and everything's okay; I still can't make it back for another day. Please give me a call as soon as you can. Thanks . . ."

I hung up and went on Patrick's computer. I typed in a search in Google: "Connecticut government officials." I scanned through the list. Sixty of them. Thirty-six representatives. Twenty-four senators. I didn't recognize any of the names. Nor could I imagine how any of them connected to Patrick's father.

I realized another hour had passed and I still hadn't heard from Elena.

I tried her one more time. Still no answer. I left another message, ending it: "Please call me back, Elena, whenever you get this message. I'm starting to get worried."

This wasn't like her. She never didn't call me back right away. The only thing that made me feel okay was that no one knew where Brandon was, so he had to be safe. Maybe the doctor had been running late. Maybe she had her phone off for some reason or had left it somewhere.

It happened.

I located Dr. Goodwin's number in my phone. It was late. Who knew if anyone was still there at this hour. I felt relieved when the receptionist answered, "Dr. Goodwin's office." I was lucky to even find someone there.

"This is Hilary Cantor," I said. "Brandon's mom."

"Hi, Mrs. Cantor," the receptionist said. "It's Claudia."

"Hi, Claudia. I was just checking up on Brandon. I haven't been able to reach my housekeeper and I know he had a five o'clock there. I know it's unlikely, but by any chance he's not still around there, is he?"

"No, Mrs. Cantor, I'm afraid he's not. But I was actually about to contact you."

"Contact me? Why?"

"To make another appointment. Dr. Goodwin said he needed to see Brandon. About the fine-motor issue. You remember, that's—"

"Of course I remember," I interrupted her.

"I thought that's why you were calling."

"What do you mean, why I was calling?" Now I could hear the worry in my voice.

"To make another appointment. Dr. Goodwin needs to see him and Brandon never showed up today."

Didn't show up.

I sat there and the phone almost fell out of my hand, all my worst fears let loose inside me.

"Is there anything I can do, Mrs. Cantor?" Claudia asked, sensing my dismay.

"No." My entire body became numb. *Where was my son?* "No, there's nothing you can do."

CHAPTER FIFTY-ONE

Mirho had kept his car hidden from the street, down the block from the empty house in Armonk. Sooner or later someone had to go by him. He'd waited all day.

His ribs were sore and his face was cut in spots, but that was nothing like what he was going to give back in return once he finished what he'd set out to do. This had started out as just a job. A job like many he'd done. Messy. Quiet. Across the lines. He was used to that kind of work.

But now it had become something more. Now there was a whole lot more at stake. More than just the money. There were too many open questions. Too many loose ends. And only one way to make sure nothing came out.

He kept his Glock hidden under the newspaper on the passenger seat and rubbed his face.

Now it had gotten personal.

Sooner or later she'd be back. There was only one reason the cops hadn't been called in so far and that was because she wanted a piece of the money too. And this time what he'd done to Rollie would be way too kind for her. He'd learned a few tricks along the way. He knew how to fillet a fish, leaving only one piece of skin.

It passed the time, just thinking about what he would do. This one had taken a few wrong turns. But in the end, things would all go his way.

He rubbed his scar. They always did.

Three twenty P.M. If no one showed, he knew where his next stop would be. Back to Staten Island. More than one way to skin a fish, he knew, right? The money, he'd find a way to make that come to him in the end.

Suddenly he saw a car go past. A clunky old white minivan. A Dodge Caravan or something. Two people in the front. He watched it wind up the cul-de-sac and make a turn.

Into the only house that was up there.

Mirho lifted the newspaper off his gun. *Well, what do you know . . .*

The garage door opened. The minivan pulled up in front. The two people in the car went inside, and one, well, one made his heart jump in delight. He drove his own car into the driveway and parked directly behind the van. He screwed the silencer on the Glock and stepped inside the open garage.

301

The door leading to the kitchen was open. He heard a woman shout in broken English. "Brandon, plees, les go. Weel be late for your appointment!"

Mirho just remained in the doorway as the woman called again. "Plees, come now."

Suddenly she came back out into the garage. She was barely over five feet. Wide as she was tall. Her dark hair pulled back.

Mirho smiled and winked at her. "*Señorita.*"

She gasped. Probably not sure if she was in danger or not. Until she saw the gun. Her eyes growing wider. Knowing she was.

The boy came around the corner carrying an iPad.

"Well, well, well," Mirho said, swatting the woman to the floor, the boy just staring at him wide-eyed. "I better stop off and play the lottery," he said, grinning, "'cause this be my lucky day."

CHAPTER FIFTY-TWO

As he drove across the bridge, the strangest thing came back to Patrick. Actually, it came back to him on the drive back from the diner. Trying to put together who his father would have been involved with.

They were blackmailing someone; that was clear now. Somehow one in the Connecticut state government.

Patrick went over everybody. Everyone it could be. It just seemed so out of character. So beyond his father. Until it hit him. From out of left field.

It was something he hadn't thought of since the funeral. A woman's voice. A door opened just a crack, only the shadow of her face visible, a look of sadness he had never quite understood.

"That means it was all for nothing then," she said simply, closing the door.

He had never understood it—what she meant. Until now maybe.

What *was all for nothing?*

It was Hilary who first put it in his mind. "Who the hell doesn't have a cell phone today?" she asked. And then bits and pieces just began to come together. How his father had been acting at the end. The calls he had made.

Who came, and who didn't come, to his funeral.

"He would have given anything for his neighbors, and he did, right, Mrs. O'B?"

Patrick went down the block and knocked on the door of the blue Victorian at the end of the street.

It took a while before he heard the footsteps coming to the door. Mrs. O'Byrne answered.

"I thought you might want some." Patrick smiled and showed her a warming dish of baked ziti. "I got it at Romano's."

"How could I turn that down?" She smiled. "Would you like to come in?"

"Sure." Patrick stepped through the door. "Just for a minute."

"It's very sweet of you," she said, taking the dish and placing it on a table, "how you're always thinking of me. I don't know how I would have made it through this without you. With Rich moved away . . ."

"It's been my pleasure, Mrs. O'B. You know how fond my dad was of you. You and Mr. O'B both. He was grief-stricken over what happened."

"As was I," Sheila O'Byrne said, "about Joe. I miss him every day. Almost as much as I do Tom."

"I know you do. I know how close the two of you got after the storm. After . . ." After Tom was killed, he meant to say, but stopped.

"Don't worry." Mrs. O'B smiled. "You can say it. Yes, your father and I talked almost every day. He was like an anchor to me. Both of you. You Kelty men have good bones." She grinned.

Patrick laughed. He had grown up looking at her as if she were an aunt and Tom an uncle. "You mind me asking something?"

"Of course not. Come in the kitchen. I'll put this on the counter. I'll warm it up tonight. All I had were some leftovers in the fridge."

Patrick followed her in. Her kitchen was far less rebuilt than his own, though he had pitched in wherever he could, run power from a generator, as the city hadn't completely restored the wiring yet. He didn't know how she stayed here in the cold. Inner fortitude or some kind of devotion. The back of their house was still open to the bay, with only a weatherproof tarp holding back the wind and the cold.

He asked, "How come you never came to the funeral, Mrs. O'B? I looked for you there. I even brought you up, about how Dad was always there in trying to help rebuild the neighborhood. Especially for you."

"Even in his condition," Sheila O'Byrne nodded. "He didn't say much. But he was tireless."

305

"He was. But I looked in the book after I couldn't find you at St. Barnabas's. I didn't see your name anywhere."

Sheila put down the warming dish on the counter. "Would you like a drink, Patrick? Listen to me, I sound like some lush. I've known you since you were three."

It was true, he'd grown up in this house as much as his own. "Maybe a Diet Coke."

"Coke? I'm having a gin and tonic. Tom always had one and we'd watch the news together. A beer? You're old enough.'

"Sure." He laughed. "A beer would be even better."

"I couldn't be there," she said. "To your question, at my age a woman doesn't want to deal with more death than she has to, and I've had my share, wouldn't you say? I'm sorry. I know I was his friend. But it's haunted me. It's haunted me for a lot of years, Patrick. Then the storm, and Tom and everyone else around here. Then Joe being killed . . . I just couldn't mourn another person. Not so soon. That's why I didn't come. I know I should have been there for him. But I think your father would understand."

He looked at her, and something he saw told him she wasn't telling him the truth. Not the whole truth, at least. Sheila had twice the inner strength of anyone else he knew. She was in this house when anyone else would have been in a hotel the city put them up in or with their family. His father had called his mother's cell

306

phone four times the week he died. And there were five calls in return. Whoever had it now.

I'm on my way back wi—

Something was going on.

"I'll grab the beer out of the garage," Mrs. O'B said. "I'll be right back."

She went out through the mud room. Patrick took his father's phone out of his pocket and pressed the number he knew by heart. His mom's old number: 917-904-9991. He could recite it in his sleep.

"I used to think I had the strength for anything," Mrs. O'B called out from the garage. "Whatever life threw at me. That I could take it, with good ol' Irish moxie. And not hate the world back. With spite. But this time life has knocked me for a good one, Patrick . . ."

The number connected. There was a pause. Then suddenly he heard a ring. Not a ring, but the trill of a familiar melody. Bach, he was told. But his mother knew it as a song from the sixties. "A Lover's Concerto": "How gentle is the rain . . ."

The melody was coming from Mrs. O'B's living room.

"I hope this is okay." She came in holding a can of beer. Budweiser.

Then she suddenly stopped, noticing the ring. Looking toward the other room, where it was coming from. Then back at Patrick. Who held up his phone to her.

"Budweiser was Tom's favorite," she said guiltily.

"What did you mean that 'it was all for nothing'?"

307

Patrick asked, pressing the phone with his thumb and cutting off the call. The house turned silent. "When I told you my dad had died in that crash, that's what you said to me, through the door . . . 'Then it was all for nothing.'"

"I knew I should have let that damn thing just die," she said, placing the can of beer on the counter. "But I kept it charged. Foolish, right? Like maybe he would call me one more time. And what happened hadn't taken place."

"My father was messaging you right before he was killed. It never went through, though."

"Messaging me? It's no crime for a friend to give an old woman a cell phone, is it now? Or is that what this country's coming to?"

"He was letting you know that he was on his way back. At first I thought maybe it was me. My mom's name was next to mine on his contacts list. But it wasn't me. It was you. He gave you the phone. He was calling you. Right before he died. Why . . .?"

"Please, Patrick. He's dead. The last thing you want to do is drum up—"

"Drum up what, Mrs. O'B? I saw what he was texting. He was letting you know that he was on his way home. But more than that. That he had something with him. And you know exactly what I'm referring to, don't you? You knew what was in the car and who he had gone to meet."

"Did you hear what I said before, Patrick? About

spite. It's not a way to live your life. I can attest. So tell me, do you want to live your life in that way too?"

"For God's sake, Mrs. O'B, he called you a half dozen times in the days leading up to the crash. What did the two of you have going on? I'm not talking as a cop now. But as his son. As someone who's known you for his whole life. He was doing something for you. Something he couldn't divulge. And it got him killed."

Sheila sat down at the table. Her face was colorless; wrinkles around her mouth that just a moment ago weren't even visible now seemed like deep canals. "You're a good young man, Patrick. Joe loved you. He idolized you when you became a cop. Don't get yourself involved in something that might tear him down now. And you. Something you'll regret."

Patrick kept his eyes trained on her, his gaze burning. "*Why?*"

She looked up at him. Her mouth twitched once or twice, or maybe she was just shaking her head.

"I know about the money," Patrick said.

She sniffed, rolling her eyes at him with a scoffing smile as if he was crazy. "What money?"

"The half a million dollars that was in the car. That he was on his way home with. But that never turned up, right, Mrs. O'B?'

She still hesitated, pushing a dish in front of her to the side. "How . . .?" Then she sat down on a chair. "How did you know?"

"It doesn't matter. What matters is that I need to know what it was about. How my dad got involved."

"That money . . ." She sniffed again bitterly and looked at him. "You think I cared two shits about the money? For what . . .? *This* . . .? This hellhole I'm left with . . ." Her eyes darted around the house, dark with scorn. "All my memories, gone. Stolen from me. My life . . . It was never about the money, Patrick. Not for a second." Her eyes grew scornful and Patrick saw something on her face he had never seen before. "It was about making him pay."

"*Who?*" Patrick stepped closer to her.

"You heard what I said before . . ." Her eyes flickered like dying embers in a fire into a thin smile. "I held it in a long time. But a mother never fully lets it go. I'm talking about spite, Patrick. It's been in there, it feels like forever, burning a hole in my belly." She patted her chest. "Every day. Since the day it happened. You want to know? Then you have to know what's been in my heart since the day my Deirdre never came home. It's been over twenty years, Patrick. Twenty years. . . ."

CHAPTER FIFTY-THREE

The night had been windy and cold, two months ago, not long after Deirdre's diary had come back, and she sat in the kitchen, wrapped in a blanket, switching channels on the small television set that an electrician friend of Patrick's had jerry-rigged.

She settled on this interview on NBC. Ann Curry talking to someone. She was about to move on—it was some official from Connecticut, that guy who was on vacation in South America or somewhere, and whose wife had been tragically killed in a fall, their kids right there.

His name was flashed on the screen. *Landry*, Frank Landry. He was a state senator up there.

Normally these stories did nothing but make her recall her own anguish, so she went to change channels, but her curiosity got the better of her and she put down the remote.

"Senator, you've remained fairly silent since the incident." Ann Curry looked at him empathetically. "But rumors are that you're considering a run for governor and that's why you finally consented to this interview . . ."

"That couldn't be further from the truth," the senator said. He was nice-looking. Maybe a little coldness or remoteness in the small blue eyes. A narrow face and light sandy hair. "It was just important to respect our family's privacy. For the sake of our kids." She liked the way he still referred to them as that. *Our* kids, as if his wife was still alive.

"You can only imagine what they've been through. But so many people have pushed, and maybe it can help avoid something else like this happening down the line. So the kids finally said, 'Go ahead, Dad. Do it.' In fact, they asked to be here now."

His two children came in and sat down next to him. A son and a daughter; both seemed in their early teens. He put his arms around them on the couch. They both looked a little awkward being there.

Then Ann leaned forward. "So, Senator, painful as it is, can you describe what happened down there, the day of the accident?"

Landry nodded, moistening his lips. He took his kids by their hands. "We hadn't been away as a family for a couple of years. So we went on this cruise to Patagonia.

312

Around the horn. It's a place my wife, Kathi, always wanted to see. And it was beautiful. We were having the time of our lives, weren't we, kids?" He squeezed his children's hands and they both nodded, kind of numbly. "We were stopped at this port, Puerto Montt, in southern Chile. We took a shore excursion for the day, a boat ride on this beautiful lake in a national park. Emerald Lake. It was surrounded by stunning mountains. Here's a picture we took . . ." Landry took out a blown-up photograph: the four of them, in bright-colored windbreakers and jackets; his wife pretty, in sunglasses, all smiles. "You can see how happy we were. We were having a great day. Then we went to visit this waterfall and rapids. It's a well-known tourist site down there. The Petrohue Rapids. It had started to rain a bit, and I remember Kathi saying, 'Maybe you guys should go ahead. I'll wait by the souvenir counters.' It seemed like the rocks could be pretty slick. But we convinced her." He pressed his lips together and paused for a while.

"But you're not alleging it was unsafe in any way?" Ann interjected.

"No. I'm not. Not in the least." Landry shook his head. "There was this pathway leading to the overlook. There were people of all ages all around. Old people. Kids. Now and then you had to step from rock to rock, and some of them were a little tricky, right, kids? I mean, my wife, Kathi . . . she's always had a bit of a

313

fear of anything like that. We used to ski when the kids were young, but then she stopped. But this was easy."

"And there were guardrails along the path. And even fences in a few spots, right?"

"Yes. There were." Landry nodded. "All around. Except . . . Except we went out on one of the outlying pathways along the side of the river. The current was raging all around. The whitewater was pretty fierce, spraying up in our faces, even twenty or thirty feet above. And there were all these huge rocks and boulders, and the current slashing all around them, spray everywhere, and then they went over these falls."

"The falls . . .," Ann asked. "How high would you estimate they were?"

"Maybe forty, fifty feet. About the same width around. And the current fed down there and was incredible. Water slamming off the rocks. And if there's one thing I do blame myself for, hold myself accountable for, it was ever going off on the trail, away from the rest of the crowd. The kids had gone up to this point where you can look over the fall with everybody else."

"So you were alone at that point. On this isolated path . . .?"

"Not exactly isolated. There were people around. You could see them in and out of the trees. Of course, Kathi said we should head back and stay with the group, but I wanted to make it out to this spot. On the way we saw another couple coming back and they said it was

314

beautiful. I was hoping we could get a picture of the kids out there on the point."

"And there was a railing on the path? Something to prevent you from just falling in."

"Yes. And most of the way it was away from the edge so the rocks alone and even some trees would hold you back from falling. But the rain began to pick up and the rocks became slick. Kathi was having trouble stepping from one to another. She slipped once and almost turned her ankle. I told her, 'Grab on to me.' I gave her my hand." Landry shook his head self-judgingly. "Believe me, it all seemed so benign."

"So what happened next?"

Landry took a breath and wet his lips one more time, and went through it slowly, methodically. With each sentence he seemed to struggle for the right words.

"What happened next was that she slipped. Off the side of this wet rock. The trail was kind of narrow there and there was a railing, but then she stumbled to the side and lunged for it to balance. But it was wet too and her hand slipped off and she went underneath it, on her side."

"Where were you?"

"I was a step or two in front. When I heard her gasp I spun around and ran to grab her. But her feet gave way on the loosened stones. I heard her go, '*Frank!*' with a gasp. And it was like there was this exposed, unprotected spot with nothing to hold her back."

Landry paused. You could see a mix of emotions crossing in his pained blue eyes. The discomfort of having to relive this in front of his kids. To the world. The horror of what his wife would have gone through.

Guilt.

Sheila thought she saw a sense of something else as well.

The camera focused in on Ann. "What did you feel then, Senator?"

Landry's eyes became opaque and he took a deep breath into his nose. "We were about thirty feet above the river. Kathi had managed to latch onto this branch of a small tree, but it was bending and about to give way. So I grabbed her. I screamed. For anybody. There were a hundred people not far from us, but the sound of the river was thundering and no one could hear. And where we were there was no one else around. I had her. It was wet. Suddenly her shoes started slipping on the rock. I could see the terror in her eyes. She said, 'Frank, pull me up. I'm—'"

"She was falling?"

Landry nodded. "Yes. I said, 'Okay, okay, get your feet over to that rock, I've got you!' But it was wet and the spray was all over us and it was like she just panicked. Her feet began to slip on the rock as she tried to cycle herself back up. And it made it harder and harder for me to hold on. I could feel her slipping out of my grasp. I looked in her eyes."

"You were staring at her?" Ann asked. "You were

316

looking into the face of your wife and you knew she was in peril."

He shook his head grimly. "I don't ever want to recall that look again. She just said, 'Oh, Frank, I think I'm going to fall. I can't hold on.' I said, 'You have to, Kathi. You have to.'

"And then suddenly I felt her just slip. She just fell out of my grasp. And I saw in horror there was nothing holding her back. Not the rocks. Not a tree. Not me. It was the worst feeling of my life. I don't even know if there was a scream; no one could possibly hear it over the roar of the rapids. I just watched her. I saw her bounce off another rock and hit the water, and her red jacket came up. And then she was carried away. She hit against the side of the rocks. I think she was headfirst at that point. I was praying she would grab on to something. I was going, 'Kathi! Please grab on!' To anything. But then she was just gone. Over the falls . . . Like that. It was just seconds. I couldn't do a thing." His daughter squeezed him and then Landry looked back at Ann. "I've been at war. Shot at . . ."

"You were awarded the Bronze Star," Ann said.

"Yes. But nothing prepares you for this. Nothing. Suddenly she was just out of my grasp. I'll never forget her look. Thank God these guys weren't with us and didn't have to see. That's the only thing in this horror I'm grateful for."

Ann actually leaned forward and put her hand

against the senator's wrist. Landry's daughter rested her head against his shoulder.

Ann said, "You loved your wife deeply, didn't you, Senator Landry?"

"Of course. We all did. Everyone who knew her did."

"And you hold yourself accountable for what happened?"

"I do." Landry inhaled a deep, penetrating breath and nodded.

"In your eulogy, you called her your rock. Your own personal salvation."

"She was. I didn't come from very much. I was kind of a rootless kid until I got in the service. The army, and my wife, turned me into whoever I am today."

"And you've had to deal with tragedy before . . ."

"Yes. My brother was killed in a helicopter crash at Camp Lejeune. When I was fourteen. He'd enlisted in the marines. And my younger brother, Todd. He died of AIDS a little over ten years ago now."

"You were raised by a single mother . . ."

"I was." Landry forced a smile. "A great lady. I grew up in New Dorp on Staten Island. My father wasn't around from the time I was six. Though we moved away to live with an uncle in Connecticut in my last year of high school, I still feel close to the place. It's something you never lose. Believe me, I never thought I would end up doing what I do. In government. No one in my family had ever even gone to college before me. We were poor. My mother had to work multiple jobs. She'd say, 'Frank, I'm doing this for you and Todd. One day you'll see why.'" He smiled; his eyes seemed to glaze over. "Well, of course she didn't exactly say '*Frank* . . . She always called me by a nickname back then. Everyone did."

"A nickname . . ." Ann Curry smiled. "Do you mind sharing what it was?" A sympathetic twinkle in her eye that Sheila knew was designed to build rapport.

Landry shrugged. "Just something silly." He looked at his kids. "I don't even know if these guys ever heard it before. I ran fast back then, in the third grade. Somehow it just stuck. They called me Streak."

At first there was simply silence, as if everyone in the world would have heard the very same thing, and Sheila O'Byrne felt like the electrical switch had turned to off in her body.

Her eyes bore in on him, almost climbing out of their sockets in shock and disbelief. *Had she heard it right?* The walls of her chest shuddering.

Streak.

She fixed on the senator's face. Did he really say what she thought he'd said? Or was it her imagination playing tricks on her, her desperate longing that had been buried inside and had been dry so long?

Streak.

She wanted to shout. Anger bubbled up like lava. But no sound came out.

She wanted to reach in and pull him through the screen into her shaking hands. He had lived in New Dorp. He was around her age. Then he moved away. She'd waited for this moment for so long. *Who else could it be?*

"Streak?" Ann Curry asked him again.

"Yes." Landry nodded. "I just ran fast, so from then on that's what everyone called me." It was almost as if he was looking directly at Sheila when he said the word one last time.

"Streak."

CHAPTER FIFTY-FOUR

"I knew it was him, and I knew, watching him, what he had done." Sheila looked up from the table, her cheeks the color of granite. "I only wish Tom, God bless him, was here to see it too."

In the kitchen, Patrick sat back, suddenly seeing how it all fit together. Mrs. O'B. His father. Landry. Deirdre.

"I knew with all my heart that he was the one. The one who had killed my Deirdre. That name. That he was from here. And how he had left. That very same year. I could see in those eyes what he was. They were so lifeless and lying. A mother can see that, Patrick, when it comes to her child. See right to the core.

"And I knew we had him cold. He had incriminated himself. Because I had her diary. It was like God had sent it back to me in the storm to bring him to

321

judgment. After all this time, I could finally make him pay."

"Why didn't you just take it to the police?" Patrick pulled out a chair and sat across from her. "Or to me . . .?"

"To the police . . .? A nickname his family used to call him. Over twenty years ago. A buried body no one even remembered but Tom and me. We knew what we had would never hold up in a trial. Not against this man, who had the sympathies of everyone. Joe said they could exhume her body and test for DNA. Maybe they could. But I could do something else. I could ruin him. I could bleed him dry like he bled me. Like I said, spite is a hard teacher, Patrick. It's a hard thing to rid yourself of when you've held it in like I had for over twenty years.

"And I could make him confess. That was your father's idea. The only reason we even asked for the money. If he paid it, it would be as good as a confession. Then we could take it to the police."

"So you went with it to my dad?"

"Who else did I have? Tom was gone. Joe would do anything to help protect me. He even claimed that the diary was his. That he'd found it at a niece's. Joe was like that, you know. Stand-up. Landry probably didn't even know that I was still alive."

"Yeah, he was," Patrick said with a smile, "stand-up."

Mrs. O'B looked at him. "Yes, he was letting me know

he had the money on his way back. Then I called and called and it just seemed like he had disappeared. When you told me he was dead, it was like God saying again, *It's your fault, Sheila. You did a bad thing.* And maybe I did."

"That's why you didn't come to the funeral? Not just because it hurt. But because you felt responsible. Complicit. In how he died."

"One way or another that storm took everything I had left that I held dear," Mrs. O'B said. "The storm, or what I held on to in my heart. But I still want him. Landry."

Patrick understood. He nodded.

"So how did you come to find out?" Mrs. O'B asked. "About the money?"

"Someone took it." Patrick told her how Hilary had come upon the accident scene. What she had done there and how she had come to him.

"Joe told them, if anything happened to him, anything, he still had a way of getting everything out. We held on to parts of it. A few pages from Deirdre's journal. As a kind of insurance. So they tracked who took their money and somehow it led to you?"

"In a way." Patrick knew now that things had changed. That this could no longer remain a secret. "If this man is a killer, Mrs. O'B, it has to come out."

"I know that. I already placed a call to the people who did that interview with him. I haven't heard back yet. But I will. It's going to get bad."

"It's already gotten bad, Mrs. O'B. Someone else has been killed. The person who first came upon Joe's accident, at least according to the police. They tried to frame his death as a suicide. But we found out. He was killed by the man who gave Dad the money. Who's done some very bad things. And they tried to get to someone else the other day. The woman who took the money, who came to me. They want the rest of what you're holding. Your insurance, as you say."

"You know what the irony is?" Her eyes were glazed over. "We were never even going to keep it anyway. The money. The money was simply his confession. Once we got it we said we were always going to hand over the rest. We were going to go to the media with the money and the diary."

Patrick looked at her. "Well, I'm afraid now it's gotten a lot more complicated than that."

He told her about Hilary and Brandon, and the part of the money she had already spent. Over sixty grand. And then about Rollie. Just a Good Samaritan who tried to help the wrong guy. Sheila crossed herself and shook her head. "That's money's got blood on it. Deirdre's blood," she said. "And it'll infect anyone who touches it."

"I'm not done," Patrick said. He told her about his sister, Annette, and the fraud she'd committed after the storm. Annette had grown up with Sheila too. And how he had paid off her debt to keep her from being charged,

324

but had implicated himself with some very bad people. The Russian mob.

"It just doesn't end, Patrick. The evil my daughter's death caused. So keep the money. I don't want it anyway. I'm glad if it can do some good for you and this girl. It won't bring Deirdre back."

"It's too late to keep it, Mrs. O'B. Now that we know what's behind it."

"I don't understand." She looked at him. "You want this to all come out?"

"Yes, it has to." Patrick nodded.

"If it does, then it'll *all* come out, won't it? Everything. What you did for Annette. The Russians."

He nodded again. "I suppose it will."

"What about your job? Your father was so proud of you. And this woman, you said she has a young son. Handicapped?"

"Asperger's syndrome," Patrick said. "It's like—"

"I know what it is," Sheila O Byrne said. "My legs may not move as they used to, but my brain still manages just fine. You said she did this to keep him in school. He'll be affected by this too?"

"He will. But too much has happened, Mrs. O'B." Patrick reached forward and took her hand. "So where are they? Those pages?"

"I can't bear that anyone else is hurt on account of them. As much as I want this man to be accountable for what he did, it won't bring Deirdre back."

"Other people are dead, Mrs. O'B. Where are they?" he asked again. "Please."

She got up and went to a cabinet above the dishwasher where canned goods and sauces were kept and reached to the back of the shelf. She came out with a wooden box. A floral design, hand painted, lacquered. "Deirdre made this. In the fifth grade."

She put it on the table and took out some photos and a few other things from inside. A piece of blond hair. Some baby shoes. Then some handwritten pages that she paged through and folded together, then handed to him. "It's all I have of her. What's in here means everything to me. But use them. Do whatever you have to. Just promise me one thing."

"Whatever you want." He nodded.

"Promise me you'll make him pay."

Patrick held it in his hands. He remembered Deirdre. She was two years older. She had sunny blond hair and blue eyes and played soccer for the Purple Eagles and liked to write. "I promise, Mrs. O'B. I knew Deirdre too."

"Not just for Deirdre." She reached out and latched onto Patrick's wrist, a different glimmer in her eyes. "There was something else I saw as I listened to what that man described and looked into those eyes. That scared me just as much as what he did to Deirdre . . ."

Patrick looked at her, and his stomach clenched as he realized what she was saying.

326

"You know that wasn't any accident, what happened up on that river. He can say it, and he can tell the world, but you can see it in his eyes, what he is, no matter how deep or how long he's kept it buried. You see what I'm saying, don't you?"

Her eyes were lit up like lava.

"You make him pay, Patrick. But not just for Deirdre." She tightened her hold on his wrist and looked into his eyes. "For that poor woman who'll never have anyone to speak for her. You make him pay for what he did to his wife too."

LANDRY

CHAPTER FIFTY-FIVE

The thought never entered my mind until I saw her dangling there.

This time, at least.

There had been a hundred other times over the years when I might have thought, what if I just let the car slip into reverse as she unloaded the groceries from the trunk, or pulled out her air piece when we were scuba diving in the Caribbean.

But then I'd stop myself. Like maybe how the rest of the world brings themselves back from fantasizing about someone they find attractive whom they've been staring at. I fought against those kinds of thoughts all the time.

And it wasn't just Kathi. It could be anyone. In the middle of a golf game. Or during a committee meeting. Or peeing next to someone in the men's room.

My thoughts just went there.

But then I'd always bring myself back. Remind myself of how crazy it was. I was a public figure. She was the mother of my kids.

Or a committee member who could help me pass a bill. Or the guy who just filled up the car.

It could be anyone.

But watching her there, latched onto that branch, seeing her helpless, her life in my grasp, everything came hurtling back.

The things that held me together fell away.

My first instinct was to pull her up. And I tried to at first. She clung to the roots of a small tree, her feet grasping for traction on the slippery rock. Nothing below her but the slashing current of the rapids. "Frank, oh my God, quick! I fell!"

I ran over and took her by the hands. Her palms were slick and wet from the soil and rain. I set my feet to steady myself. I even yelled out, "Help! Anyone, Jesus, is anyone there?"

I wanted to save her.

But no one heard me over the thundering roar of the falls and the echo of the rapids.

"Pull me up! Frank, pull me up, for God's sake, please!" Kathi begged. Fear lit up her eyes.

I had her in my grasp and started to pull. "Just hang on."

Then something came over me. Something I always tried to push away. Banish.

I looked around. Through the trees, I could see specks of bright-colored jackets back at the point where everyone was observing the falls.

"Help me, Frank. Pull me up. I'm slipping. Please, don't let me fall, Frank. Don't."

I just looked in her eyes. That's when I knew that this time was different.

I know I gave a hoist, Kathi whimpering, her legs cycling to catch some footing on the rock, which made it harder for me to lift her up.

I felt it again.

Like a fingernail brushing ever so slightly across my skin. A tingling down my arms and into my thighs. I knew it would put everything I'd built in my life at risk. Completely wrong, self-destructive. The devil talking.

Yet as I watched her dangling there, her life in my hands, I knew it was the one course of action I would take.

I just snapped.

"I'm not gonna make it, Frank. I know it," she whimpered in the grip of panic. "Please, pull me up. Please . . ."

She looked down.

It was as if a hypnotist had snapped me out of a spell. I tried to push the thought away, but this time it didn't leave. Until I was no longer Frank there, the architect of this new, successful life. The father of these kids. With my beautiful wife.

But John.

John. Who I was before. And all the things he had done.

"Frank, what are you doing? I can feel myself falling. I—"

Our eyes met. Hers white and large with fear. Mine, I knew now, filled with something else. I felt her slip. Suddenly I stopped trying to pull her upward.

333

In that moment I think she saw me. She saw me for the first time. Not Frank.

But someone she had never met. Or even knew existed.

She screamed, "Frank, can't you see I'm—"

I just let her go.

There was a shriek, a piercing, stretched-out "Noooo . . .!" as she toppled out of my grasp and disappeared into the foam. I watched her come to the surface, her red Windbreaker sticking out from the white, frantically trying to grasp something as the river carried her away. People no doubt seeing her now, pointing.

Over the falls.

And I felt something as I watched. Watched her disappear. The sensation far too brief, too short-lived.

Not a thrill. Or what you might call pleasure.

Or a sense of horror at what I'd done. Or even remorse.

All of that came a bit later; it just took time.

What I felt was something that I hadn't felt in years, maybe since that hot August night on Staten Island in the shadow of the Goethals Bridge. My blood racing. My heart alive.

And it brought the tiniest smile to my lips as I saw people running, shouting, pointing toward the falls.

I felt like myself.

CHAPTER FIFTY-SIX

"I know who's behind it!" Patrick said, his voice fired up. "And why."

My cell had rung and I'd picked up expectantly. I'd been trying to reach him for the past hour, to no avail. "*Who?*"

"It's that state senator from Connecticut whose wife fell into the river in South America. Landry. He's the one up in Hartford Charlie's working for. I know what he's done and what it is he wants to keep quiet."

I wanted to interrupt him and say, "Patrick, I've got something you have to hear!" I was desperate to tell him about Brandon. But I found myself answering almost involuntarily, "What is it?" And "How did you find out?"

He told me about his neighbor, Mrs. O'Byrne, the

one who'd lost her house and husband, and the murder of her daughter, twenty years ago. How Landry had been there as a kid on Staten Island, and the nickname he was called by back then. *Streak*. The only name her murdered daughter knew him by and had written in her diary.

How an interview on TV after his wife's death had brought it all back.

"They were using Deirdre's diary to extract the money from Landry with Mirho as the go-between. That's what he's really looking for, Hilary—that book. Or at least the pages from it that tie Landry to that murder. Just raising the possibility of it could cause people to investigate and blow apart any chance of him becoming governor."

"Patrick, that's good. It really is. But there's something you have to hear . . ."

"This has to come out, Hilary. Whatever happens, the money doesn't matter anymore. Because it doesn't end with that murder. There's more . . ."

"What do you mean, there's *more* . . .?"

Patrick paused. "There's what happened to Landry's wife in South America."

I thought back on what I knew about that horrifying accident. A man watched his own wife fall out of his hands, into a river and over a fall. His kids nearby. And then the reality of what Patrick was suggesting came clear to me, like something icy pressed to my skin. "Oh

God, you're saying he killed her. That it wasn't an accident? What kind of monster could let his wife fall to her death in front of her own family?" My stomach turned at the thought.

"The same kind who can kill an innocent eighteen-year-old girl who was heading off to start her life. Someone who doesn't think or feel like you or me. Who doesn't have an ounce of remorse or sympathy inside. Someone psychopathic. That's an animal out there. I'm sorry. I'm going to turn this over to the authorities now."

"Patrick, *wait!*" My voice rang with panic. "We can't bring this to the police! Something else has happened . . ."

I told him about Brandon not showing up for his doctor's appointment. And how I hadn't been able to reach Elena. For the past couple of hours. "That man's got him. I know he has. The one who tried to kill me. Charlie. I can feel it, Patrick. I'm going out of my mind. He's just an innocent boy. The man mentioned my son when he was trying to find me at the yard. I know he's got Brandon."

"Hilary, we don't know *what's* happened. It could be any of number of things. Maybe her phone isn't working. Maybe she lost it. She could be—"

"*No!* She would never have missed that appointment. We'd just spoken about it earlier in the day. She's never ever done anything like this before. So we can't bring

337

in the police. At least not yet. Not until we know. We have his money. We can give them back the missing pages. We can—"

I heard a beep. My phone vibrated. Another call coming in. I checked the screen. My heart surged in relief.

Elena.

"My God, it's her! Thank God!" The panic of a moment ago now turned to elation. "I'll call you back in a minute. Let me talk to them. Then we'll decide what to do."

"All right. Call me right away."

I pressed the green answer button and the call switched over. I didn't give her a second to answer. I shouted, *"Elena!* Elena, I was so worried. What happened? Why didn't you go to Dr. Goodwin's?"

But in that very second my elation collapsed. Another voice answered me, a voice I'd heard for the first time only yesterday calling out for me in the darkened shed of the boatyard. And all he said was, about as calmly as a person could say such words:

"Do you ever want to see your son alive again?"

CHAPTER FIFTY-SEVEN

I froze. A scream rose in me that tried to make its way up my throat, but remained bottled up inside. "Don't you hurt him," I said. More like begged. "He's just an innocent boy. Don't you hurt him or I'll make you pay. I swear I will."

Tears rushed into my eyes.

"You'll make *me* pay? That right?" The man said with a chortle. "Darlin', I think you've got things a bit reversed, though all the passion is admirable. I figure this is an unsettling time. But that isn't what I asked you, is it?" He waited. It was clear he wanted me to say the words.

"Yes, I want to see him," I said. The phone was shaking in my hands.

"*Alive?* I wouldn't be mistaken in assuming that would be the preferred state?"

"Yes, please, *alive!* Alive!" I said, the tears on my cheeks now turning from ones of anger to helplessness. "I beg you, please, don't hurt him."

"And the nanny? I figure you'd probably like to see her again too?"

"Elena. She's got a family. She's a religious woman. She'd never hurt anyone. Yes. Both of them. Please . . ."

"Then what do you say we get right down to business. You know what we want from you, right?"

I nodded, clutching the phone with both hands. "Yes. I know."

"I mean, all of it, right? You do know what I'm talking about, don't you?"

"Yes. I know what it is you're looking for. The missing pages from the diary." I swallowed and said, "We have them."

"Good. And we can never forget about the money, can we?"

"I have the money too."

"Well, good then. So grab a pen. Here's what you have to do."

I ran into Patrick's kitchen and searched around frantically for a pen. I found one in a drawer and scribbled everything down on the back of an envelope.

"You know Bruckner Boulevard? In the Bronx?"

"Yes." In the South Bronx. It was one of the routes for leaving or driving into Manhattan going north. It fed into 95 North from the Triboro Bridge. "I know it."

"There's an entrance ramp. On 138th Street? It feeds up onto the expressway . . ."

"Yes," I said again. "I know it." It was a run-down area of auto-body shops and check-cashing storefronts. At rush hour, there was always a backup there to get on the expressway. But the area would be deserted at night.

"I want you to be there at two A.M. That's in five hours. Pull onto the access road that's adjacent to the entrance ramp leading to the expressway. Park there and turn your headlights off."

"I got it. I understand, 138th Street."

"Put the money in a plastic garbage bag and the pages in a clear folder so I can see them."

"Okay."

"Just yourself. No cops. No heroes. I hope I'm making myself a hundred percent clear on that."

"Yes, I hear you," I said. My heart was pounding. "I know what you're asking for. I understand."

"I see any sign of the police, or even anyone in particular who might hail from Staten Island . . . One stupid act, darlin', and you're going to regret it for the rest of your life. He seems like a sweet boy. Not a good thing to see your son's life come to an end right in front of your eyes. Or maybe worse, to never know what happened to him."

"No, I understand, please . . . All I want is for him to be safe."

"Good then. You have that all down? I'm counting on you being as smart as you are pretty. What did you say your name was . . . Jeanine?"

Jeanine. My middle name. That was the name I had given Rollie. That was somehow how he found me.

"Yes." I took in a breath. I knew what I said next would shock him. "I have it all perfectly, Charlie."

There was only silence. It seemed for a good ten seconds. I'm sure I knocked him for a loop, telling him I knew his name too. I just wanted him to know that there were stakes for us both. If *he* did something stupid. It was all I had. "Well, someone's been busy, busy, busy . . ." He sniffed admiringly.

"I just thought you should know there are stakes for you too. In case *you* decide to do something stupid. And for the state senator as well."

"You are really walking a dangerous path with that one, hon . . ."

"All I want is my son back. And Elena. After tonight, nothing that's happened here even concerns me. Just give me back my son. It'll all be something no one will ever be able to prove."

"Just so we're clear, you or your boyfriend get any different ideas, that boy of yours will be a bloody mess, so help me God."

I steeled myself with a breath. "I hear you."

"So two A.M. then. And that's all the warning you

get. Don't bother calling this number back. I'm pulling the battery."

"Then how will I find you?" It would be dark and mostly deserted near that underpass. You could shoot someone there at that hour; no one would even hear the sound.

"Don't worry. I'll find you."

CHAPTER FIFTY-EIGHT

Patrick didn't make it back until around ten.

I'd called him as soon as I hung up, pretty much out of my mind with panic, imagining Brandon being held by that man, my sweet little boy, and Elena, who didn't even know what she had stumbled into.

All I could think of was how afraid Brandon must be.

When I finally saw the car lights pull up in front of the house and then heard the key in the front door, I basically ran into Patrick's arms, hurling myself around him and burying my face in his chest, unable to stop the nerves and tears.

"I know," he said, brushing my hair gently. "It's going to be okay."

"We can't let him hurt him, Patrick," I said, afraid to

lift my head and look him in the eye. "Whatever happens, I just want my son. Nothing else matters."

"And we're going to get him," he said. "I promise." He put his hands on my shoulders and gently eased me away. What I saw was a confident smile. "Okay?"

Not even sure I believed it, I nodded.

"Okay. So we have less than five hours. Let's figure out what we're going to do."

"You have the pages?"

"I have them." He took out a clear plastic folder. Inside I could see three water-stained, handwritten pages, clipped out of the original diary. The last days of a girl murdered over twenty years ago. I looked at the one on top. I saw the name written with a kind of squiggly, girlish underlining underneath it.

Streak.

"These are all there are?"

"This is what they kept as insurance so that no one would come after them. My father told them they would be released. According to Mrs. O'Byrne, they were never even going to keep them. They were going to turn them over to the police with the ransom. The ransom was basically Landry's confession. They figured that would be enough to exhume Deirdre's body and check for Landry's DNA. For twenty years she had no idea who her daughter's killer was until she heard that interview." He set the folder down on the coffee table. "The diary was lost in the storm. If it hadn't washed up on the

345

Jersey shore, and some couple brought it back to her, she'd have no proof."

"I'm sorry." I brushed the tears out of my eyes. "I'm sorry for what she had to go through all these years. I'm sorry that we got mixed up in it. She deserves a whole lot better than just turning these back over to that bastard just to get back my son."

"All she asked was that no one else be hurt on account of these . . ."

"I understand how she feels. I hope I get to meet her one day."

"You will."

He sank into the chair across from me.

"Patrick, he said if he saw any sign of the police, he'd kill them both. I can't take that risk. Once we have him back, I don't care what we do. We have to turn ourselves in. But now . . . I just want the two of us to get out of this and not do anything crazy."

"You mean the three of us," Patrick said.

I shook my head. "He said just me, Patrick. No one else. Even you, he said, otherwise he'd show me what it was like to see my boy killed in front of my eyes." My eyes flooded up again. "That's too much for me to risk."

"You know there's not even a chance that I'd let you go there alone." Patrick's blue eyes shone resolutely. "He'll kill you, Hilary. And then he'll kill the nanny and then your boy. You can tie him to Rollie's murder. I want Brandon back safely as much as you, but there's just no way."

"I can't lose my son, Patrick. I can't."

"We're not going to lose him. Landry wants those diary pages as much as you want Brandon. But I'm not going to let him walk away either. And not just for Deirdre."

"What do you mean?"

"Knowing what we know now, is there any way that what happened down in South America looks like an accident? It's entirely possible this guy is covering up at least *two* murders. Not to mention Rollie McMahon. So we have to decide how we get your son back and still do what's right. To Landry. Because that's the price. That's all Mrs. O'Byrne wanted for her daughter's memory. To make him pay. So that's what I'm gonna do . . . Get your son back, hopefully without landing us in jail. And get him. Both of them. Wait here . . . I'll be right back."

Patrick got up. I heard him open a door and go down to the basement. A minute later he came back up carrying the nylon bag with the money in it. He dropped it to the floor. Then he went into the kitchen and came back with a large black garbage bag.

"We have a lot to go over," he said, unzipping the case and transferring the bundled cash into the garbage bag. "So let's get prepared."

From his waist he also took out a gun and placed it on top of the diary.

347

"I hope you know what you're doing," I said, nerves shooting down my spine.

"I hope so too."

"You ever use that?" I asked, pointing to the gun on the table.

"Not in years." He finished transferring the cash, then looked at me. He smiled, I knew trying to bolster me, but there was resignation in it, and duty; we were crossing a line in the sand for him too.

"But fortunately I know a bunch of people who have."

CHAPTER FIFTY-NINE

Mirho strapped the boy and the Latino nanny into the Escalade. Their hands were bound. The kid kept babbling in these nonsensical sounds. Weird. Like he was touched in the head. The nanny kept praying in Spanish and trying to comfort the kid. "Relax, soon it'll all be over," Mirho said. "One way or another, you'll be out of my hair."

That didn't stop her.

"Just shut the fuck up," he tried, glaring at them.

Finally he just taped their mouths shut.

"Now that's an improvement."

He drove, an hour before the meet time. He had other plans to finish. I'm sorry, he thought, but it just ain't gonna end good for anyone. He rubbed his nose;

he figured it was broken from the boatyard. It had swelled up to twice its size. And his ribs ached. It hurt to breathe, much less talk. The bitch was going to regret she had ever stumbled into this mess. He owed her.

He covered the HK 9 millimeter that was on the seat next to him.

"I know it's past your bedtime," he said as he came down the Bronx River Parkway. "Don't let it worry you," he said to the nanny, meeting her wide eyes in the rearview mirror. "You'll all be catching up on your sleep real soon."

He pulled off the parkway and onto the Bruckner. It was dead this time of night. A totally abandoned part of the city. You could give money away and you'd have trouble finding anyone to come around.

His cell rang. Clearly it could be only one person. "Mirho," he answered.

"Where are you?" the senator asked.

"Getting you back a good night's sleep, what you hired me to do. I've got the gal coming with the cash and the journal. Give me an hour. You'll have what you want."

"That woman's only a part of it," the senator said. "Those pages came from somewhere. There are still two others out there who know. You think there's still a way to keep this quiet?"

No, there was no way to keep this quiet anymore, Mirho knew.

"Just what are you up to?" Mirho asked.

"Let's just say I'm doing what comes naturally. However this goes, it's all going to end tonight."

CHAPTER SIXTY

At close to two in the morning we made it to the Bruckner in twenty minutes. We drove separately, me in the Acura, which Patrick had had a friend check out and remove from it a GPS device, and Patrick in his truck. We pulled onto a deserted side street in the Bronx just across the RFK Bridge, about ten blocks from the meet site.

The area was dark and abandoned, graffiti all over the empty row houses, and an abandoned lot. I'd have been petrified to be here at this time of night were it not for Patrick. We parked, he came over and got into my car, and we went over the plan one more time.

He'd be in the cargo compartment hidden from view until Brandon and Elena were safely in the car. I had the money in the plastic bag next to me on the passenger seat and Deirdre's diary pages in a clear plastic folder.

"Whatever you do, don't get out of the car," Patrick instructed me, I think for the third time. "Hand him the money first—and don't hand over the diary until Brandon and Elena are safely in the car. Ask to see his hands if he keeps one of them hidden. You're not armed; you want to know what he's hiding. Say you're uncomfortable otherwise. If you see anything resembling a gun, say something like 'That gun is scaring Brandon.' Anything. Just so I'll know. Remember, he wants those pages as much as you want your son, so keep your wits about you and just make it an exchange of goods. If it's anything else, I'll be here. As soon as they're back in your car and you've handed him the pages, hit the gas and get the hell out of there. You'll be facing north, so jump on the expressway as fast as you can."

"What's going to happen to him?"

"You don't have to think about what's going to happen to him. All you have to do is keep your wits about you and you'll have your son. If he makes a wrong move, I promise, it'll be his last."

"Please let me do this alone, Patrick. I'm scared. What if he sees you in there?"

"He wants his merchandise, Hilary. If he doesn't get it, you can nail his boss's ass for murder. Just don't give him the journal pages before Brandon and Elena are safely back. Whatever he does. This is what he does for a living. You have to stay strong."

"I'm so sorry that Brandon has to go through this," I said.

"I know. But it'll all be over soon."

I checked the time. It was eight before two. My heart was beating about three times its normal rate. "Now put down the rear windows." Patrick gave me a squeeze on the arm. "I'll climb in back. Are you okay?"

"I'm okay." I heard the crack in my voice. Then I shook my head. "No. I'm not okay. I'm scared to death. For Brandon."

"C'mere . . ." He leaned across and gave me a comforting hug. I didn't want it to end. I wanted to wake up from this and find out it had all been a dream. A horrible one. He let me go and he held on to my hand. He squeezed it. "I promise. He's gonna be okay."

I sucked in a breath. "Okay . . ."

I lowered the rear windows. Patrick went around and climbed into the back. He pulled a blanket over himself, and some shopping bags I had back there, and a mat I used for exercise. My windows were darkened, so there was no way anyone could see.

Five of two now. My heartbeat picked up another gear. My stomach started to turn.

"Ready?" he said.

This time I nodded. "Yeah, I'm ready."

"Just remember, one last time . . ."

"I know. I know." I nodded. I knew that this time he

meant it only to put me at ease. "Whatever happens, don't get out of the car."

He put his hand on my shoulder. "I was going to say remember the best day you ever had with your son, because that's exactly what it's gonna be like with him tomorrow."

I met his eyes in the rearview mirror and put my hand on his. "Thank you, Patrick. For everything."

The clock read 2:58. "Okay, let's go."

I started up the car and drove the ten or so blocks up to 138th Street and came around in front of the ramp to the expressway, which rumbled directly above us. The body shops and check-cashing places and bodegas were all shuttered. A transmission repair garage had the aluminum siding pulled down. It was dark, the traffic was sparse. Two or three cars crossed 138th, probably heading to the Hunts Point produce market, which was not far away but didn't open for a couple of hours. The elevated Bruckner Expressway rumbled intermittently directly over our head.

It was time, Hilary.

It flashed in my mind. How Robin had described it. Welcome to the other side of the road.

CHAPTER SIXTY-ONE

A car drove by and my heart climbed up my throat, the car's headlights washing us in light. I froze and tried to draw any saliva, but my mouth was completely dry.

Anyway, it continued on its way.

"Take it easy," Patrick cautioned from the back. Every car light flashing by, every sound I heard, I sucked in a breath, certain that it was him, aching to see my son. I tried to remember the bravest thing I'd ever done. Once I confronted some clearly off-his-rocker guy as he was harassing a woman on the subway, and I remembered thinking, telling the guy to get on his way, *This is crazy, Hil, he could have had a gun or pulled a knife. You could be a story on the news tomorrow morning. You hear about these stories all the time.* Whatever happened, I chuckled to myself darkly, this had definitely risen to the top of the list now.

On the hour, my phone rang.

Elena.

"I'm scared," I said to Patrick in the back. The nerves were crazy in my stomach. It rang again. I was too frightened to even answer.

It rang a third time and I hadn't moved.

"It could always be Bloomingdale's about the house-goods sale tomorrow." I met Patrick's eyes in the mirror. "If you don't answer, you'll never know."

A fourth time. I nodded and drew in a breath.

"Ask to speak to your son. He's waiting for you. I'm right here."

I nodded and took the phone with both hands and answered. "Hello."

"Are you where I told you to be?" the familiar voice said, a syringeful of ice shooting through my veins.

"Yes. I'm at the access ramp," I said. "Just like you asked."

"Change of plans. I want to you to drive straight north, fifteen blocks, to 153rd Street. When you get there make a slight left and pull up directly under the expressway. There'll be a vacant lot under the overpass. When you're there shut off your lights. Do you have it?"

"Yes, 153rd."

"I'm giving you two minutes."

"Two minutes?" I tightened in fear. "I want to speak to my son."

"I wouldn't worry about your son right about now. He won't be around to speak to you ever again if you're not here. I'd get rolling. You're down to a minute and forty-five."

The phone clicked off and my heart started to go crazy. I spun around and looked at Patrick. "He's at 153rd Street. He said I have two minutes."

"All right, go!" he said, glancing around outside. "Go!"

I threw the car into drive and jammed my foot on the accelerator.

The light was red and I sped right through it. I didn't give a shit. There was no one else around; 153rd was fifteen blocks away and all I could think of was him pulling away with my son. For good.

No, I remembered what Patrick had said. *He wants that diary as much as you want Brandon.*

"Take it easy," Patrick said. "He'll be there. You don't want a cop to pull you over."

At 149th I caught another red light. This time I had to stop. If it was dark and deserted ten blocks south, it was like a desert up here. A black, empty, steel-trestled burnt-out desert. There wasn't even a streetlamp on. The odd businesses amid the vacated storefronts were auto-repair shops and a closed-down bakery. Maybe a homeless guy or two huddled up in a blanket under the overpass. If you wanted to make a drug transaction

358

with no one to see you, this was probably the cushiest address in the city.

Or kill someone, I was thinking. I was sure Patrick was too.

"Come on, come on, come on!" I shouted at the light.

"Stay calm," Patrick said. He could probably see that I was losing it. "Remember what we went over. The money first and not the diary. Until you have Brandon safely in the car."

"Okay! Okay!" I shouted at him, my nerves frayed.

Finally the light changed and I hit the gas again; 153rd was just four blocks away. When I reached it, nothing around, not even a fucking light, I turned left as he'd said and came up under the expressway.

There was an empty lot under the overpass, completely abandoned. The expressway clattering with the occasional cars thirty feet above. I didn't see anyone.

"Oh God," I said, looking at where we were, my hands shaking. This was the kind of place where anything could happen. Where people could just disappear.

I shut off my lights as he'd instructed.

CHAPTER SIXTY-TWO

I waited, my heart bouncing back and forth off my ribs like a metronome set to high.

I didn't see anyone anywhere. Once in a while, a rumble came from the expressway as a car went over us above.

My mouth had the feel of sandpaper. I wanted to say something to Patrick but I was petrified it would give us away. Every second felt like an eternity. Just my heart keeping time in my chest.

Three full minutes passed.

A ripple of fear snaked through me. Suddenly I wasn't sure: *Did I have the right street? He did say 153rd?* I looked for the street sign, indecision worming its way into my brain.

That was when a car slowly pulled around the corner

from a block north in the southbound lane, the lot we were in situated directly in the middle.

An SUV. A Cadillac Escalade. It turned under the overpass and pulled alongside us. The driver's window directly across from me. The windows were tinted. I searched for Brandon through the darkened glass. I couldn't see into it.

Which scared me.

Please, please let him be here, I tried to reassure myself. *But what if he wasn't? What if he was at some other location? What then?*

My heart came to a stop as the driver's window slowly went down. Suddenly I was staring at the same smirking face that had lunged at me with that boathook as I tried to get away at the boatyard.

A round jaw. Large nose. Short, light-colored hair. Narrow, haughty eyes. The sonovabitch was enjoying this.

"Hello, Jeanine." He grinned. "Pleasure to see you again. Sorry about that window the last time we met. How about if we keep it on your insurance, if that's okay? Oh, and by the way, Rollie said to say hi!"

"Where's my son?" I said and glared at him.

"He's here. Aren't you, Brandon?" He glanced behind. "Quite a kid. Doesn't say a whole lot, though. You notice that as well? I have to ask, you sure that school is really working for him . . .? The nanny doesn't say a lot herself—at least not in anything resembling English.

361

Can't get ten words out between them. Just a bunch of gibberish. Of course, it's not exactly their fault right now. Is it, guys?" He turned his head. "What with the tape over their mouths . . ."

"I want to see him," I said.

"You want to see him? Sure, why not?"

He rolled down the rear driver's-side window. I saw Brandon in the backseat on the far side. Mouth taped. He looked terrified. Terrified and confused. *What had I gotten him into?* I had to restrain myself from leaping out of the car and running over to him.

"Hold on, honey." I smiled. My heart was breaking just watching him. "You're gonna be back with Mommy very soon. I promise."

His eyes seemed to brighten at my voice. I know he was trying to talk to me. My eyes flicked to Elena, who looked just as frightened and helpless. I winked a sign of support to hang in there. Then the window went up again.

"Aw, that's a nice thought," Charlie said. "You brought everything just like I said?"

"I have it." I showed him the large garbage bag on the seat across from me.

"And the rest? You know what I'm talking about, I think."

"It's here." I raised the clear plastic folder.

"Good. Rollie said you were a sight to look at. And he was right. About that part maybe. And hopefully you're just as smart. So here's what you're gonna do. You're gonna put those pages in the bag with the money, open your door, and hand it over to me."

I shook my head. "Not until my son and Elena are in the car."

"*Sorry?* Are we negotiating here, Jeanine? You don't mind if I call you that, do you? So very clever. Do you want your son back in one piece or not? Your call . . . I can just drive off with my little packages in the backseat and we can call it a night."

"*No!*" I reminded myself that he wanted what I had as much as I did what he had, and there was no way he would leave without them. "Take the money first. You let Brandon and Elena climb in the backseat here. Then you get the diary pages . . ."

He smiled. Not a smile of agreement. A smile that conveyed he was not being amused. "I must not have made a very strong impression on you, Jeanine. Guys"— he turned around—"I don't think she really wants you back at all. Neither of you." He turned back to me and his eyes glimmered. "What's the matter, you don't trust me, doll?"

"I'm not your doll." I glared at him. His left arm rested on the open window; his right arm was hidden. "You're making me nervous. I want to see your hands. Both of them."

Sweat had soaked through my top. I sucked in a breath to steady myself. I told myself I was doing fine.

Just to hold it together, like Patrick would say. If I really believed it.

"Take it out and bring it over to me," he said, no longer with any mirth in his tone. "We're wasting time."

"I can't." All I could do was wait him out. "You can have the money. *Here . . .*" I moved it nearer to me. "I'll give you the diary pages next. Once I have my son and Elena. Look, we better get on with this. If someone comes by . . ."

He looked at me. "All right. Take it around and put it in the back of my car. Then you can have the nanny."

"I'm not getting out of this car."

Somehow I didn't feel so scared anymore. I knew that was probably a gun in his lap. He could pull it out and shoot me at any time. But I wasn't afraid. I wanted to look around at Patrick. It took everything I had not to. I just prayed that he had everything covered.

"Okay"—he seemed to relent—"let's get on with this. Hand it to me."

I picked up the bag of money and cracked open my door, just enough to get it through, and moved it across the narrow space between us with two hands. I don't know how I lifted it. It must have weighed thirty pounds. Charlie glanced around. Making sure no one had come on the scene. It was still just us. Then he opened his door and took the cinched bag with his left hand. He stuffed it inside his car and threw it on the seat across from him.

"One down. *Señora,* you want to go and visit with your *matron* over there . . ." He lowered the window and grinned to Elena in the back.

I heard the automatic locks release.

Elena wouldn't come. She shook her head and then she looked at my son. I knew what she was saying. She wouldn't leave Brandon. She wouldn't go until he did. My heart went out to her.

"Brave little woman. So that takes care of one part of it." He looked back at me and smiled. "What about the rest?"

"You mean the diary pages," I said, and held them up. Maybe we would get out of here. Everyone. With our lives.

"No, not the diary . . ." Charlie shook his head, grinning. "I mean about the guy in the back there. You know, the one holding the gun on me."

CHAPTER SIXTY-THREE

I froze. Like an electrical switch had gone off in my heart. And then like it had been kicked off a cliff.

"Well, I guess that makes us kind of even, doesn't it?" Charlie reached back around and seemed to unbuckle Brandon's seat, grabbing him by the jacket, and yanked him virtually into the front. He put his gun to the side of his head, his eyes bright with rage. "Hello, young man. Now get out of the car and bring me those diary pages!"

"No." I heard Patrick's voice, coming from behind me. "I'm afraid I can't let her do that, Charlie."

"Well, well . . . what do you know, the police are on the scene. We can all rest easy. *Charlie*, huh?" He sneered. "You've all been busy bees. I already had a dim view of the NYPD, but you just managed to drop it a notch lower."

I looked across at my son. "Brandon, don't worry, honey. Don't worry about what he says. We're going to have you out of there in a minute."

"Yeah, right, you just keep believing that, kid." Charlie pressed the gun into his skull. "I know it's past your bedtime and all, but your mom here's gonna have you dead before the Smurfs come on."

I held myself from lunging through the car window and putting my hands around his throat. My blood ached just knowing Brandon had to hear him say that. He must be so scared.

"It's just a transfer of merchandise, Charlie," Patrick said. "Give us the boy. You get the diary pages. We can all go home. No one hears from each other again."

"Just a transfer of merchandise, huh . . ." Charlie pulled back the hammer. "Let's see."

He brought Brandon's head up, as if to shoot him in front of me.

"No. No. No!" I screamed. "He's only a boy."

"Didn't think so. Now, what I want you to do is extend your arm forward, slowly, please, and drop that gun onto the seat in front of you, and we'll see if we can get on with things. My way. And quick now. Every vegetable truck in the city will be driving through here if we stay any longer."

For the first time I began to feel that maybe it wasn't just the money and the diary he was after. But me. For what I'd done to him at the yard. Or to eliminate anyone who knew what those pages meant. I looked across to the Escalade and met Brandon's wide-stretched eyes. I couldn't bear to think that this would be how it would end. I no longer even cared about me. I was past that. Only for my son. And for Elena, who I'd dragged into this even though she was completely innocent. Who wouldn't leave him there.

"What's the point, Charlie?" Patrick asked. "If we wanted the police brought in, they'd be here already. It's clear we want to end this as much as you. Landry gets the pages. Then even if we want to say something, we can't prove anything, right? You did your job. Everyone wins . . ."

"Everyone wins, eh?" I could see the intent that was in his eyes. What he was here to do. His brain ticking. Blood would spill. Definitely. I caught Patrick's eyes in the mirror. *Please, don't let it end like this . . .*

And then maybe Charlie seemed to finally come to the belief that, what was the point? He didn't want to die here any more than I did, or Brandon. I saw him smile. He flashed a wink at me, like, *oh, what the hell.* He pressed a button and I heard the rear doors unlock.

"Brandon, get the fuck out of the car," he said, and pushed him into the back. "You too, *señora.* Fun's over. You go around and take him, *por favor. Comprende?*"

Elena nodded. "Jeanine, hand those pages across to me." He reached a hand out of the window, the other still pointed at my son with the gun.

Elena opened her door. Her wrists were bound with wire. She ripped the tape off her mouth and shot me a relieved but still worried look. Then she ran around the back of the Escalade to help Brandon out.

"Fast," Charlie said. "Now."

I glanced at Patrick. He had his gun trained on the Escalade.

"Give me those fucking pages!" Charlie said. "Or so help me I'll hit the gas now and you'll never see him again."

Elena was around the side. She'd opened Brandon's door. He was still wrapped up in the seat belt. She unbuckled him.

My gaze found Patrick's again. This time he said, "Go ahead, give him what he wants."

Through the window I could see Elena take hold of Brandon and slide him out of the seat. She slammed the door. Then they were running back to us.

I thrust the plastic folder into Charlie's hand. He grabbed it while I waited for Brandon and Elena to come around. Patrick lunged forward and opened the rear door.

That's when I saw it! What was going around in Charlie's mind. His smirk suddenly morphing into something a lot more deadly. He raised his hand with the gun toward me, everything going in slow motion, Brandon and Elena finally reaching our car. Then it wasn't in slow motion. It was as if time stood still. And I saw that it wasn't me he was aiming at. But Brandon. Patrick had reached out a hand to him, pulling him in.

"Mommy!"

"Say sayonara, Jeanine," Charlie sniffed, smirking at me.

"*No!*"

I heard a shot. "Brandon!" I screamed. Not one shot, but two in rapid succession. Maybe three. Like fire-crackers. I looked for the spark from Charlie's muzzle, the one that would have killed my son.

But there was none.

Patrick was shielding Brandon and Elena with his body.

Then I saw Charlie spin and grab his shoulder and side, his outstretched gun clattering onto the street. "*Son of a—!*"

And men advancing toward his car. Not cops—or anyone I had seen who looked like a cop. One in a dark leather jacket and jeans. Another in jeans and an Adidas-style warm-up top. No lights flashing everywhere. Or commands barked.

All I heard was "Mommy, Mommy, Mommy!" And Brandon crying.

Charlie hit the gas and his car lurched forward. Just as quickly three black SUVs came out of nowhere and blocked his path. He slammed on the brakes and threw it into reverse, but there was nowhere to move and he smashed into the concrete stanchions of the overhead expressway.

He went forward again, then saw he was completely pinned in, almost parallel with me again. His eyes were like some mad cornered animal's. "You stupid fucks," he said to me, "I warned you not to call the police."

"I didn't call the police," Patrick met his eyes and said.

Five or six men surrounded his car, carrying semiautomatic weapons. One of them kicked open the door and Charlie stopped, spun around toward them in fear, then looked back at us with a glower of anger and resignation.

The largest of them was the size of a tank and had big bushy hair. Only then did it hit me who Patrick had called. The large one seemed to be in charge and he barked out some commands. In Russian. He went into the Escalade and came back out with the garbage bag of cash, Charlie going, "Hey . . .!" as the big guy smacked him across his face with the butt of his gun.

Then he came over to Patrick. He grinned. "Sergei Lukov thanks you for generous interest payment on the loan."

"Don't take this the wrong way," Patrick said, "but I hope I never hear from him again."

"He who has no money needs no purse," the Russian

said. "Here." He handed Patrick something. "I don't think he'll be in need of these."

It was the diary pages.

"Thank you, Yuri."

"You better get out of here," the Russian said. "What happens next is not a sight for little children."

Brandon had snaked up front and I squeezed him with everything I had and smothered him with kisses, so grateful I actually had him in my arms, my cheeks burning with joyful tears.

"Hilary, we have to get out of here," Patrick said.

I hit the gas, Brandon still in my arms, and we drove away from the underpass. Through the rearview mirror I saw the men drag Charlie out of his car.

"By tomorrow morning, he'll probably be stuffed in an oil drum somewhere," Patrick said, "at the bottom of Sheepshead Bay."

I turned and said over my shoulder to Elena. "Are you okay?"

She nodded, harried, but gave me a grateful smile. "*Sí*, missus. I am okay."

"Thank you" was all I could say. And then the tears started up again. I couldn't stop them.

This time tears of joy.

A mile north on the Bruckner I pulled over. "He tried to hurt me," Brandon said. "And Elena too, Mommy."

"I know he did, baby," I said, burying my face in his

hair. "But he can't hurt you anymore. Not ever. It's okay, it's okay now," I kept telling him. I looked past him at Patrick. And he smiled back at me. I just kept saying, "It's okay, baby, it's okay."

CHAPTER SIXTY-FOUR

She was dreaming. Of daffodils.

It was a clear cold night and the moon was full over the bay. A cone of soft white light left a sheen over the towers of lower Manhattan, a flowery light on the dark water all the way to the bridge.

Almost like daffodils.

She waited for the call.

The call that would let her soul finally breathe easy. That the boy was all right, and the bastard who had taken him to protect that animal who had killed her Deirdre had been dealt with. Then it was what to do with the one who had done this. Who had opened the gates and let in all this hell.

But the call never came.

Around two, her eyes grew heavy and she had to

close them for a moment. She didn't even put her two fingers to Tom's picture on the night table as she did every night. Or recite a Hail Mary to the memory of her daughter, which she'd done before she closed her eyes for the past twenty-two years.

Sheila had drifted off, to a sleep as sweet as any she'd had in years, daffodils falling from the sky and landing in the palm of her little baby's hand—maybe five then—when she first heard the noise.

Just a creak, at first. On the floorboards downstairs. She didn't even open her eyes. The house made a million noises. The walls seeming to shift with every change of the wind.

And there were surely no looters around here, though the house lay partially open. With so many cops and firemen, you had to be crazy to come here with malice on your mind.

She drifted off again and was almost back in the same sweet dream when she heard it again.

This time on the stairs. Closer. She opened her eyes and checked the clock. Ten after two. Still no word. Maybe soon. She listened, and then there was nothing, nothing for a long time but the wind and the flapping of the tarp fastened to the roof.

Again she shut her eyes.

Her daughter's face was the prettiest thing she ever saw. Who knew what she could have done in life? She wanted to be a vet. She might have gone far. Most of all she was happy. She had a smile like green meadows peeking through a cover of clouds, like the sun shining, Sheila fell back into her dream, on the pretty hill with—

This time her eyes jumped open. She felt something, a creepy presence that knifed through her like a chill. In the room.

This time the creaking of the floorboard went right through her. Sheila spun around and tried to let out a scream.

It never got out. There was a person directly above her on the edge of her bed and he cupped his hand tightly over her mouth.

She knew him—his face was like an indelible image in her mind since she had first seen it, first heard the name, only a month before.

The devil's face.

Her first thought was to go for the gun Tom always kept in the top drawer of the night table, but his hand held her back so firmly she couldn't move.

Her next thought was of her husband. That today would be a good day for Tom, in heaven, for she would surely see him soon.

"It's nice to finally meet you, Mrs. O'Byrne . . ." The man on the bed smiled. "You may not know who I am, but I was a friend of your daughter's."

CHAPTER SIXTY-FIVE

"Oh, Jesus, no . . .," Patrick exhaled grimly from the back.

I spun around.

"Hilary, turn around, quick," he instructed me. "I need to get back to my car."

We were still pulled over on the side of the expressway near the housing projects, Brandon buried in my arms. The worry in Patrick's voice was clear.

"What's happened?"

"I just got a couple of texts from two of my neighbors. There's been a fire at Mrs. O'Byrne's house. They think she's still trapped inside."

"Oh, Patrick, no. My God!"

"I have to get back there," he said. "Hilary, listen, drop Elena off back at her house, but I don't want you going back to yours. Is there somewhere you can go? A friend's? A hotel? Anywhere?"

"It's two thirty in the morning, Patrick."

"Just until I'm back. I'll be in touch with you as soon as I can. Tomorrow, we'll go to the police with what we have on Landry."

"Please, Mrs. Cantor . . .," Elena injected in her broken English. "You can stay with me. At my house."

"I'll figure something out," I said, tenderly grasping her arm. Brandon was stirring. "Here, baby." I buckled him in the seat next to me. "Stay over here."

"Just promise me you'll do that." Patrick's gaze was resolute. "I don't want you going anywhere near your house."

"Okay, I won't." I nodded. "I promise."

It took no more than three minutes to get back to Patrick's truck near the RFK Bridge. We passed the spot beneath the expressway where we'd just been with Mirho. The Russians' vehicles were gone. So was Charlie's. There was no sign of him. No doubt Patrick was right. He probably had a bullet in his head by now.

We didn't stop for a single light as we made our way back to the truck. When we got there, Patrick jumped out. He smiled, happily, at me; Mirho was dead, I had my son. Everything had worked out. But it was a worried-looking smile at the same time, looking at me with Brandon. "There's something I want to say . . ."

"Okay . . ."

"Not now. I'll call you when I know something."

"Patrick, I hope she's all right."

"I know. Thanks. You know I hoped we could just bury all this—that's why I called in Yuri. Handle it *privately*." He smiled. "Now I know that can't happen."

"I understand," I said. His hand was wrapped around my lowered window and I placed mine over his. There was almost sorrow in his eyes.

"You know what that means, don't you, if we go after Landry?"

It meant an investigation. It meant coming clean on all I'd done. And all that came with it.

Patrick too.

I nodded.

"I love my son. But I'm with you, Patrick. I'm ready for whatever it is."

He smiled wistfully and wrapped his fingers around my hand. "I have to go." There was something in his eyes. Something both unsettled, yet pleased at the same time. Looking at me with my hand over Brandon's face, my son leaning into me. As if it was almost like the one certain thing in the face of everything uncertain that was about to happen. Almost freeing.

His life was about to come crashing down too.

He had squeezed my arm and taken a step away when he suddenly came back and put his hands on my cheeks and leaned in and gave me a kiss. A brief one, but one that was full of life and alive with what lay ahead. Warm with possibilities.

"Mom of the Year." He pointed as he went back to his truck. "You've got my vote locked."

"Thank you for what you did," I said. "For everything."

"*Remember . . .,*" he said.

"I got it, Patrick. I won't go back home. I'll let you know where I am when I figure it out."

He jumped in his truck. He started it up and pulled out into the street ahead of me. I followed him for a couple of blocks, amid the all-night gas stations and shuttered-up auto shops, until it was time for me to turn and head north, and for him to go onto the Triboro Bridge, then the BQE, which led across the Verazzano. I kept an eye on his truck in my mirror until it turned out of sight. Then Brandon murmured in the seat next to me, "Where are we going, Mommy?"

I didn't know where we were going. Until someone entered my mind. Somone I knew I could call. I took my phone out. I didn't know how much longer I'd be able to be there with him, my beautiful little angel. "We're almost there, Brandon. Just one more day and then we can go home."

I prayed.

CHAPTER SIXTY-SIX

I had to do it, of course.

She knew. She could bring me down. Even without the diary. I had to protect my kids, right? They'd been through so much. I couldn't let it all come out. Not with what was now on the line.

Not now.

It was strange as I pressed the pillow over her face and held it there. Feeling her legs thrash and kick. There was still a lot of life in her for an old bitch. Stubborn. I said to her, why resist? That she would see her daughter soon. What was left for her here but to damn me? Still, she didn't want to die.

I was struck that all these years later, it was pretty much the same way I had done it to her daughter. Who I rarely thought of these days. And as I felt her resistance start to wane, her fists lose their power against me, her legs slowly give up the fight, it brought me back. All the way to where it all started for me. Here in Staten Island. Under another bridge. Well, maybe not where it all started . . . It had already begun a long time ago. Todd. That mangy, little dog Jerry. I'd always had that dark edge, my mother always said. I thought I was free of it, but truth be told, I might as well have ended up in that hole next to Deirdre. Stuffed into that drum. Smelling of rot and decay. Food for the rodents and spiders. Because that's how it's been for me.

All these years holding it in.

So it had to be done. I mean, I couldn't let her ruin me. I had to burn the house. The fire was just a diversion. To cover what I'd done and just in case there were any remnants that could incriminate me. But there was also another purpose. Even more important.

As a lure.

To draw him here.

Charlie had his job to do, but I had mine.

So I had to do it. I had to protect my family. She knew. They all knew.

CHAPTER SIXTY-SEVEN

We might have gotten away with it, Patrick thought, climbing the steps of his father's house. Two hours had passed. The street was still ablaze with lights from the smoldering fire and EMTs and fire crews.

We might have gotten away with it if it wasn't for Mrs. O'B.

Mirho was history. Gone without a trace. Hilary had paid off her debts. Patrick had paid off his too. Who would ever even know, if they just wanted to keep it all quiet?

But there was Mrs. O'B. He recalled the last thing she had ever said to him.

"You make him pay, Patrick." Make him pay.

He'd watched in silent rage after he'd rushed to the house and saw it burn. The house he had been inside a thousand times. Almost like his own house while he was growing up. He had to be restrained like the rest of the street to stay behind the perimeter. As he watched, knowing she was still inside, he had no idea if Landry had been behind this or not. Or whether it was a cigarette she hadn't put out before falling asleep, as Patrick always warned.

But he suspected Landry was. And there was no way he could let him get away with any of it now. Now that they knew the whole story. Now that they had the one thing that could connect him back to Deirdre. Come morning, it would all have to come out. Whatever happened would happen, he and Hilary agreed.

That was clear when he stood there watching the last of her house burn down.

Deirdre, Tom. The last of her possessions.

They'd almost gotten away with it, but there was no hiding it now.

He was there when they finally carried her out. A small mound on the EMS stretcher. He was able to stop them for a second before they put her into the van. "Family?" they asked. "Yes," he said. She *was* almost like a second mother to him. He was as close as she had there. Maybe fifty people from the neighborhood gathered around to watch. Friends, neighbors. He was able to touch her hand, which had fallen out from under the sheet.

Make him pay.

On his father's porch, Patrick turned and saw a thin orange light start to creep over the towers of lower Manhattan. In a million years he would never have thought it would come to this. He'd spent his whole life doing what was right. He'd gotten himself into a good school, joined the force out of college when he could have done almost anything with his life. Rose quickly through the ranks. Took the community job when it was offered. Lots of cops crossed the line, committed crimes. But he was the last one he would ever have imagined doing it. Now he had and he would have to pay. Even if it had been for a good reason, helping out his sister. Just like Hilary had.

The right reasons maybe, but still a crime.

And now, when it was light, he would put a stop to it. They'd go to the police and turn themselves in.

He opened the door and stepped into his family's home. The back deck was still partially open and Patrick felt a crisp breeze as he looked out at the bay. He had to call Hilary. He saw she had called him twice in the past hour and texted him where she was. At her friend Robin's, she said. He was glad she was safe.

As he looked out, he saw in a flash how everything was linked. As if part of a vast chain, a chain that had linked so many unsuspecting and disparate parts. His dad. Mr. and Mrs. O'Byrne. Deirdre. Hilary. Even Rollie.

A car that drove off the road leading to an unsolved murder twenty years ago.

All connected to a storm, a storm that at first took everything they had and then washed some of it back onshore. He saw it that way, maybe for the first time.

He took out his phone and went to text Hilary back.

He never felt the person who came up from behind him. Only the hand that wrapped across his face, wrenching it backward, the blade driven deep into his side, unleashing a shock wave of searing pain.

He let out an agonizing gasp.

He was trained to protect himself, though he'd been behind a desk for many years. And maybe if he hadn't been preoccupied he would have heard him and swung around. Or at least faced him, the person who was about to rob him of the one thing he'd sworn to do.

Make him pay.

But his killer had been trained too. For a lifetime.

Patrick reached back around him, the phone falling out of his grasp. He stabbed for his gun, but his strength leaked away, like water slowly circling down a drain. His assailant's hand was viselike across his throat. The other hand removed the gun from Patrick's belt and kicked it aside.

"You should have just left it all alone," the man said into Patrick's ear. "It was just a stupid little diary. It didn't mean anything to anybody anymore. Just some old bitch . . ."

He dug the knife in deeper.

Patrick's knees buckled. *Yes, it did.* It did matter. He

reached for his side and felt the thick pool of blood matting there. *It did!* With a gasp, summoning everything he had, he bent and lifted his assailant into the air, staggering to keep upright, fighting the pain and his sagging strength, and rolled him over his back and onto the floor. He faced him, his legs jelly, the knife still in his abdomen.

Deirdre's killer.

"It does matter," Patrick said. *It does.*

He wanted with everything he had to show him just how much. Instead, he dropped to his knees. He dug at the knife, trying to pull it out. Everything grew gauzy.

He had to make him pay.

Landry got up. Patrick felt him come up behind him. He put his foot on Patrick's back and pushed him onto the floor—*Oh, Jesus, he wanted so bad to be able to show him*—but now his gaze faced no farther than the man's shoes.

"You're probably wondering," Landry said, "so I'll tell you. It hardly matters now. I set the fire. After I killed her, of course. But I doubt they'll ever know. I had to. I couldn't let her bring me down. Or *you*, right? I mean, there were only three of you who knew. Who knew what those pages meant. The old woman. And we don't have to worry about *her* anymore. You . . ."

He paused.

Hilary. Patrick flashed to her with trepidation. He wanted to say, *No, no* . . . He deserved this maybe, but she, *no* . . .

But by that time all his strength had pretty much emptied from him and he was able to make out the band of morning light growing brighter over the sky through the open doors.

He heard a voice that sounded very far away as Landry picked up his cell phone.

"Now there's just one more . . ."

CHAPTER SIXTY-EIGHT

I opened my eyes, the morning sun shining into Robin's guest room. The feeling swept over me that something wasn't right.

I jumped up and made sure Brandon was still next to me.

He was. Curled up on the other side of the bed. Still in his clothes. Where we'd lain down just a few hours earlier.

Thank God!

He murmured, his eyes blinking narrowly. "What's wrong, Mommy?"

"Nothing. Nothing's wrong." I stroked his face. "Go back to sleep, honey. It's still early."

I reached for my cell and saw it was 8:26 A.M. Then it hit me what all my nerves were about.

Five hours had passed since he left me, and I hadn't heard back from Patrick.

Today was the day we said we'd go to the police with everything that had happened. My phone showed the two calls I'd made to him during the night, unanswered, and the text, telling him that I was at Robin's, whom I'd woken up at three in the morning after dropping off Elena with the tale that I had Brandon and that I couldn't go home, and who said to me, "Please, Hil, don't say another word, come on over. With the kids away, I have a couple of extra rooms."

My last message to Patrick was at 4:26 A.M., after I'd sat up with Robin for a while, explaining some of it, as little as I could actually, before finally dropping off to sleep. He would have gotten back to Staten Island around 3:30 A.M. He said he'd call me as soon as he knew something about Mrs. O'Byrne. That was five hours ago. This wasn't like him. I'd been a little concerned before I'd fallen asleep.

Now the concern had ratcheted up to worry.

Something wasn't right.

I left Brandon in bed and threw on my jeans. I went into the bathroom and peed, and tried Patrick again.

The call immediately connected to his voice mail.

I left a message, my third: "Patrick, I never heard back from you. Are you okay? I'm at my friend's. Everything's okay here, but I'm worried. Please call me when you get this message." I went downstairs.

Robin was in the kitchen, drinking a cup of coffee,

dressed in a beige and red sweater that picked up the color of her long auburn hair. "Coffee's over there," she said, pointing to the counter. "Want some?"

"Sure." I sat down at the counter.

She poured one out. "Sugar's here and milk's in the fridge."

"Thanks."

"So how'd you sleep?"

I had told her the basics early this morning when we arrived. Leaving out Landry, and that I'd just had a gun pointed at me in the act of bartering back my kid. And that I'd probably played a hand in getting someone dropped in the river. Just basically that I had taken some money and I was scared to go home. *You remember when I told you I had a way to get some money . . .*

"Rob, I can't thank you enough for letting Brandon and me come here."

"Don't be silly." She waved it off. "I probably would have been up anyway to pee. I just hope everything works out, hon. Is there anything I can do?"

"No, nothing." I shook my head. "I'm just a little freaked out that I haven't heard from Patrick."

She had the news on, the CBS morning show, and I was hoping something might be on about the fire and Mrs. O'Byrne when it was time for the local news. Maybe Patrick was just too exhausted and had passed out at his house like we had here. What if he ran into the flaming house? What if something had happened and he was injured? *Or worse . . .* He loved that woman like his own mom. I glanced at the time: 8:43 A.M. *Eight or nine minutes or so to the local news.*

To my surprise, Brandon shuffled in, rubbing his eyes. "What time is it, Mommy?"

"Why don't you go back to sleep, honey? You're not going to school today."

He climbed onto a stool at the counter. "I'm hungry."

"There's some cereal in the cabinet," Robin said. "The kids still love it when they come home."

I said to him, "Why don't you go into the family room and put on the TV? I'll bring some in . . ."

"Cap'n Crunch," Robin helped me out.

"You love Cap'n Crunch, don't you?"

I walked him out and he curled up on the couch with a pillow and put on the large-screen TV. The Cartoon Network came on.

"Just stay in the TV room," I said. "I'll be right in, okay?"

I didn't want to upset him, any more than he'd already been. But I knew things were about to change. It was no longer possible, or more so, right, to keep what had happened over the past two days hidden any longer. When Patrick called in we had decided he would arrange a meet with friends of his in the NYPD and we would lay it all out to them. About the money, about what happened to Rollie. Charlie. Landry. By the end of the day, who knew if I'd be booked on charges or even held in jail? It was no longer about just taking the money; it was that people

392

had died. Innocent people. I had no idea where that would leave me with my son. But it was too late for that.

When I got back in the kitchen, Robin was tying up a bag of trash. "I have a business appointment I have to run out to. Is that okay? I could always cancel it and stay, if you need me."

"No, Robin, you go about your day." I went over and gave her a warm hug.

"I'll just take this on the way out." She pulled out and opened the bin. "And where the hell's my bag? I just had it somewhere. Maybe it's back in my room. I'm always crazy these days. How about I call you as soon as I finish up?"

"Okay. *Robin . . .*" I caught her as she was about to head out of the kitchen. I smiled, both worried and appreciative. "I don't know how to say thanks."

She smiled. "Things are gonna work out, honey. You'll see."

She left and I went into the cabinet and took out Brandon's cereal. I found a bowl in a lazy Susan and a tray leaning against the wall. I brought it in and thought I heard the door close as Robin called out, "Talk to you later!"

Brandon was already immersed in some Transformers cartoon.

I went back in the kitchen and checked my phone again. Still nothing. I watched the news for a minute, something about a woman who was helping homeless people get off the street; I was growing more and more concerned. I

393

noticed the garbage bag still on the floor. Robin must have forgotten it. The TV announced the local news would be on in sixty seconds. I closed the bag and took it out to the garage where I assumed the trash containers were. I opened the door and saw the trash bin next to Robin's car.

My heart almost exploded.

Robin.

She was on the garage floor, crumpled against her car, her head slumped to the side. In horror, I fixed on the flower of dark blood pooling on her sweater. Her jaw was slack and her eyes were open and fixed in a horrifying expression.

I screamed.

I ran toward her, knowing it was too late, unable to believe the horrifying sight I was facing.

And then the most paralyzing shock of fear stabbed me. *Brandon.*

My eyes darted back into the house.

"*Brandon!*" I screamed, knowing instantly what had happened and that he was in danger. I ran back inside through the kitchen and into the TV room. The TV was still on, the Transformers on the screen. The cereal bowl was still on the tray where I had left it.

He wasn't there.

Oh my God! Panic ripped through me. I ran back into the hallway, shouting throughout the house. "*Brandon! Brandon! Where are you?*"

Why wasn't he answering?

I hurried to the front door. It was shut. My heart was beating like crazy. I spun, looking frantically in every direction. I knew who it was. I also knew it wasn't Brandon he wanted.

Then I fixed on something and stopped.

The outside doors to the patio were open. They hadn't been a minute ago. And there was something there I also hadn't seen. A metal can with a long spout. Like an oil can.

My eyes fastened on it as my heart started beating in escalating terror.

I sprinted through the house, screaming in every direction, *"Brandon!"*

Suddenly, *"Mommy,"* I heard him call. *"Mommy,* in here!" It sounded like it was coming from the living room.

I ran down the hall. "Brandon, where are you? Answer me, honey. *I—"*

He was there in front of a love seat next to Robin's couch. My first instinct was to let out a breath in relief. That he was okay.

But the breath never got halfway out of my chest.

Landry was sitting next to him in the love seat, a hand tucked around my son's waist.

His other hand had a gun in it.

The muzzle was pressed so tightly underneath Brandon's jaw, it forced his face upward.

CHAPTER SIXTY-NINE

"Brandon and I were just talking," Landry said, nudging him with a smile. "Right, buddy?"

"I know you told me to stay there." Brandon looked at me apologetically. "I'm sorry, Mommy."

"That's okay, honey," I said, trying to appear together. Though my heart was beating out of control. I forced a tremulous smile for him. "It's okay."

Then I fixed on Landry's icy, almost mocking eyes. "Leave him alone. Please." I took a step toward them. "He's innocent. He doesn't know anything."

"Nice little guy . . ." Landry jostled Brandon amiably. He looked larger than I'd imagined. Sandy hair. Slightly balding on top. A narrow face. "We've been talking. Seems we might have some things in common, right? Do you always need to act out on your urges, Brandon?

Do you want to show people what you're made of inside? Violence doesn't bother you. In fact, you even kind of enjoy it, don't you? Watching it occur. Even stepping on an ant, you don't much care, do you, Brandon, when you extinguish life?"

"*Stop it!*" I glared at him. "He's nothing like you. Nothing."

"Oh, I'm not so sure. I know it when I see it. The problem is, little guy," Landry jostled him again, good-naturedly, "I'm not sure we're ever going to fully find out."

That shot through my blood like ice. I knew at that moment that everything was all on me. Patrick was on Staten Island. Robin was dead. No one was going to come. I took another step. "What do you want?"

"Let me see. What. Would. I. Want?" Landry let out a sigh. "I think you know what I want, Hilary. Can we start with those diary pages?" He motioned to the couch. "By the way, if I were you, I might sit down."

I stood there, my eyes drifting around the room. Trying to identify anything I could possibly use against him. I spotted an iron poker next to the fireplace. On the coffee table, I saw a kind of animal horn mounted on a wood base, like a zebu or an African cow.

If I could even get to them.

Landry looked at me and pushed the muzzle deeper into Brandon's jaw. "I said, sit down."

Brandon was strangely calm, just standing in Landry's

arm, blinking. Not showing any outward signs of fear. I stepped back toward the couch. "Whatever you think you're going to do, you won't get away with it. We know. We know about Deirdre O'Byrne. And I'm not the only one."

"You mean the old hag?" Landry shrugged with a snort. "Nothing to worry about there. She's gone. Oh, and your boyfriend? Kelty's son . . . You probably mean him too. Solid guy. Whatever happened to Charlie, anyway? I really would like to know. Anyway, don't waste away your precious time thinking he'll be coming round any time soon to save you . . ."

My heart picked up with worry. "What do you mean?"

Landry winked. "He ran into a little situation after the fire. He's dead too."

I shook my head and felt my knees start to wobble. "No."

"Afraid so. Here, check out the phone . . ." Landry lowered the gun, keeping his hand tucked tightly around Brandon's waist, and took out a cell phone from his jacket pocket and tossed it at my feet. I felt my heart constrict. I was almost afraid to pick it up and look. I shook my head back and forth, staring at Landry with both heartbreak and anger. *"No!"*

"Go on . . . I'm afraid, yes, it's his. And thank you very much for those texts you sent, which made it easy to find you." He brought the gun back to Brandon's jaw and smiled. "His gun too."

No . . .! I felt the blood rush out of my head and my knees start to buckle. *It couldn't be.* Landry couldn't have killed him. Patrick was more than a match for him. It had to be a lie. Suddenly I felt like a thousand pounds was pressing me into the floor and I would drop.

Oh, Patrick, I thought, tears filling up my eyes.

I fell back on the couch.

Landry chuckled. "I told you to sit, didn't I? And so, you see, you are . . ." He smiled, seemingly satisfied, at me. "You *are* the only one left to worry about."

"*You* son of a bitch!" I glared. The tears ran unstoppably now.

Patrick.

"I told him he should've just left well enough alone. Taken the money. It wasn't the money I ever really wanted. You know that. Though now that I mention it, I wouldn't mind it if you gave me a clue as to where the hell it all went?"

"You're a fucking monster." My glare burned into his eyes. "You killed Robin. She was innocent too. You killed that old woman and her daughter. You even killed your own wife!"

That seemed to sting him a bit. He nodded, letting out a breath that actually seemed contrite. "You know what I'm talking about, don't you, Brandon? It's hard to explain this to someone on the outside. Who doesn't know."

"Stop it!"

"It seems easy, doesn't it, to point a finger? But that wasn't me."

"*It wasn't* you . . .?" Mucus and tears slid down my face. Tears of grief and hatred.

"No." He shook his head. "It wasn't. Tell her what I mean, won't you, son?"

"Mommy, Mommy, I don't want to be here . . ." Brandon tried to pull away.

"Please, *please*," I begged. "For God's sake, let him go."

Landry held him back and turned to me. "So where are they? You know what I mean."

"You can do what you want to me. Just let him go. I'm begging you. You have children. I saw them. You understand. He can't do anything to you . . ."

"The pages," Landry said again, his eyes unblinking. He pressed the muzzle on top of Brandon's yellow hair. "I think one thing's been made clear, don't you agree? I won't have a lot of hesitation about pulling this trigger. And take it from me, I don't think that's a sight you care to see."

"*Mommy!*" Brandon started squirming in his arms. "Mommy, don't let him hurt me." Landry tightened his hold.

"*Please!*" I was dying. I knew any minute my life could end. Brandon's too. I had to do something. No one was going to come. Listening to my son imploring me was killing me.

"I have them," I said. "They're in my purse. Just, don't! *Don't.*" I put up my palms. "Please."

"All right." I'd left my bag at the table by the front door. "Bring the bag over here. And don't do anything foolish or you'll watch your son's brains splatter all over the fancy upholstery."

I got up, my legs jelly. Time was running out. Soon as I showed him those pages, I had no idea what he would do. I went and grabbed my handbag by the straps and took it over to him. I stopped about five feet away. "*Here . . .*"

"Open it," Landry said. "Let me see."

I pulled out the plastic folder Patrick's Russian friend had given us. I wished the man was here now. The three pages were visible through the clear binding. Landry seemed satisfied.

"I knew that fucking nickname would come back to haunt me one day." He shook his head. "Stupid, huh? I would never have let it come out, even after all these years, if I knew this silly diary even existed. Hard to believe, how that girl managed to point the finger at me after being stuffed in a hole all those years. I loved her, you know . . ."

"Just like you loved your wife. Like you love your kids."

"I did, though." He shrugged. "I still do."

My gaze drifted to the fireplace. The iron poker leaning there. "What are you going to do?"

401

"There is a plan, such as it may be. You saw that oil can over there?" I involuntarily glanced toward the open doors. "It has a little fuel left in it. Just enough . . . And identical to what they might find accelerated that fire in Staten Island last night.

"And *this* . . ." He showed me Patrick's gun, lifting it away from Brandon. "Your police boyfriend's gun . . . Which when found here ties you to both those crime scenes from last night. The fire *and* Kelty."

"Who do you think is going to believe that?" I asked.

"It's not perfect. I admit." He squeezed Brandon by the shoulder and stood up. "But there will be a trail of inter-action between the two of you, and somehow they'll tie it to the money—cops are good, you know—wherever it may be. To me, it'll seem like you told the son you'd taken it from his father and the son was threatening to turn you in. You killed him and the woman, and then yourself. Oh, and your friend, in the garage. I admit, it's a bit rough. But the good news is, I don't see how any of it points toward me. Especially"—he grinned and glanced at the pages in my hand—"without that diary . . ."

Suddenly all my grief for Patrick fell away and I knew I couldn't let it happen like this. "What about Brandon?"

"*The boy?* I'm sorry." He stood there, smiling, stroking Brandon's hair. "But I'll be doing the world a favor when they find him here. He's just like me."

"*Mommy!*" Brandon tried to pull away, but Landry yanked him back.

402

"*He's not like you!*" I glared at him. "*Here* . . . take them!" I took a step and held out the diary pages to him. "Do what you want with me. Just let me have my boy. Please . . . *please* . . ."

Landry didn't bite. He just stood there.

"*Here,*" I said, again. "Take them. All of them." I opened the clear folder and hurled the pages at him.

Instinctively, he reached out to grasp them.

I'm not sure the thought occurred to me even as much as a second before; it was just instinct.

But that's when I spun.

With a loud grunt, I whirled into a perfect roundhouse kick that I'd executed in the gym at least a thousand times. It completely surprised Landry, catching him on the upper chest and shoulder, knocking him backward into the stone hearth, the gun clattering to the floor. He staggered for a second in shock, and I followed it with a powerful forward-thrust kick that sent him reeling over the love seat and onto the floor.

I yelled, "Brandon, get away!"

I searched frantically on the floor for the gun. It was like a race, who would find it first. I didn't see it, and didn't know whether Landry had landed on it or if it had been swept under the love seat. I didn't have the time. I leaped and took the iron poker from the fireplace stand and came at him with the point down into his chest, not knowing if he had the gun and it would be the last thing I would ever do.

403

He didn't.

With a scream I drove the poker into his chest. Landry put his legs up and blocked it away, the tip slicing into his leg. He let out a roar. He thrashed his hand about, trying to locate the gun. I lunged at him again.

"*Brandon, run!*" I shouted. "Just get out of here. Run to one of the neighbors. Then call the police. Go!"

I tried to drive the poker into Landry, but he wrapped his hands around it and tried to twist it out of my grasp. He was stronger than me by far.

"*Run!*" I yelled again to Brandon. I felt Landry guiding the point away from his midsection. Brandon hadn't moved.

"*Please, Brandon, run! Get out. Now!*"

He just stood there, seemingly transfixed.

I didn't know how long I could keep Landry at bay. I kept begging Brandon, "Please, go to the neighbors! Tell them to call the police!"

Landry was gradually wrestling it away from me. I strained with everything I had, but it wasn't enough. I was losing. Soon he'd have it from me.

"Please, honey, go now. I'm begging you, go!"

"I'm sorry, Mommy." Finally Brandon took off.

I heard him run to the foyer and open the front door. A part of me felt uplifted, that no matter what happened here, at least my son would escape. That maybe in the end Landry wouldn't get away with it.

"You don't actually think he's going to get away, do

you?" Landry mocked me, his eyes ablaze. He pulled me to him, one hand releasing the poker, and the next thing I felt a punch to my face. My head shot back, blood bursting from my lip. He hit me again. I kept pushing with everything I had, trying to ignore the blood and the pain, but I knew it was futile. Again, he hit me. I was almost done. Finally he drove my arms to the side and rolled on top of me, ripping the poker from my grasp. My head hit against the coffee table and I almost blacked out.

I tore at his face, trying to rip off whatever I could take hold of. Lips, cheeks, eyes.

Landry screamed in pain.

Blood streamed down his face. He had reversed it now and he was over me on the floor, pressing the shaft of the steel poker into my larynx. Forcing the air out of me. I fought back, sucking air into my lungs.

But I couldn't hold him off any longer.

"You really think I'm going to let that little toad just get away? I'll find him. I will. How does that feel?" He dug the iron rod into my throat. "How does it feel, knowing I'll get him as soon as I'm done with you? Enjoy it to the max, please . . ." His voice crackled with rage. "'Cause it's the last thing you're ever going to feel."

I tried to squeeze air into my heaving lungs. I felt my arms grow weak, no longer able to fend him off.

Run, Brandon, please, I said to myself. Angry. Angry

that Landry had won. Angry that he had killed Deirdre and Mrs. O'Byrne. And Patrick. The only prayer I had was that my son would get away. *Just run . . .*

I felt my strength waning.

Then I looked past Landry over me and my one remaining prayer was dashed.

It was Brandon. He was there. Behind Landry.

No, no, no, no, no!

I wasn't sure if it was real or if this was some kind of near-death delusion they say happens at the end of life.

I was almost crying. *Why are you here? Why are you here . . .? You have to get away. Get away . . .*

"Mommy," he said, his arms in the air. "Don't be afraid."

The next thing I knew he brought his hands down and the tip of something sharp and shiny came through Landry's neck. He uttered a garbled scream, not a scream really, more of a strangled gasp.

It was the tip of the large cow's horn coming through him.

His face twisted in shock and anguish, his eyes grew angry and wide. So wide I could see the blood vessels in the whites like swelling red rivers.

He threw his arms back and flailed at Brandon, who stepped back, the horn stuck through Landry's throat. Landry's hands wrapped around it. He grabbed the exposed tip, gargling in agony, not sure how to remove it. His eyes fell on me as if somehow I would help him.

Three words went through me: *Make him pay.*

He thrashed around like some wounded animal, his hand slapping the floor until his hand found the poker. He wrapped his fingers around it and almost had it up to strike. Me? Brandon?

Then a heavy wheeze came out of him, his breaths short and hacking. He looked toward Brandon and dropped the rod. And if you didn't know it was death taking hold of him, his final act, you might have sworn he had uttered a laugh.

He fell over. He let out two or three more resigned, hacking breaths.

Then he was quiet.

I lay on my back, too exhausted, too in shock, to even feel a thing. I sucked precious air back into my starving lungs. And then my gasps turned into sobs. Tears alternating between exhalations of joy and grief.

"Brandon . . ." I pulled him onto me. I brought him close with everything I had, but my arms were so weak and heavy, all I could do was just feel him close to me and laugh.

You made him pay, darling. You made him pay.

Then I noticed that he wasn't even looking at me. He was just kind of staring blankly. His head on my chest. His gaze fixed on Landry.

Not crying as I would have thought, after the horror of what had happened. Or aghast. Or even with joy that we were somehow alive and he had rescued me.

But something more detached. Staring at him with those transfixed blue eyes.

"Brandon, baby, he's gone. He's gone," I said. "Don't worry anymore." I squeezed him. "He can't hurt you now." I pushed myself up. "I know that was terrible."

He just remained there, staring. His eyes calm, almost pleased. Then finally he turned to me, and said in a way that he might have if he was playing a video game. "It wasn't terrible. I cut off his head, Mommy. I cut off his head."

Epilogue

Six months later.

The air never smelled so sweet or the sky seem so blue as the day I walked out of the minimum security prison in Beacon, New York, and back into the arms of my family.

"Mommy! Mommy!" Brandon shouted, running up to me as I came through the gates. My folks, who had been taking care of him these past months, came up and put their arms around me as well. They'd brought him up to visit most weekends during the time I was inside. Which surely made it easier for me. But it wasn't the same as having him in my arms and knowing no one was going to separate us for a long while.

"You're coming home now?" Brandon looked up at me. "For good?"

"I'm coming home, guy." I picked him up and kissed him on the cheek. "For good."

Home. That was something else that was no longer the same since I'd been inside.

I'd served three months of a negotiated two-year sentence, after pleading guilty in New York state court to two counts of grand larceny and trafficking in stolen property. Because of what we had been through, and for my help in bringing to light the unsolved murders of Deirdre O'Byrne, Rollie McMahon, and Kathy Landry, the U.S. government declined to prosecute, though they could easily have added various federal charges ranging from money laundering to defrauding the banking system.

In addition, I was given a thirty-six-month window to repay the sixty-three thousand dollars that I'd actually spent by making restitution to a state-sponsored victims' fund. Brandon's school agreed to return next year's tuition, and even more helpfully, allowed him to remain in school.

I willingly agreed to the terms.

So much had taken place while I was inside. First it was just dealing with the people I'd lost. Patrick. Robin. Poor, poor, Robin. We put the house in Armonk up for sale. Jim had tried contacting me several times before I went in, but I never called him back. Instead, I served him with papers under the state's "deadbeat" laws for back alimony and child support, and it ended up he had a few dollars more tucked away than he had let on, so as part of that settlement he committed to paying for Brandon's school at least through the next year, and all the house payments and taxes until it was sold. He even restored my alimony for one year.

Which meant that the *second*-best call I got while I was inside was that a buyer had put a no-contingency bid on the house for a hundred grand above the mortgage. Which would barely put $20,000 in my pocket, after commissions, but what it did do, at long last, was get me out from under it. I rented an apartment in Stamford where Brandon and I were going to live once the house closed.

The best call I got while I was away was from Steve Fisher of my old firm, who said that Ralph Gelfand, the company's CFO who'd been with him for twenty years, advised him he was planning to retire in three months' time and would I be interested in the job?

I almost didn't have the words.

"You know you'd be hiring a felon," I said from the phone bank in the visitors' center, at the same time grinning from ear to ear.

"As long as you promise not to steal the staplers and the coffee mugs," he replied. "The job opens up in October, Hilary. By then, you'll have done your time. I can't think of anyone who would do a better job for us."

"Yes . . ." I sat down and thought of all that had happened in the past six months. "I have done my time, haven't I?"

And Brandon . . . I mussed his silky blond hair in the parking lot and smiled into those dusty blue eyes.

He'd undergone a round of counseling after the incident with Landry, both concerning the trauma of what had happened and the thing I saw inside him that I feared.

All the psychologists said he was handling it well. When I brought up what he'd said, staring at Landry's body, they all told me it was just his way of compartmentalizing such a harrowing event. That it was nothing to worry about.

Still, after the lights went out, in my bunk at night I must have relived that moment a million times. That dissociative, clear-eyed stare. And what Landry had said about him. *Brandon and I, we're two of a kind.* I read whatever I could on the subject. Books, clinical studies. On trying to identify the patterns of psychopathic behavior in a child. Wondering, worrying . . . Was that what Landry's dying smile was about?

Was Brandon one like him?

"We've got the car over here," my dad said. "Let me take your bag."

I put my arm around Brandon. I would always worry.

There's this, poor Robin once told me. There's love. Health. Family. *And then there's the other side of the road.*

I'd been on both.

It was nice to be on this side for a while.

And then there was Patrick . . .

There wasn't a day in the last six months that I hadn't

412

thought of him. That I hadn't brought his face to mind. The way he shook his head and asked if I wanted a drink at Red's, and how that cut right through my fears and made me soften inside. His inner goodness and gentleness. From the moment I heard him at the funeral speaking about his dad, I knew he was a good soul.

I'd asked myself at least a thousand times, if I'd never gone there after my house was broken into, would Mirho have found him? Would he still be alive?

And each time I asked myself, I couldn't answer. He saved my life and got me back my son.

He got me back everything.

And it cost him his life.

It took me another three weeks before I could gather up the nerve.

I had to get Brandon back in school; get the house ready to close; put some of my things in storage. Get myself ready for my new job.

But on a warm, clear day at the end of September, I drove back out to Baden Avenue.

For the most part it looked as it had when I was there the last time. It was now nine months since Sandy and homes there were finally well under construction.

I parked across from Patrick's blue Victorian. There was a FOR SALE sign out in front. I knew how hard Patrick had worked to restore it, and it made me sad to think of someone else living there. I went up the front stairs, recalling that coffee we'd had on the porch. "I can see you're not a volunteer . . .," he'd told me, finally smiling at my shoes. I looked down now. My Tod's knockoffs. I'd worn them especially for the occasion. I knocked on the freshly painted door.

No one answered.

After a few moments, I went around back. The deck was finished. It smelled of fresh pine. I went up and peeked inside the new glass doors. The floors were new too. The sliding door was open, so I stepped inside. There was no furniture. The kitchen was new as well. Nice. It was all nice. He would have liked it.

"Oh, Patrick . . .," I whispered, on the fireplace hearth, the tears starting to come.

Was it here? I looked at the front door. In the living room, as he came in? It had happened at six in the morning, as the sun came up over the harbor. He was found on the floor. Was that his last sight as he overlooked the bay?

In a corner, perched as if it had been placed there just yesterday, I saw the little stuffed bear. Someone had placed it here. "He watches over the place," Patrick had said. He named him after his dad.

"Joe," I said, as if he could answer me. Now I couldn't hold anything back.

The tears came. They ran and ran and I mashed them against my cheeks. Tears for the little time I'd known him. And for how we'd been robbed of what might have been.

414

How many people do you meet in your life who you knew would stand up to anything for you? *Anything*.

I looked at Joe the bear and then out at the bay.

I'd known one.

At the end of the street, Mrs. O'Byrne's house had been razed. What the storm hadn't taken, the fire had. There was a construction sign in the front and a new wooden frame being raised. A couple of men were at work. I went up and asked one of them who was rebuilding it.

"New owners," the man replied. "It's been sold."

New owners. I'd never met the previous one, but our lives had surely touched.

"Mind if I go around back?" I asked.

"Be my guest."

I went around the side. The house was at the end of the street, closest to the bay. The water was blue-gray and calm. The sun was gleaming off the towers of lower Manhattan, across the harbor. An American flag hung limply on the flagpole.

I recalled how Patrick said it was during Fleet Week, as the ships came gliding past.

Glorious.

I went down to the seawall, the water lapping against the edge. I knew, knew as surely as that the tide would roll in tonight and another would follow tomorrow, that my life would hold together.

Thanks to Patrick. And this woman I had never met.

Mrs. O'B.

I took out the diary pages from my jacket. They had caused it all, Landry had said. These three handwritten pages of a girl's last dreams.

Mrs. O'B said she never wanted anyone to be hurt again because of them.

I took them out of the folder and I stared at the water for a while. Then I tore each one into small pieces. I held them for a second in my palm, like ashes, as if I had some prayer. Then I kneeled and cast them into the bay. For a while they just bobbed in the tide, almost reluctant to finally leave, then started to scatter and drift apart, some carried back in, others out to the bay.

I stayed and watched, a hand above my eyes against the sun, hoping nothing brought them back this time. *She pointed a finger at me, even from the grave,* Landry had said.

They had already done enough.

And as I watched, I knew that hope, like dreams, sometimes hangs in the balance of an instance, a glint of light angling through skyscrapers, diffused over the water, under the span of a tall bridge, shining brightly for a moment, a moment you can't get back, and then gone, and ultimately out to sea.

Acknowledgments

This story came about from a newspaper article on a man who admitted to killing his girlfriend and burying the body on Staten Island, New York, twenty years ago. Combine it with a magazine article on the subject of C-U (callous and unemotional) kids, and the many poignant stories that came out of Superstorm Sandy, some from friends, and the novel began to take shape.

Writing it, I have taken a few geographical liberties with my setting in Midland Beach on Staten Island. You cannot see across to Manhattan from there; from most homes, you can't even see the Verrazano-Narrows Bridge, only a couple of miles away. The street described as Baden Avenue may be more like a street you would find in the communities of South Beach or Shore Acres. Yet Midland Beach became a kind of hallowed ground to me, in that eleven people lost their lives there during the storm. So forgive me the small tinkering with fact; the book needed to be set there.

Two sources were keenly helpful on the subject of C-U kids, who may manifest the early signs of psychopathic behavior, as well as children who suffer from Asperger's syndrome and autism. "When Is a Problem Child Truly Dangerous?" published in the May 13, 2012, edition of *The New York Times Magazine*, and the groundbreaking study *Far from the Tree: Parents, Children and the Search for Identity*, by Andrew Solomon (Scribner, 2012), recommended to me by my friend Margery Mayer. I couldn't have written this book nearly as well without them.

A quick thanks to my editing and agenting team, Henry Ferris, Julia Wisdom, and Simon Lipskar, who know the unconventional and sometimes maddening way this book got done, but in the end, gives birth, I hope, to something of lasting value. And to Cole Hager and Joe Volpe, who really keep these departments moving.

And to my sister, Liz Scoponich, who showed me how a boatyard looks in winter, which I, keeping in character, trashed.

My wife, Lynn, and my kids always pitch in with my books, sometimes by helping to problem-solve and talk things out, sometimes by just being there. But I'd like to take this moment to give a long-overdue shout-out to my son, Nick, who first spoke to me about Florida pill mills as a possible subject for a thriller (which grew into *15 Seconds*), and showed me an article from *Playboy* on the bloody drug wars in the Sinaloa province of Mexico, which became what you might call the MacGuffin, or driving plot device, for *No Way Back,* and whom I managed not to mention in two previous acknowledgments. So here's to finally correcting that oversight, my tall, savvy son, though, at long last, you've had absolutely zero to do with this book!

And speaking of MacGuffins, this book is dedicated to the memory of Michael Palmer; ours was a late-blossoming friendship, but one that I will miss. He used that term more than anyone I know in his talks on how to construct a thriller, and were it anyone with less warmth or passion you might go, "All right, all right, would you stop with all the MacGuffins already . . ."

And so I will.

THE BLUE ZONE

THERE ARE NO RULES IN THE BLUE ZONE.

They were the perfect family. And he was the perfect family man.
One day changed it all.

Arrested for racketeering, Ben Raab must take his family into
America's Witness Protection Programme. Only his eldest daughter,
Kate, chooses to stay on the outside. But the Programme's perfect
success rate is about to come to a shocking end. A case agent is
tortured to death and Ben vanishes. The one person who
might be able to find him is Kate.

Pursued by killers, forced to question everything she knows about
her life so far, Kate is plunged into a terrifying existence
for which nothing has prepared her.

Most people would call it certain death.

The FBI calls it The Blue Zone.

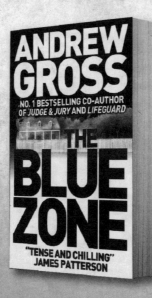

THE DARK TIDE

GET UP. KISS YOUR FAMILY GOODBYE.
GO TO WORK. DIE…

They say bad luck comes in threes. But for Karen Friedman's
family, bad luck is just the beginning.

It starts with her husband Charlie's investments going wrong
and the sudden death of a much-loved family pet. Then one
morning Charlie takes the train to work – straight into
a lethal terrorist blast. For Karen and their children,
all that remains of Charlie is a shared past.

Or is it? When the Friedmans begin to receive terrifying threats,
Karen turns to Detective Ty Hauck for help. Hauck's family fell apart
too, after a tragic accident he still blames himself for. Now he's
determined to keep Karen's family safe. But what Hauck
doesn't know, is that the people who investigate Charlie
have a way of ending up dead…

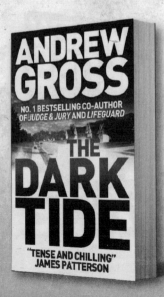

RECKLESS

THE SENSELESS SLAUGHTER OF A FAMILY.
A FINANCIER'S TRAGIC SUICIDE.
A SIMPLE PHONE CALL WITH TERRIBLE CONSEQUENCES.

Three seemingly separate events – that may be linked. From small-town America, through Wall Street to Central Europe and London, the threads of evidence can be followed – if you're good enough. Fortunately, Ty Hauck is. Ty, a former police detective uncomfortable with his new status as a 'security consultant', also has a powerful personal motive: a promise to one of the dead, April Glassman.

Joining forces with Naomi Blum, a beautiful, ambitious US Treasury trouble-shooter, they dig deep into the dark heart of what might be one of the cleverest – and most dangerous – conspiracies the world has ever seen…

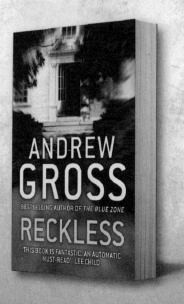

KILLING HOUR

A YOUNG MAN'S SUICIDE.
AN ELDERLY WOMAN'S MURDER.
A CONSPIRACY STRETCHING BACK DECADES.

Dr. Jay Erlich's life is perfect: a wife and children he loves; a successful career. But a call comes that changes everything. His troubled nephew, Evan, has killed himself and Jay's brother is in despair.

Jay flies to California to help out, and is soon convinced Evan's death was no suicide. The police want him to leave the matter alone but he is determined to dig deeper. When his investigation takes him on a journey into his brother's shady past, Jay finds himself caught up in a world of dangerous secrets and ruthless killers…

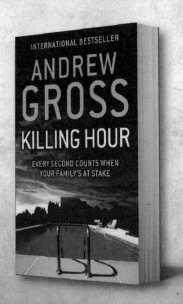

She's seen too much, now there's…

No Way Back

**'STARTS AT FULL
THROTTLE AND
STAYS THERE
TILL THE END'**
Linwood Barclay

A chance encounter with a stranger in a New York hotel ends in
a shooting. Wendy Gould was an average mother – now she's the
sole witness to the murder she's being framed for.

YOU CAN RUN

What she saw makes Wendy the top target for a deadly network
of powerful men. They want her silenced. They will take no prisoners.
How can she clear her name?

YOU CAN HIDE

Lauritzia Velez is a suburban nanny with a tragic past – and a terrifying
future. After another attempt on her life, she once again leaves
behind everything she loves to go on the run.

THERE IS NO WAY BACK

Both women know too much – except how to escape from this
nightmare alive. To survive, they must find each other fast,
or there will be no way back…